LOVE YOU TO DEATH

ROWEN CHAMBERS

INKUBATOR
BOOKS

Published by Inkubator Books
www.inkubatorbooks.com

Copyright © 2025 by Rowen Chambers

ISBN (eBook): 978-1-83756-493-4
ISBN (Paperback): 978-1-83756-494-1
ISBN (Hardback): 978-1-83756-495-8

Rowen Chambers has asserted her right to be identified as the author of this work.

LOVE YOU TO DEATH is a work of fiction. People, places, events, and situations are the product of the author's imagination. Any resemblance to actual persons, living or dead is entirely coincidental.

No part of this book may be reproduced, stored in any retrieval system, or transmitted by any means without the prior written permission of the publisher.

PART 1

CHAPTER ONE

"How'd I do?" Logan yells from the kitchen. "You like it?"

I look down at the ham salad on my plate. I do not like ham salad. It's this hideous shade of pink, for one, and then there's the consistency. It's chewy, but also creamy and a little fluffy. And why is it sweet?

"It's very good!" I yell back, trying to gulp down another bite of the fluffy pink mixture.

My poor husband. He's been working so hard to take care of me. I don't have the heart to tell him that the ham salad he made is horrible. He said he followed the recipe, which apparently I printed out, but I can't imagine wanting this enough to print out a recipe for it.

I take another bite, cringing when I feel the texture against my tongue. Why would I have ever thought this was good? The neurologist told me it's common to wake up from a traumatic brain injury and find your likes and dislikes have changed, but I feel like I'm a totally different person.

"I brought dessert," Logan says, sounding proud of

himself as he comes into the guest room holding a plate of cookies. His smile drops to a frown when he sees my nearly untouched ham salad. "You've barely had a bite."

"Honey, I'm sorry." I set my fork down. "I know you worked really hard to make it, but I think I've lost my taste for it." I look at the pink fluffy blob. "Honestly, I can't imagine ever liking this." I glance up at Logan and see the disappointment on his face.

"You used to love it." He sits across from me on the bed.

"I tried to eat it. I really did. It's just... not very good."

His lips purse, then begin to tremble. Oh no, is he going to cry? He never cries. I can't imagine he'd cry over ham salad.

"Logan, I feel terrible. I know you went to a lot of work to—"

He bursts out laughing. "You don't have to apologize. It's disgusting. I don't blame you for not eating it."

"You knew it was bad?" I sit back. "Then why'd you make it?"

"Because you really did used to like it, but you made it differently. It was chunkier. I put it in the blender, which made it more like thick soup."

"So you're not upset I didn't eat it?"

"Of course not." He leans over and kisses my forehead. "I'll make you whatever you want, and if you don't like it, just tell me. You won't hurt my feelings."

"You really had me fooled. I thought you were about to cry."

He laughs again. "I was just seeing how long you'd keep apologizing for not eating that disgusting ham salad." He picks up the plate of cookies. "Try these. I think you'll like them much better."

I take a cookie, which has chunks of peanut butter and chocolate candy poking out of it. "You made these?"

"I'd like to take credit for them, but Rachel brought them over."

"How nice of her." I take a bite, making sure to get some of the gooey chocolate. "They're wonderful. Tell her thank you."

Rachel and her husband, Connor, live next door. I don't remember them, but Logan said he occasionally goes golfing with Connor and that the four of us used to go out for dinner or take turns having backyard cookouts.

"You can tell her yourself," Logan says. "She's coming over later. Or if you don't feel up to it, we can do it another time."

"I'm up for some company," I say, noticing I'm feeling much better than I did earlier in the week. The new pain meds I'm on seem to be working. "Is she coming to visit?"

"Actually, it's more than that." Logan scoots closer to me on the bed. "Honey, you know I love taking care of you, and I'd continue to if I could, but—"

"Logan, you don't have to explain." I set what's left of the cookie down on the plate. "I know you need to go back to work. I didn't expect you to stay home with me for however long it takes me to get better. I'll be fine on my own."

"No." He shakes his head. "It's too soon. You could get dizzy and fall or have one of your headaches and pass out. I wouldn't be able to work if you were here alone all day. I'd be worried sick."

"So what are you proposing?"

"Rachel will come over during the day and help out. It'll only be two or three days a week, depending on my schedule. I'll be here as much as I can. I just can't be here every day with the new housing project starting and my city council role ramping up."

"And Rachel's okay with this?"

"Yes. In fact, she offered to help. I know you don't remember, but you two were good friends, and she's missed having you around to talk to."

"And you're comfortable with this? I mean, I'm sure Rachel will do the best she can, but she's not a nurse. What if something happens?"

"She'll call for help, just like I'd do if something happened. Honey, if you want me to find someone else, I will. I could hire a nurse if that would make you more comfortable."

"I don't think that's necessary. I just worry that Rachel's taking on more than she realizes."

"I've spoken with her about it. She knows what's involved, what to look for, what meds you're on. I told her she can change her mind at any time if it gets to be too much."

"Or maybe someone else could help. Like Edith. She's home all day."

"I wouldn't feel good about that. Edith is old and frail. I'd worry about both of you getting hurt if she were here."

"She's not frail. She's out working in her garden every morning."

"Caring for a few tomato plants is not the same as caring for someone with a traumatic brain injury and autoimmune disease." Logan gets up, signaling the end of our discussion. "Let's see how Rachel does and go from there."

"What time will she be over?"

He checks his watch. "I told her to come later this afternoon, but she could be over sooner if you'd like. I wasn't sure if you'd want to rest after lunch." He glances at my tray. "I need to make you something else. What would you like?"

"Can you make grilled cheese?"

"Yes." He smiles. "Just so you know, I'm not a bad cook. I might even say I'm good at it."

My eyes dart to the ham salad.

"Oh, come on," Logan says, noticing me holding back a laugh. "You can't judge my cooking skills based on that ham salad. I followed the recipe exactly."

"I'm just kidding. I'm sure the grilled cheese will be much better."

"Coming right up." He leans down to kiss me, then picks up the tray and heads back to the kitchen.

Logan is such a wonderful man. I couldn't ask for a better husband. He's been by my side since the moment I woke up at the hospital. He looked so frightened, and I understand why. I almost died. He almost lost me. Coming home and finding my lifeless body on the kitchen floor was bad enough. But then, to find out that I had swelling on the brain and needed emergency surgery? It's the last thing either of us ever thought would happen.

Logan has been through so much with me. The past couple of years, I've had one health problem after another. I don't remember that time, but Logan told me about it. He said the doctors diagnosed me with an autoimmune disease but that they couldn't name it or offer me a cure. Basically, they were telling me they didn't know what was wrong with me and couldn't make me better.

It's not the answer Logan or I wanted. This isn't how our lives were supposed to be. But at least we have each other.

And no matter what happens, Logan will always be there for me.

As we said in our wedding vows, we'll be together for better or for worse. Through good times and bad. And, most importantly, in sickness and in health.

CHAPTER TWO

"Avery." Rachel comes into the bedroom holding a white ceramic vase overflowing with flowers. "How are you feeling?"

"Better than I was a few weeks ago." I smile as she sets the vase on the dresser across from the bed. "Those are gorgeous."

"Hydrangeas. They're from Edith. I told her I was seeing you today, and she insisted I bring you some of her blue hydrangeas." Rachel walks over to the chair beside the bed and sits down. "I think she might be losing it."

"Why? Did something happen?" I ask with concern. I enjoy having Edith as a neighbor. She's a little odd, but in a good way. And she's very generous with her garden surplus. I remember her bringing us baskets of vegetables when we first moved into the house.

"She called me Vera," Rachel says. "That's her sister's name."

"She probably just misspoke. I mix up names too sometimes."

"It's not just that. She also asked how my cat was doing. But I've never had a cat. She was obviously thinking of someone else."

I furrow my brow. "I hope she's okay. I'd hate to see her have to go into a care center. She loves being in that house and having her garden. Maybe she just saw a cat in your yard and thought you'd adopted one recently. I can't imagine her mind failing that much since I saw her last."

"You haven't seen her in over a month. Isn't that right? Wasn't it before your accident?"

"Yes, but I've spoken to her on the phone. She seemed fine. She wanted to come by, but Logan doesn't want me having visitors yet. He thinks it's too stimulating for my brain and will make my headaches worse."

She nods. "He told me that. I assured him I'd keep things quiet around here so you could rest, meaning no visitors and limiting your time chatting on the phone."

"He's being overprotective. When the doctor said to avoid stimulating environments, he meant crowded stores or sports arenas, not my own home. But Logan thinks merely having a conversation could be too much for me."

"He just wants you to get better. It's sweet. It shows how much he loves you."

She's right, and I'm grateful to have a husband who loves me as much as Logan does. But it's frustrating not being able to go out or have visitors. I spent two weeks in the hospital and then the past two weeks at home, mostly in bed because Logan worries I'll fall again if I get up and walk around.

As I'm thinking that, Logan walks into the room. He's so handsome that sometimes I wonder how I was lucky enough to marry a man who's not only kind and loving but also very good-looking. With his broad shoulders and strong, chiseled features, he's always getting attention from women, including Rachel, who watches him as he comes over to me.

"How's it going in here?"

"I was just telling Rachel that you're being overprotective," I say with a smile so he knows I'm not upset with him.

"I just want you to get better," Logan says.

"I promise to take good care of her," Rachel says, smiling at Logan.

"Have you two gone over the schedule?" he asks her.

"Not yet," she says, making me wonder what they're talking about. I'm a little annoyed Logan didn't consult me before setting up this arrangement with Rachel. She seems nice, and apparently we were friends, but until my memory returns, this woman is basically a stranger. Logan said she moved in a year ago, which is within the time period I can't recall.

"What schedule?" I ask.

Rachel turns to me. "I'll come by in the morning, right before Logan leaves for work, and stay until he gets home. For now, I'll plan on being here Monday through Wednesday, and Logan will be here the rest of the week."

"Three days is a lot," I say. "I really don't need someone here that much. Maybe we could try one day to start and see how it goes."

"Honey, no," Logan says. "I'd be worried sick if you were here alone all day. I'm sorry, Avery, but I'm not backing down on this. I can't risk something happening to you while I'm at work."

I'm not going to win this argument, so I decide to go along with their plan for now. Maybe after a week or two, I'll convince Logan I don't need someone babysitting me all day.

"Won't you be bored?" I say to Rachel. "Just sitting here all day?"

"Not at all. I have some freelance projects I can work on when you're resting or don't need me."

"What is it you do again?"

"I'm a writer. A journalist, or I was until all the news agencies laid everyone off. Now I mostly write fluff pieces for online."

"She's a very talented writer," Logan says. "You've read a lot of her stuff."

"Sorry, Rachel, I don't remember," I say. "I didn't even remember that you were a writer." I look down, feeling hopeless, like I'll never get my memories back.

"Honey, don't be so hard on yourself." Logan sits down on the bed. "The doctor said it could be weeks before your brain heals enough for your memories to return."

He also said that they may never come back. What's strange is that most of my memories are still there. I remember my childhood, my teen years, going to college. I even remember our wedding and the first year of our marriage. It's only the past two years that I'm struggling with. My neurologist said that's unusual but not unheard of, and that every brain injury is different, with some patients losing days of memories and others losing years.

"Honestly, the stuff I've written lately isn't that memorable," Rachel says with a laugh. "Even for people who haven't had memory loss."

"I'll let you two chat," Logan says, getting up. "I just wanted to check how things are going. Do either of you need anything? Something to drink, maybe?"

"I'm fine, but thank you," Rachel says.

"I'd take some tea," I say.

Logan smiles at me. "Coming right up."

Rachel watches him leave, then says, "You got a good one."

"He's great. But so is your husband. Connor, right?"

"Yes." She smiles. "Did you remember that?"

"No, Logan told me. He said they go golfing sometimes."

She nods, then looks down, seeming uncomfortable.

"Is something wrong?" I ask.

"It's nothing." She shakes her head, then glances up at me. "Let's talk about next week. Is there anything you'd like me to do? I'm happy to help out with the laundry. Do some light housework. Whatever you need."

"You don't have to do any of that. You're not here to be our maid. You really don't have to do anything other than make sure I don't fall."

She reaches over and puts her hand over mine. "We're friends. I'm here to help you, so please, let me help."

"Well, I would like something to read." I lower my voice so Logan won't hear. "My overprotective husband thinks reading will hurt my brain, but I'm not asking for a novel. I just want a few fashion magazines to flip through and maybe some home magazines."

"Done!" Rachel says, like she's thrilled I asked her for something. "Anything else?"

"Yes. No matter what Logan tells you, don't ever make me ham salad. He claims I used to love it, but I don't now."

"Got it. No ham salad."

Her phone rings. She picks it up and silences it.

"You could've answered that," I tell her.

She shakes her head. "It was Connor. I can talk to him later."

"Is everything okay? You seem upset, but if you don't want to talk about it, I get it. I don't mean to pry."

"We're having issues," she says with a sigh.

"What kind of issues?"

"I don't want to get into it. But it's gotten to the point that all we do is fight. I'm wondering if Connor and I should even be together."

"Oh, Rachel, I'm sorry."

"I'm not saying we're getting divorced, but I've thought about it, especially when I see you with Logan. It makes me think that I should have that too."

"Have what, exactly?"

"A husband who loves me the way Logan loves you. I know you don't remember, but Logan has taken such good care of you the past year as you struggled with your health. Connor would never do that. If I got sick, he'd be gone."

"I doubt that. A lot of guys really step up when their wives get sick. I think you'd be surprised what Connor would do for you."

She smiles. "That's sweet of you to say, but you don't know him like I do. Everyone thinks they know someone, but really all you're seeing is what they let you see."

As she says that, a chill goes through me and I shiver.

"Are you cold?" Rachel asks. "I could get you a blanket."

"I'm not cold."

"You were shivering."

But it wasn't that kind of chill. It was the kind that tells you something is wrong. That you might be in danger.

Was I imagining it? Maybe it was a side effect of one of my medications. But I don't remember feeling it before.

CHAPTER THREE

"Have you been looking through pictures?" Rachel asks, noticing the stack of photo albums on top of the dresser.

"Logan and I were looking at them together. I thought it might help with my memory."

"And did it?"

"I'm not sure. The tricky thing about memory loss is that sometimes you're not sure if you're remembering something or simply latching on to someone else's memory."

"What do you mean?"

"Like this morning, Logan was showing me photos of a trip we took last summer to Napa. He said I fell and broke my arm. I feel like I remember that, but then I wonder if it's an actual memory or if I'm just taking Logan's memory and making it my own."

"I remember that trip. You two had to come home early because of your arm."

"Yeah, that's what he said. He's been telling me about all the health problems I've had the past couple of years. I'm a little surprised he's still with me."

"He loves you," Rachel says. "He's one of the few men who's actually following through on his vows."

"In sickness and in health," I mutter, remembering the day Logan said those words. Out of all the memories I still have, I'm glad my wedding is one of them. Logan looked at me with so much love when he said his vows. Then later, as we shared our first dance, he gazed at me and told me how happy he was to have me as his wife. I was in pure bliss, knowing I'd get to have forever with this wonderful man. It was a perfect day. The perfect start of what I knew would be a loving and happy marriage.

"Did you remember anything else?" Rachel asks. "After looking at the photos?"

"We only went through a few. Logan doesn't want to overwhelm me. I kind of have a memory of my birthday last fall, but again, I'm not sure if I'm making up a story to go with the pictures or if it actually happened."

"Did you ask Logan?"

"No, I want to let the memory sit with me longer. If Logan tells me about that day, I won't have a chance to recall it myself."

"Maybe it's better if you don't. Logan said you get headaches when you try really hard to remember something."

"But I need to still do it. The only way my brain will get better is if I give it a workout."

"I'm not sure Logan would agree with that."

"Did I hear my name?" Logan says, coming in with my cup of tea. He sets it on the nightstand.

"I was telling Rachel about the time I broke my arm."

"You remember that?" Logan stands beside my bed, his

brows drawing together, the wrinkles in his forehead deepening.

"No, I was just telling her about the photos from our Napa trip and what you said happened."

He looks over at Rachel. "It was a very stressful day. We were out in a vineyard with no medical help for miles."

"Yes, I remember Avery telling me about it when you two got back."

"And how did I fall?" I ask Logan. "You said I tripped?"

"I'm guessing you did. I didn't see it happen. I was a few feet ahead of you."

"I'm surprised it was a hard enough fall to break my arm. Falling on dirt should've cushioned my fall. It's not like I fell on concrete."

"Sometimes it's all about the angle," Rachel says. "You hit the bone at just the right spot and you break it."

"I guess."

But it doesn't sound plausible. I was walking, probably at a slow pace. It's not as though I was running or fell from a height. I can't imagine hitting the ground with enough force or momentum to break a bone.

"You look tired," Logan says, rubbing my shoulder. "Why don't you try to get some sleep?"

Rachel gets up. "I'll head out."

"You don't have to leave," I tell her, thinking it was nice having someone new to talk to. I love Logan, but after two weeks with him, stuck in this house, we're running out of things to say. All he wants to talk about is my health and how I'm feeling, which I know is because he's worried about me, but enough is enough. I need a break.

"I'll be back on Monday," Rachel says, smiling at me.

"For now, get some rest." She glances at Logan. "You two have a nice weekend."

"We will," Logan tells her. "I'll walk you out."

They leave, and Logan closes the door behind him. I hear them walking to the door, then the sound of them talking. I wonder what they're saying. Is Logan telling her to make sure I stay in bed all day? If so, it's not happening. I need to get up and move around if I'm ever going to get my strength back.

They're still talking but keeping their voices low, probably to make sure I can't hear. I don't like that they're talking about me. If Logan has something to tell her, he should've done it when Rachel was here in my room.

Shoving off the covers, I sit up and move to the edge of the bed, pausing a moment to make sure I'm not dizzy. I feel okay, so I slowly stand up, then pause again, noticing my legs feel weak from not using them. I head to the door using slow careful steps. When I reach it, I turn the handle and open the door enough to hear Logan talking.

"I worry something will happen," he says in a hushed tone.

"Nothing will happen," Rachel says, her voice barely above a whisper. "I'll be right here."

"And you can assure me you won't let her—"

"Yes. I'll make sure of it. Logan, I need to go. Connor will be home soon."

"Tell him I'm sorry I can't golf on Saturday, or any Saturday for the foreseeable future."

"He already knows that. He knows your priority is being with Avery."

The door opens, and I hear Rachel leaving. I close the

door to the bedroom but then feel it being pushed from the other side. I stumble back, catching myself before I fall.

"Avery!" Logan races up to me, gripping my shoulders. "What are you doing?"

"I want to go to the living room. Watch some TV."

"You have a TV in here."

"I'm tired of being in bed. I want to sit on the couch."

I look up at him, noticing his eyes are narrowed and his jaw is clenched. He's still gripping my shoulders, his fingers digging in.

"You're hurting me," I say, glancing at my shoulder. "Let me go."

He loosens his grip, but his hands remain where they are. "You can't be doing this, Avery."

"Doing what?"

"Putting yourself at risk. You nearly fell and hurt yourself."

"Because you shoved the door open when I wasn't expecting it."

"You're blaming *me*?" he says, raising his voice. "I told you to stay in bed!"

"Logan, I'm a grown woman. I can get out of bed if I want."

He laughs, a deep throaty laugh that startles and confuses me.

"What's so funny?" I ask, my heart beating faster.

"You can't remember what day it is, or what foods you like, or where we went for Christmas last year. Do you really think you're capable of making decisions about your health?"

His harsh words, and the condescending way he said them, take me by surprise. He's never acted this way, grabbing me with so much force, talking down to me. I don't like it, and I'm not going to allow it.

I shove his hands off me. "I'm going to the living room. I'm going to watch TV and come back here when I'm ready." Turning away from him, I slowly walk to the door.

"Avery, wait!" Logan comes up beside me. "I'm sorry. I shouldn't have spoken to you that way."

"No, you shouldn't have." I turn to him. "I know you're only trying to help, but I can't have you telling me what to do all the time. I need to get up and move around. I can't sit in bed all day."

"I understand." He smiles a little. "Can I at least help you to the living room?" He offers me his arm.

"I guess that'd be okay." I wrap my arm around his, and we make our way to the couch. I sit down, and Logan settles in beside me.

"I'm sorry for how I reacted," he says. "I just panicked when I saw you almost fall."

I turn to him, my eyes moving over his face, noticing he looks completely calm now, a stark change from the man I saw in the bedroom moments ago.

"You can't do that again," I tell him. "I didn't like seeing you like that. It's almost like... like you were someone else."

"I'm sorry, honey." He pulls me into his arms, gently holding me. "I just love you so much. I don't want anything to happen to you."

"I know," I whisper. "I love you too."

But I can't stop thinking about what happened in the bedroom. Why did he look at me that way? Why was he gripping my shoulders so hard? He had to have known he was hurting me.

I'm probably overanalyzing it. It was just such a big change from how Logan normally acts that it surprised me. That wasn't the Logan I know. The one I'm with now, lovingly holding me in his arms, is the man I married.

CHAPTER FOUR

"Maybe I could come there later this month," Mia says. "I could talk to my boss. See if I could work remote."

"You don't need to. It's too far. And I'm fine. Really. Logan is taking very good care of me."

"Hey, Mia!" Logan yells.

"Tell him I say hi," she says. "Or actually, put me on speaker."

"She wants to talk to you," I say as I press the speaker button. "Okay, go ahead, Mia."

"Is my sister really doing okay?" she asks. "Or is she just pretending so I won't show up at your door?"

Logan walks closer to the phone, smiling at me. "She's doing much better, but she's a very difficult patient. I tell her to rest and then find her walking around."

"I'm walking to the living room," I tell Mia. "He makes it sound like I'm walking around the block, which I'm pretty sure I could do if he let me."

"Absolutely not," Logan says. "It's too soon."

"Have you been out at all?" Mia asks.

"No, and I'm going crazy," I say, looking at Logan. "I haven't left the house since getting home from the hospital."

"Logan, you should take her for a drive," Mia says. "Just to get her out of the house."

"Yes, maybe we'll do that," he says. "But not today. It's getting late, and I have some things I need to do before I go back to the office tomorrow."

Logan works for a company that contracts with the city to build low-income housing. San Francisco is known for being one of the world's most expensive cities, leaving people with lower-paying jobs few options for housing. To address the problem, two Silicon Valley tech billionaires started a company to build innovative housing solutions with affordable rent. Logan's worked at the company for three years now and was recently promoted to executive director in charge of planning and development. He's received numerous awards for his dedication to reducing homelessness and recently got a seat on the city council. I'm so proud of him and the work he's done.

"You have someone coming over, right?" Mia asks. "To help Avery?"

"Yes, Rachel will be here," Logan says. "Avery doesn't remember, but she and Rachel did a lot together before..."

"Before I broke my brain," I say, deciding enough time has passed that I can joke about it. It's not funny, but I'm tired of everyone being so serious around me. I feel the need to inject some humor into the situation.

"Does she have any medical training?" Mia asks.

"No, but she doesn't need it," I say. "If anything happens, she can call my doctor. But nothing's going to happen. I'm doing much better."

"Logan, do you agree?" Mia asks, assuming I'm lying to her.

"I do, but I still want her to rest more."

"You really should, Avery."

"Okay, enough ganging up on me," I say, smiling at Logan. "Go do your work stuff," I tell him. "I'm going to talk to Mia some more."

"Bye, Mia!" Logan leans down to give me a kiss, then says, "Let me know if you need anything."

"I will." I take the phone off speaker as Logan leaves and goes down the hall to his office. "Okay, it's just you and me now."

"Sounds like Logan's taking good care of you."

"He is, but he's so overprotective. It's getting to be annoying. I'm looking forward to him going back to work so I can do stuff without being told I need to rest."

"He seems really worried about you, which I guess makes sense given what happened."

"I still can't believe I hit my head hard enough to cause that much damage."

"I can. Hitting a granite counter is like slamming your head against concrete. And then you hit the tile floor when you fell. That's two really hard blows to the head."

"Logan told you I was doing laundry when this happened?"

Mia sighs. "Avery, why do you keep asking me this? I read an article that said reliving a traumatic experience is like going through it all over again. You don't need that kind of stress when you're trying to get better."

"I don't remember it, so I'm not reliving it. I'm just trying to figure out what happened."

"Nobody really knows. You were alone when it happened, but from the way you were found, it looked like you were on your way to the laundry room when you slipped, fell backward, hit the granite island, then landed on the floor."

"And this happened on a Thursday," I say, confirming what I've been told.

"Yeah, probably sometime in the morning is what the doctors think, based on the condition you were in when you got to the hospital."

"That doesn't make sense. I never do laundry on Thursdays. I do it on Wednesdays and Sundays. I've been doing that since college."

"Maybe you didn't have time on Wednesday, so you decided to do it Thursday."

"Or maybe I spilled something on a shirt and was doing a small load to get the stain out."

"I don't think so. Logan said there were clothes all over the floor, like it was a full load. Avery, you gotta let this go. You can't change what happened, no matter how many times you go over it in your head."

"But if I know the story, I can prevent it from happening again."

"Accidents happen, even when you try to prevent them. But I do think you should slow down. You're always in a hurry. You've been like that since we were kids. I'm thinking that day you hit your head, you were probably walking too fast, hit a slick spot on the tile, and fell."

"Was the tile wet?"

"I don't know. If it was, it would've dried by the time Logan got to you."

"And that was at five?"

"A little after four. He left work early because he hadn't heard from you. He was worried."

"So I was lying there unconscious for what... four hours?"

"Around that. Okay, this is going to make me cry. Let's talk about something else."

"Mia, I'm fine now. You don't have to be sad."

"I get sad when I think of you being there all that time without help. What if Logan hadn't come home early? What if... what if I lost you?" She sniffles. "I can't go through that again, Avery."

She's referring to the loss of our brother, John. He died a few years ago when his woodworking shed went up in flames. The fire department said the fire was most likely caused by some stain-soaked rags being exposed to a flame. Cigarettes were found at the scene. John had given up smoking years ago but had started up again after his girlfriend broke up with him.

"It's almost his birthday," I say. "Are we going to do anything?"

"Like what? You aren't able to fly, and I can't make it back there just for a day."

Soon after I got married, Mia got a job in London and moved away. She's so busy with work that she's only flown back here once in three years. She flew to Seattle for John's funeral but was only there a few days, then had to fly back.

"Logan and I could drive up there. Go to the cemetery. Leave some flowers."

"Logan wouldn't want you that far from your medical team," she says. "I'll have flowers sent to the grave. I'll send some for Mom and Dad too."

Our parents are buried in Seattle, where we grew up.

When John died, he was living here in the Bay Area, but we buried his ashes next to our parents' graves. Mia and I will be there too someday. My parents bought spots for the whole family so we'd all be together. I thought it was really morbid when they did that, but now I'm glad they did. I feel some peace when I go to the cemetery and see John's name next to Mom's and Dad's.

Logan comes into the living room, stopping next to the couch. "You're still on the phone?"

"Yeah. Why?"

"You've been talking for almost an hour. Maybe you could call her back some other time."

"Is that Logan?" Mia asks.

"Yes, he thinks talking on the phone is somehow going to hurt my brain." I smile at him.

"Okay, I'll let you go."

"No, Mia, we don't have to hang up."

"It's fine. I have some stuff to do anyway. We'll talk later."

"Yeah, okay. Bye!" I end the call. "Logan, this really needs to stop."

"What needs to stop? Me looking out for you?" He folds his arms over his chest as he stares down at me on the couch.

"You're treating me like a child. Telling me when to go to bed. Making me take naps. Rushing me off the phone."

"Those are all things that will help you get better. Isn't that what you want? To get better so things can go back to normal?"

"Yes, but that's not going to happen if all I do is sit in bed all day. Even the doctor said I should be up and moving around by now, and he definitely never said I can't talk on the phone."

"He said to avoid stress, and unfortunately, your sister causes you a great deal of stress."

I laugh. "Mia? We get along great. She doesn't cause me stress."

"She did. You just don't remember."

"Is this a joke? Because Mia is the absolute last person who would stress me out. Talking to her gets rid of my stress. She calms me down."

"Maybe when you were younger, but things changed after we got married."

"What do you mean?"

He sits down beside me. "You really want to hear this?"

"Yes," I say, because I have no idea what he's talking about.

Mia and I have always been close. She's my best friend as well as my sister. I confide in her. I look to her for advice. I trust her and trust her opinion. We may argue sometimes, but over little things, nothing big. So why is Logan saying these things? What does he know that I don't?

CHAPTER FIVE

"You haven't been as close to Mia the past few years," Logan says.

"What do you mean by that?"

"You felt you couldn't tell her things anymore. She was trying to tell you what to do and wouldn't listen when you told her to stop."

"That doesn't sound like Mia."

"She changed. You don't know because you don't remember. But she changed after..." Logan pauses.

"After what?"

"After John's death. With your parents gone and then John, you're really all the family she has left, so she became very protective of you." Logan rubs his hand over his jaw. "She got to be very controlling. She was telling you what to do and even how to think. It got so bad I asked you to stop talking to her, to give you a break."

"And this happened when?"

"A few months after John died."

"Which I can't remember," I say, frustrated that my

memory loss goes back that far. I remember John's death, but I don't remember fighting with Mia or her telling me what to do.

"The symptoms of your autoimmune disease were getting worse," Logan says, "and I thought it might be because of the stress Mia was causing you, so I tried to lessen that stress by getting you to take a break from her."

"And did I?"

"No. You insisted she wasn't the reason you were feeling sick, but I disagreed. I could see how upset you were after talking to her. Some nights you couldn't even sleep."

"I don't understand. That doesn't sound like Mia at all."

"I know. I was surprised too when she started being so controlling, but I really think it was a response to her grief. Not just her grief over losing John but also your parents. She was afraid she might lose you too. Controlling you was her way of trying to make sure nothing happened to you."

"Kind of like you're doing now?"

He takes my hand and holds it in his. "I guess I am being a little too forceful, telling you to rest all the time, but it's only because I don't want to lose you."

"I know." I smile at him. "And I love you for that."

He looks down. "There's more. About Mia."

"What is it?"

"I don't know if I should tell you. Maybe it's best to forget it."

"No. Tell me. What did she do?"

"It's not what she did. It's what she said." His eyes rise to mine. "She blamed me for John's death."

"Wait—what?" I laugh because the idea is so completely crazy. "Mia wouldn't do that."

"But she did." Logan pauses. "John died on a Sunday. I

was with him the day before, on Saturday. I went over there to see the table he was working on. I knew someone who might want to buy it, so I went over to take some pictures. I was there for maybe an hour, and then I left."

"I don't get it. Why would Mia blame you for John's death? You weren't even there that day."

Logan lets go of my hand and looks down at the floor.

"What is it? What aren't you telling me?"

"The cigarettes. I'm the one who bought them." Logan looks up at me. "John asked me to bring him some. I knew I shouldn't, but I also felt bad for the guy. Lori had dumped him that week, and he wasn't taking it well. He'd missed work. He was sleeping all the time. I figured a few cigarettes couldn't be that bad if they helped him get through a rough time."

"That's why Mia blamed you for his death? Because of the cigarettes? You bought them. You didn't make my brother smoke them."

"I know it doesn't make sense, but Mia was looking for someone to blame, and I was it."

"When did this happen? When did she accuse you of this?"

"After the investigation closed and it was decided that it must have been a cigarette that ignited the rags and caused the fire. Mia called me and asked what happened the day before he died, the day I went to see him. I told her I saw the table he was making, took some photos, and left. That's when she brought up the cigarettes. She said she'd talked to him the night before he died, and he'd admitted he was smoking again. He told her I'd brought him a pack when I came over."

"Okay, but that's no reason to blame you for what happened."

"And I told her that. I told her I was sorry and that I never should've bought them, but I wasn't taking responsibility for something I didn't do. Like you said, I didn't make John smoke that day, and if I'd been there, I never would've let him smoke in the shed, where he was surrounded by flammable chemicals."

"He wasn't thinking straight," I say, feeling horrible that I wasn't there for John like I should've been. "He was devastated when Lori left him." I pause, my eyes tearing up. "He was going to ask her to marry him, and then she dumped him. I wish I'd gone over there that weekend. Maybe things would've—"

"Avery, stop." Logan turns to me. "It wasn't your fault. It wasn't mine either. John was hurting and made some bad decisions. There's nothing we could've done."

I don't agree. I could've been with John that weekend. I could've helped him get through the pain of losing the woman he loved. I didn't because he was someone who liked to work things out on his own. Even as a kid, he'd want to be left alone when he was sad. So I'd decided it was best to not bother him and let him work through his feelings.

"Why didn't you tell me?" I ask. "About the cigarettes?"

"I did, after Mia told you I was to blame for John's death. I didn't want to tell you before that because I didn't want you to know. I felt horrible, Avery. I still do. I know it's not my fault, but I still regret ever buying them."

"If he really wanted them, John would've bought them himself. The outcome would've been the same."

He nods, but I can tell he still carries that guilt with him, just like I still carry my guilt for not being with John that weekend.

"Going back to Mia," I say, "how did you two get past this? You seem to get along with her now."

"She eventually realized I wasn't to blame and that she was hurting her relationship with you by making me the bad guy. But it was too late. The damage was done. You told me you didn't feel you could tell her things anymore, like things about us. You said she was trying to break up our marriage so she'd have you all to herself."

"Mia said that?" I ask, shocked.

"She didn't say it. You just sensed that's where things were headed. She even suggested you both move back to Seattle and get a place together. She never once mentioned how I fit in that plan."

"That must've been her grief talking. I'm guessing she was really lonely, feeling like I was all she had left."

"I think so too. Anyway, things gradually got better, and you two became close again."

"Yeah, she seems fine when we talk." I smile. "And she has nothing but good things to say about you."

"I've been giving her regular updates about your health. I think that's what got me back on her good side. She can tell how much I care about you."

"You've been talking to her without telling me?"

"Usually, it's over text. Honey, I know I should've told you, but I didn't want to upset you, especially now, while you're recovering."

"When did this start? How long have you been sending her updates?"

Logan leans back on the couch. "For almost two years."

"Two years?" I turn to him. "You've been hiding this for two years?"

"She didn't want me to tell you. She knew if I did, you might tell me to stop. She was concerned for you, Avery. She knew you wouldn't tell her the truth, so she came to me instead."

"I can't believe she did this," I say, getting up. "And I can't believe you went along with it." I walk around the living room, too angry to sit still any longer.

"Avery, come on. Think about it from her perspective. If your sister was having health problems, wouldn't you want to be updated on how she was doing?"

"Yes, but I wouldn't go behind her back to find out. I'd just ask her, and she'd tell me."

"But you wouldn't." Logan gets up and comes over to me. "You didn't want to worry her, so you kept things from her. Like the time you passed out and didn't remember it. You asked me not to tell her about that, but how could I not? She's your only family. She deserved to know."

"That was for me to decide. Not you." I go around him and to the kitchen, to the slider door that leads to the patio.

"Avery!" Logan calls out as I go outside. "Get in here!"

I ignore him and sit down on one of the lounge chairs, breathing in the fresh air, trying to calm myself.

Logan appears beside me. "What are you doing?"

"I needed some air."

He sits in the chair next to mine. "I'm sorry you're angry, but I don't think what I did was wrong. She needed to know, and it's not like I went into detail. I tried to keep it as generic as possible."

"She never should've asked you to do that."

"She didn't. I'm the one who started it. It was during the

time when you were so tired you couldn't get out of bed. I know you don't remember it, but it was bad. The doctors weren't helping, and you seemed to be getting worse. I didn't know what to do. So I called Mia. I told her what was going on. She couldn't do anything to help, but she was incredibly grateful that I'd called and told her. That's when she asked me to keep her updated on how you were doing."

I'm still angry, but maybe I shouldn't be. I'm all Mia has left. She's not married. She doesn't have kids. It makes sense she'd be worried she might lose me and be left with no one. I just don't understand why I didn't tell her myself how I was doing. Why would I keep that from her? From what Logan said, it sounds like I'd gotten past whatever problems Mia and I were having after John's death, so why wasn't I being more open with her?

Something about this doesn't make sense.

CHAPTER SIX

"Yes, I got it," I hear Rachel say. "I'll make sure she takes them with food."

It's Monday, and Rachel's here to stay with me for the day. I'm a little sad I won't be seeing Logan until tonight. I've gotten used to having him around, even though he did annoy me at times with his need to watch over me every second of the day.

Now he's in the kitchen with Rachel, telling her when I take my meds. I don't know why he's doing this. I know when to take my meds. He must think I'll forget. I keep reminding him my memory of the present isn't a problem. It's the recent past I can't remember.

Logan comes into the living room with Rachel following behind. "I think we're all set. I told her as much as I could and left some notes, too."

"He was very thorough," Rachel says, smiling at me. "And very knowledgeable about your care. I think your husband should've been a doctor."

"He'd hate that," I say with a laugh. "He can't stand the sight of blood."

"True," he says. "I almost passed out when I found you that day. There was so much blood." He shudders.

When I hit my head on the granite counter, it tore some of the skin on the back of my skull, exposing it to even more damage when I then hit the tile floor. Hours later, when Logan got home, there was a pool of blood around my head. He thought I was dead. I would've thought so too. I honestly can't believe I'm still alive. The doctors said it was a miracle I survived.

"You should go," I tell Logan. "You're going to be late for work."

"We'll be fine," Rachel assures him. "I have your number. I'll call if I have any concerns."

Logan comes over to me on the couch and kisses my forehead. "Have a good day."

"I will. I'll see you tonight."

As he leaves, I feel an uneasiness come over me. I don't know what's causing it. Am I already missing Logan? I felt better having him around. I knew if I fell, he'd be able to help me up. Rachel's tiny, barely over a hundred pounds. If I fell with her here, she'd have to call someone for help.

"You're really lucky to have him," Rachel says, sitting on the chair across from me. "Most men wouldn't be that dedicated to their wife's care." She huffs. "Mine definitely wouldn't."

"How are things going with you two? Sorry, is that too personal? I know you said we were friends, but I don't know how close we were."

"It's fine. You can ask. Everyone will know soon anyway."

"Know what?"

"Connor and I have decided to separate."

"Oh, Rachel, I'm sorry."

She shrugs. "I knew it would happen."

"Maybe counseling would help," I say.

"We've talked about it, but Connor doesn't want to go. He thinks counseling is a waste of time. I think separating is our best option for now."

"Is he moving out?"

She nods. "He has already. Last night. He's staying with a friend." She gives me a sad smile. "Could we talk about something else?"

"Sure, although I don't have much to say. I haven't left the house in weeks, and I haven't watched the news, so I'm behind on current events."

"Oh!" She jumps up from her chair. "I forgot the magazines! I left them at the house. Is it okay if I run back there?"

"Go ahead."

While she's gone, I notice her purse on the table. There's a metal key chain attached to the strap. As I look at it, my chest tightens, and my pulse speeds up. I almost feel like I'm going to be sick. What's causing this? Why am I reacting this way to a key chain?

"Okay, I'm back," Rachel says, coming into the house with a stack of magazines. She sets them down on the coffee table. "I've got fashion ones, home decor, celebrity gossip, and then some food ones. I thought you could flip through and find Logan some recipes to try." She smiles. "So he doesn't make you ham salad again."

"Yeah, that was terrible." I pick up a fashion magazine. "Where'd you get all these?"

"I just went to the store and bought them."

"What do I owe you? I think Logan has some cash in his office."

"Don't worry about it. They're technically mine. I'm just letting you borrow them." She winks at me. "Since your husband won't let you have them."

"It's so ridiculous. Does he really think looking at a magazine is bad for my health?" I look up at Rachel. "I noticed that key chain on your purse. Where's it from?"

She glances at it. "There was a fundraiser for the homeless. They gave out gift bags with the key chain and some other stuff. I used to keep my gym key on it. I guess I could take it off now. I don't belong to that gym anymore."

"Do you go to a lot of those types of events?"

"No, and I didn't go to this one, but I heard it was well done. They hired one of the city's top event planners." She leans back and crosses her legs. "I've thought about getting into event planning. I worked in PR for a few years, so I have some events experience."

"Did I know that?"

"You did," she says, meaning before my brain injury wiped out the past couple of years. Sometimes I feel like parts of my memory are coming back, but it's more of a feeling than an actual memory. Like with that key chain. When I look at it, I feel anxious and sick to my stomach, which doesn't make sense. Why would I feel that way?

"Was I at the fundraiser?" I ask, thinking maybe that's where my memory of the key chain comes from.

"Yes," Rachel says. "In fact, Logan's company is the one that organized it."

"I'll have to ask him about it. It's so strange not knowing this stuff. I lived it, yet I can't remember it."

"I'm sure that's frustrating." Rachel gets up and grabs a

magazine from the stack, then sits back down. "You think it'll come back?"

"My memory? The doctors think it will eventually. They just don't know when or how much. They said everyone is different." She nods and flips through the magazine. I take a moment to look at her, at her styled hair and perfectly done makeup. She seems like someone who can't leave the house without making sure she's immaculately put together. Like today, she's wearing dark wide-legged pants and a silky beige blouse with a scarf-like tie at the top. It looks like something you'd wear to the office not to sit around the house all day.

"I like your blouse," I say. It's not my style, but it looks good on her.

"Thanks!" She glances up from her magazine. "I just got it, along with my pants. And my purse." Rachel laughs. "I'm kind of a shopping addict."

The doorbell rings.

Rachel sets the magazine down. "Are you expecting someone?"

"No. Maybe it's a delivery guy."

She gets up and walks to the door. "Who is it?"

Why is she asking? Why doesn't she just open the door?

"It's Edith," says a gravelly voice.

"Avery can't have visitors," Rachel says. "She's resting."

"I'm not resting," I say. "Let her in."

Rachel turns to me. "Logan said you're not to have visitors."

"Logan isn't the boss. Please open the door."

I'm annoyed that Rachel is so insistent on doing whatever Logan says. I'm a grown woman, two years older than

Rachel. This isn't going to work if she keeps treating me like a child. Right now, I'm not even sure I like her.

CHAPTER SEVEN

Rachel lets out a sigh as she unlocks the door and opens it. "Hello, Edith."

"What are *you* doing here?" Edith says, in a tone that makes me think she doesn't like Rachel.

"I'm keeping watch over Avery until her husband gets home. Did you need something?"

"I brought Avery some of my famous banana bread."

"I'll take it." Rachel reaches for it, but Edith holds onto it.

She shoves her way through the door, smiling when she sees me. "It's good to see you up."

"She's not to have visitors," Rachel says, shutting the door.

"That's Logan's rule, not mine," I say as Edith comes over to me. She's wearing faded jeans that hang on her thin frame and a lime green sweatshirt. Her long gray hair is pulled back in a ponytail, and dirt-stained sneakers cover her feet.

"You look good," Edith says, standing in front of me with

the banana bread. "From the way your husband talked, I thought you'd be spending all your days in bed."

"When did you talk to him?"

"Last Saturday. I wanted to bring over my banana bread then, but he told me not to. He said you weren't well. That you were confused and wouldn't know who I am."

"I don't know why he said that. It's not true. Of course I know who you are."

"You can't stay," Rachel blurts out. "Avery needs her rest."

Edith pretends not to hear her. "You want to try a piece?" She holds up the bread. "I made it fresh this morning."

"I'd love some! You want me to show you around the kitchen?"

"I know my way around. I've been in there many times. Be right back." She takes off, walking fast for someone her age, which I'm guessing is eighty-something.

Rachel comes over to me. "She's not supposed to be here. Logan gave me strict orders to keep it quiet around here, meaning no visitors."

"Logan doesn't get to decide who I see. I feel fine. Having Edith here isn't going to do any harm."

"She's old," Rachel says in a hushed tone. "What if she falls and then you fall? I can't help both of you."

Edith returns with two slices of banana bread slathered with butter.

"I'm not going to fall," she says, shooting a dirty look at Rachel. "I can walk just fine."

Rachel's mouth drops open. "How did you—"

"I'm old, not deaf," Edith says. She sits down beside me. "Here you go. Let me know what you think."

I pick up the banana bread and take a bite. "Oh, wow, this is really good."

Edith smiles. "It's your favorite! Do you remember?"

"I'm not sure." I take another bite, and as I do, an image flashes in my mind of a loaf of bread in a wicker basket. "Did you ever give this to me in a basket?"

Edith's face lights up. "Sure did! It was Easter. You weren't home, so I left it at the door with a card."

"You remember that?" Rachel asks me.

"She just said she did," Edith snaps. "Weren't you listening?"

"I'm surprised, that's all." Rachel looks at me. "Do you remember anything else?"

"No. Edith, when did you give me the basket?"

"Let's see." She pauses. "I think it was the Easter after you moved in."

"Then of course she remembers," Rachel says. "That was over two years ago."

"I'm only foggy on the last couple of years," I say to Edith. "So yeah, it makes sense I'd remember the basket."

Rachel's phone rings, and she jumps up from her chair. "I need to answer this. I'll be right back." She goes to the door and races outside.

"I don't know why you're friends with that woman," Edith says.

"What do you mean?"

"She's a fake. One of those people who pretends to be nice when she's really not. You know she'd rather be shopping or getting her nails done than hanging out here all day."

"Well, to be fair, a lot of people are like that," I say, thinking about the volunteer work I did in my twenties.

Some people genuinely wanted to help, but others were only there because they thought it made them look good.

I met Logan while I was volunteering. We were building a house, and I had no idea what I was doing. Logan saw I was struggling and showed me what to do. He was so kind and helpful. I immediately liked him and was thrilled when he asked me out.

"That husband of hers is a fake too," Edith says. "But he's a salesman, and I've never trusted salesmen, so there's that."

"Why do you think he's fake?"

"The fancy suits. The expensive car. Those two don't have money for that. Rachel doesn't even work."

"Maybe she doesn't need to. Salespeople can make a lot."

Edith leans closer and lowers her voice. "I think he got fired."

"When?"

"About a month ago? I can't say for sure, but that's when I noticed him being at home all day instead of going out to work."

"Maybe he quit."

"Who quits a well-paid job when he was the only one working?"

"So you don't know that he was fired. You're just guessing."

"I know what I see, and the evidence tells me he was fired. I think it happened when you were in the hospital. He came home, and Rachel and he got in a huge fight. I was outside and could hear them from inside their house."

"Could you hear what they were saying?" I say, suddenly intrigued.

"No, just a lot of yelling."

"Logan is friends with Connor. He would've told me if Connor had been fired."

"Would he?" Her brows rise.

"Why wouldn't he?"

She shrugs. "Men don't always tell their wives everything. Mine used to lie to me all the time. If he hadn't died, I was going to kill him and bury him in the garden."

I keep quiet, not sure how to respond to that.

She laughs, a deep throaty laugh. "I'm joking. I thought you could use a laugh."

"Maybe we should change topics," I say, feeling uncomfortable with her so-called joke. I'm also annoyed that she implied Logan is lying to me. I thought Edith was a nice old lady, but maybe I was wrong about her.

"So how long is she here for?" Edith asks, glancing outside to where Rachel is still talking on the phone. "All day?"

"Yeah, for a few times a week."

Edith's eyes widen. "You hired her?"

"No, she's doing it for free. Because we're friends, although I really don't remember her."

"If I were you, I'd tell her to take a hike." Edith huffs. "I'm happy to come over and help out. My schedule's wide open, and I can guarantee I'm a better cook than her."

"I'm sure you are, but Logan already worked it out with her and... well, it's not a bad idea for her to have something to do right now, given her situation."

"What situation?" Edith asks, a sly grin on her face, like she's looking forward to hearing some juicy gossip.

"Nothing. I shouldn't have said anything."

"Oh, come on. Tell me. You know I'll find out eventually."

"I really can't. Hey, I think she's coming back."

The door opens, and Rachel walks in, her eyes red and puffy.

"What happened?" Edith asks. "Someone die?"

The woman has no filter. She blurts out whatever pops in her head.

"No." Rachel gives her a funny look. "I just had to take a call."

"It couldn't have been good news if you look like that." Edith points to her.

Rachel sits down across from us. "You know, Edith, sometimes it's best to keep your thoughts to yourself."

"When you're my age, you say what you want." She glances at my empty plate. "You want some more?"

"No, but thanks. It really is delicious."

Edith turns back to Rachel. "Who was on the phone?"

Rachel picks up the magazine she was reading. "It doesn't concern you, Edith."

"I'm just making conversation."

"So, Edith," I say so she'll leave Rachel alone, "how's your garden this year?"

"Not the best. Those darn birds keep eating my seeds. I tried covering them with garden fabric, but some critter ripped it right off. I'm guessing it was a squirrel, but who knows?"

"Sounds like the wildlife doesn't want you having a garden this year."

"Seems like it, doesn't it?" She folds her arms over her chest. "My son put some cameras out there so I could see what's going on."

"Some what?" Rachel asks.

"Cameras. So I could see what those critters are up to when I'm not around."

"That seems a bit extreme," Rachel says.

"It's just for fun. My son thought I'd get a kick out of it. Like watching my own nature documentary."

"And what have you seen?" Rachel asks.

"Nothing. Honestly, I forgot they were even there until I just mentioned it."

"It looks like you have a lot of stuff growing," I say to Edith.

"Not as much as I'd like. By this time of year, I should have an entire bed of lettuce and some radishes coming up."

Edith continues talking about the perils of growing vegetables while Rachel reads her magazine, occasionally glancing up at Edith with annoyance, like she wishes she'd hurry up and leave.

She finally does around noon, but not before making me lunch. She made me the absolute best grilled cheese, which had me wanting to take her up on her offer to replace Rachel as my caregiver. But I know Logan would never accept that.

CHAPTER EIGHT

"I didn't think she'd ever leave," Rachel groans, sitting beside me on the couch.

"I liked having her here. It was nice to have some company." I see Rachel's hurt expression and realize that sounded bad. "Not that you aren't company. I just meant... I don't know what I meant. Sorry."

With my brain injury, sometimes I can't find the words to finish my thoughts, or I'll forget what I was going to say in the middle of saying it.

"No need to apologize." She forces out a smile. "Edith can be quite entertaining. The stories she comes up with are so outrageous you just have to laugh. I hope she doesn't truly believe them, because if she does, she should probably be in a home."

"What stories?"

"Like what she says about the neighbors. Pure fiction, but she tells it like it's fact. When I first met her, I actually believed her. It wasn't until I talked to you that I found out her stories were made up. I think she does it to get attention, or maybe she's just losing it."

"Did she tell you stuff about me?"

"Of course. She had stories about everyone."

"What did she say about me?"

"I really shouldn't tell you. It's not true, so why talk about it?"

"Because I want to know."

"Okay, well…" Rachel sighs. "She said you and Logan were having problems and that she'd heard you fighting."

Edith just told me the exact same thing about Rachel and Connor. I assumed it was true, given their separation, but maybe she'd made it up. She definitely made up the stuff about Logan and me. I'm sure we fought now and then, but every couple does. That doesn't mean our marriage was in trouble.

"What else did she say?"

"I think that was it for you and Logan."

"But it wasn't true. We weren't having problems. Were we?"

"Of course not. Forget Edith. She just wanted to gossip, so she made up stories about everyone."

"But what if we *were* having problems? And Logan didn't tell me?"

"You weren't. Believe me. I know you two better than crazy old Edith does. Connor and I hung out with you guys all the time, and I can't remember you two bickering or saying even one unkind word to each other."

"I'm sure we did. No one's perfect."

"Well, obviously, you could've argued when I wasn't around, but I doubt it. Logan is crazy about you. And you're crazy about him. What would you have to fight about?"

I really can't say since I can't remember the past two years. I know we argued a few times during our first year of marriage, but it was never over anything serious. What if that changed? What if Edith was right and Logan and I were having problems? But what problems? And how long did they last?

"If I were you," Rachel says, "I'd stay away from Edith. She loves stirring up trouble, and the last thing you need is more stress. She's a nosy old lady with too much time on her hands. I hate that she lives right behind us. If I'd known about her before we moved here, I would've picked somewhere else to live."

"On the plus side," I say, wanting to lift the mood, "her banana bread is the best I've ever had."

"I wouldn't eat anything that woman made. I'd assume she'd ground up one of her poisonous plants in it."

"She has poisonous plants?"

"Probably. Her garden's like a jungle. She grows everything back there, even pot."

"Edith has marijuana plants?"

"She had them even before it was legal, or that's what she told me, but knowing her, that story was probably true. I'm telling you, Avery, the woman is nuts. You should stay away from her."

I think she's nice. And I like her stories, even if not all of them are entirely true.

"I'm going to take a nap," I say, getting up.

"Good idea!" Rachel says, like she was hoping I would so she'd get some time alone.

I'm not sure this arrangement is going to work. We're half a day in, and I'm really not comfortable around her. Our conversations seem forced, and she seems annoyed that she has to be here. She keeps checking her watch like she can't wait for the day to be over.

MY NAP LASTS for three hours, and when I wake up, I hear talking in the other room. As I listen closer, it sounds like Logan's voice.

"She just needs some time," he says.

"Maybe this isn't a good idea," Rachel says. "I don't think I'm—"

"You are. And this is what we decided. I'll talk to her. Don't worry about it."

"Okay, then I guess I'll see you later."

I hear the door open and close, then Logan's heavy footsteps as he walks to my room. He peeks past the door.

"I'm awake," I tell him. "I just woke up."

He walks over to me. "How was your day?" He leans down to kiss my forehead.

"It was okay."

"I just talked to Rachel. She said you had a visitor."

"Yeah, Edith. She brought over some banana bread. The best I've ever had."

He sits down on my bed. "I thought we talked about visitors."

"We did, and we don't agree. If Rachel can be over here, why can't other people?"

"Rachel is your caregiver. Other people are just tiring you out and carrying germs into the house."

"Logan, I'm not sick. I can be around germs."

"They drilled a hole in your head," he says. "You want to risk it getting infected?"

"It won't." I point to the side of my head. "It's covered. How are germs going to get in?"

"Why risk it? You want to end up back in the hospital?" He says it with anger not concern, almost like he blames me for landing myself in the hospital.

"What's going on with you? Did you have a bad day?"

"No, not until I got home and found out that my wife let some crazy old woman spend all morning here."

"It was only a few hours, and I liked having Edith here. All we did was talk. What's wrong with that?"

"I'll tell you what's wrong." He gets up from the bed. "For one, she's been arrested multiple times. I don't want a criminal in my house."

I look at him in disbelief. "What was she arrested for?"

"Protesting. Smoking pot. I don't know the whole list, but I'm sure she'd be happy to tell you. She's proud of her arrests, which should be enough of a reason not to trust her."

"Protests and pot? That's it? Pot's not even illegal anymore."

"It was when she got arrested."

"Okay, but that's not enough of a reason to ban her from coming over. What are your other reasons?"

"She makes up lies." He folds his arms over his chest. "About you and me."

"What about us?" I ask, seeing if his story matches Rachel's.

"She used to tell everyone that we were having problems. She claimed she heard us fighting, which maybe she did, but what couple doesn't argue now and then?"

"Why do you care what she says?" I challenge. "Neighbors gossip about each other all the time. It's annoying, but not uncommon."

"I'm in the public eye. I'm on the city council now. Do you really think I want some old lady spreading rumors that I don't get along with my wife?"

"So that's what this is about? You're worried what people will think?"

"Of course I'm worried. Do you know the scrutiny a politician is under? People watch our every move. If I so much as look at someone the wrong way, it could end up in the papers."

"Nobody reads the paper, Logan. And I don't think people are that interested in some city council member. It's not like you're the mayor or the governor."

"And I never will be if people like Edith go around spreading lies about me."

"Are you saying you want to be mayor?" This is news to me.

"It's the next logical step. I could do a lot more if I were mayor. Just think of all the housing projects I could get approved. I'd actually make a difference."

"You already make a difference," I remind him. "And the plan was never for you to be in politics. You were going to work your way up at your job, which you've done."

"And I'm finding it takes years to get through all the red tape simply to put up one building. I've realized I have to be on the inside."

"You're saying you'd quit your job to be a politician?"

"I obviously couldn't run a city this size and still keep my job," he tells me, as if I was failing to keep up. "And if I decided to run for governor, I'd need to devote time to fundraising and events."

"You're joking, right?" I say with a laugh. "You're not actually considering being the mayor? Or the governor?"

"Why is that funny?" he says with an edge to his tone. "You don't think I can do it?"

"I'm just surprised. You've never mentioned this before."

"We're getting off track. The point I'm making is that we need to surround ourselves with people who support us, and Edith isn't one of them."

"You mean support *you*," I say, getting annoyed with him.

"If that's how you want to think of it, then fine. But the way I think about it, we're a team. We help each other out. And that means staying away from people who are trying to sabotage us."

"Edith is not trying to sabotage us," I insist. "She's a kind and funny old lady."

"Why are you being so difficult?" he says, his voice increasing in volume. "I ask you to do one simple thing, and you refuse!"

"Logan, stop it. Stop yelling at me."

He looks down, rubbing his hand through his thick dark hair. "You're right. I'm sorry. I shouldn't have yelled." His eyes rise to mine. "And I shouldn't be fighting with you." He sits beside me on the bed. "It's my fault. I had a tough day, and I'm taking it out on you."

"What happened?"

"I couldn't focus." He sighs. "I had a million things to do, and I couldn't get a single one of them done."

"Because you've been gone for so long?"

"Because I felt like I shouldn't be there. I kept thinking about you. Worrying about you. Feeling guilty that I left you."

"Logan, I'm fine. If I wasn't, they wouldn't have released me from the hospital."

He rubs my hand. "I don't want to lose you, Avery."
"You won't." I smile at him. "You're stuck with me."
He smiles back. "I'm a lucky man."

CHAPTER NINE

It's Friday, and the first day all week that Logan's been home with me. I'm not surprised. I knew once Logan was back at the office, he'd get drawn into projects and meetings that couldn't be done remotely.

I'm glad he's home today. I'm getting used to Rachel, but I'd still rather have Logan here. Truthfully, I'd rather be alone so I could do what I please and not be so closely monitored. Rachel follows me around and is constantly asking me how I feel. It's too much, and I've told her that, but she doesn't listen. She's doing what Logan told her to, like he's the boss and she's simply following his orders. It makes me wonder if he's paying her to do this.

"You're up," Logan says, coming into the guest room.

I've been staying in this room since I got home from the hospital. Logan didn't want to risk sleeping next to me and accidentally bumping my head. But I doubt he'd bump me hard enough to cause any damage. Even the doctor said we'd be fine sleeping in the same bed, but my overly cautious husband insists we sleep apart for at least a few more weeks.

"I was watching a movie and wanted to see the end." I pick up the remote and turn off the TV.

"Did you take your meds?"

"Yes, and they're making me drowsy. I think I'll take a nap."

"That's a good idea. I'll be in my office if you need me."

"Do you have a meeting?"

"I do." He checks his watch. "It starts in a few minutes. I wanted to see if you needed anything before I got on the call."

"I'm good for now." I smile at him. "How long is the meeting?"

"Probably an hour, although it could be done sooner. Why do you ask?"

"I just wondered." I yawn. "I'm really tired. The meds are kicking in."

"Get some rest. I'll check on you after my meeting."

"You don't need to. You might wake me up."

"I'll make sure to be quiet," he says as he closes the door.

I wait until I hear him go into his office, then I shove the covers off. I'm not taking a nap. I'm sick of napping. It's all I do. I'm bored out of my mind. Even movies and magazines aren't entertaining me anymore. I need to get outside, go to a restaurant, ride in a car. All the things I used to take for granted or think were dull, ordinary activities now seem like exciting adventures. I've begged Logan to take me out, but he thinks it's too soon.

I make my way down the hall to the master bedroom. I want to look through my things and see if any of them jog my memory. Logan would tell me that doing this will stress my brain, which is why I'm doing it while he's on a call. I have to take advantage of what little time I have to myself when Logan isn't hovering over me.

When I'm in our room, I go over to the dresser that Logan and I share. His drawers are at the top, and mine are on the bottom. I carefully lower to my knees, then sit down on the floor. I don't need to be this cautious, but I'm doing it because I'm so afraid of falling again. At least the bedroom is carpeted, making me feel more stable than I do on the tiled floors.

Pulling out the bottom drawer, I see stacks of heavy sweaters appropriate for fall or winter. Opening the drawer above it, I see more sweaters and some pairs of flannel pajamas. This must be where I store my out-of-season clothes.

Taking out a sweater, I unfold it and hold it up. It's a deep purple color with a thin silver stripe going down each arm. It doesn't look like something I would like, but I must have thought it was pretty or comfortable or something, or why would I have bought it?

Pulling the sweater to my face, I close my eyes and sniff the fabric, seeing if the scent will conjure up any memories. I read online that some of our best memories are linked to our senses, like the smell of your grandma's cookies baking in the oven. I'm hoping the sweater will hold a scent that might trigger a memory, but as I hold my nose to it, all I smell is the lavender sachet that was in the drawer.

Setting the sweater down, I take another one out. It's bright red, like something I might have worn at Christmas. Closing my eyes, I bring the sweater to my nose, but again I smell nothing but the lavender from the sachet. Tossing it aside, I take out another sweater and then another. Not a single one of them looks familiar.

How is that possible? I have memories from a few years

ago. I'm sure I had these sweaters back then, unless I completely changed my wardrobe over the past two years. But I can't imagine I'd do that. I've never been someone who's into fashion trends. If I find something I like, I keep it for years, even if it's not the latest style.

When I've cleared out the drawer, I look at the sweaters spread around me, trying once again to connect a memory to any of them. But there's nothing, not even a feeling that might go along with the memory.

It's so frustrating. Even when I think the memories are there, I discover they're not. Like the other day, I was in the kitchen and had a sudden memory of making dinner. I saw myself pulling salmon from the fridge and cooking it in a skillet. I was wearing a black apron, jeans, and a cotton shirt with the sleeves rolled up.

When Logan got home, I couldn't wait to tell him. I was beyond thrilled. I assumed that was just one of many memories that would soon come flooding back. But then Logan told me I've never cooked salmon in the entire time he's known me. I must've been so desperate for a memory that I made it all up. Or I might've seen someone on TV making salmon and created a memory of myself doing it.

The mind is a tricky thing, especially when it's been injured. It can create false memories to make up for the real ones. My doctor warned me this could happen, and unfortunately, it's happened several times. The salmon memory was just one of many I thought was real but wasn't.

As I'm folding up the sweaters and putting them away, I remind myself that recovery is a process, and everyone's experience is different. The doctors said it could take months before my mind releases the memories trapped inside it, but they assured me they're still there. I guess that's a reason to be hopeful. At least they're not gone forever.

"What's this?" I mutter to myself as I pick up a business card. It must have fallen out of the pocket of one of my sweaters. "Harris Row Shelter?"

Turning the card over, I see something written on it. It looks like a phone number, but the ink is smudged, so I can't make out the numbers. Why did I keep this? Did I want to volunteer there? Or maybe I did and don't remember.

Holding up the card, I consider tossing it, but then decide to keep it. Maybe when I'm able to, I'll go down there and ask about volunteer opportunities. Given all my health problems, I doubt I'll be going back to a regular job anytime soon.

What's strange is that the symptoms I had before the accident seem to be gone. According to Logan, I used to have stomach problems, joint pain, and extreme fatigue, but I haven't experienced any of that since my accident. It's as if the trauma to my brain somehow fixed my autoimmune disease, but that doesn't make sense. Maybe the medications I'm taking are helping.

Hearing Logan's footsteps in the other room, I hurry and put the sweaters back into the drawer, along with the card. I didn't get a chance to look through the other drawer. I'll have to do it later. I shut both drawers and get up to my feet just as Logan walks in.

"What are you doing in here?" he asks, his brows drawn together.

"Getting my earrings," I say, opening the jewelry box on top of the dresser. Logan wouldn't be happy knowing I was just on the floor, pulling open a heavy drawer, so I'm going to keep that to myself.

"Why do you want your earrings?" he says with a slight grin. "You planning to go somewhere?"

"Could we?" I walk over to him. "I've been cooped up here for weeks. I need to get out. Let's go to dinner. It can be somewhere close. Isn't there that cute Mexican restaurant down the street?"

He pauses, his eyes examining me, then says, "You remember that? The Mexican place?"

"I think so. Does it have a pink flamingo out front?"

"Yeah. It does." His face breaks out in a smile. "Honey, you just remembered something! That's amazing!" He leans down to hug me. "Why aren't you more excited?"

"Because it's been there for years," I say with a sigh. "I remember going there the week we moved into the house."

"Well, at least you remembered it," Logan says, trying to remain positive. "You love their guacamole. You order it every time we go."

"Really?"

"Yeah. Why?"

"I remember not liking it. It was too salty, and they added way too much garlic."

"They must've changed the recipe, because now you love it."

"Let's go there now. We can order the guacamole, and I can see if I still like it."

"Honey, no." Logan sets his hand on my shoulder and leans down to me. "I understand you want to get out of here, but it's too soon."

"Why? It's just dinner. It's not like I'm doing anything strenuous."

"I don't want to take any risks. You've been doing so well. Why hinder your recovery?"

"I'm not—" I stop myself, knowing it's pointless to argue. No matter what I say, he'll tell me I'm not ready to go out.

"What if we order it in?" he asks. "Would you like that?"

"Sure." I smile at him, appreciating his effort. I know he's trying to cheer me up. It's not easy being my caretaker, especially when he works full-time and serves on the city council. "Could we order now? I know it's kind of early, but I'm hungry, and Mexican sounds good."

He gets out his phone. "Let me pull up the menu."

"Hey, do you know anything about Harris Row Shelter?"

"Of course I know about it," he says like I'm an idiot for asking. "It's part of my job. I know all the shelters in town."

"Yes, I didn't mean it that way. I meant, do you know if I ever volunteered there?"

"If you did, you never told me. Why do you ask?"

"I found this—" I stop, uncertain as to whether I should mention the card. Something inside me is telling me not to, but I don't know why.

"You found what?" Logan asks, his head cocked to the side.

"A listing of volunteer jobs," I say, not sure why I'm lying. "The shelter was one of the places listed as being in need of volunteers."

"Avery, you are not volunteering. You're still recovering."

"I know, but later, when I'm better, I'd like to volunteer."

"No. I don't want you doing that. Those shelters are in dangerous areas. I will not allow you to put yourself in harm's way."

My brows rise. "You won't allow it? Logan, I'm not a child. I can go wherever I want."

"You're my wife, and I won't have my wife going to

sketchy parts of town to hang out with a bunch of homeless women."

His sharp, judgmental tone takes me by surprise, along with his insistence that I not volunteer. We met volunteering. It's something we both value.

"Logan, these are the people you're trying to help. Why wouldn't you want me to help them too?"

"We're not discussing this. There's no point. You're not even close to being ready to volunteer given your health and what you've been through." He looks back at his phone. "I've got the menu here. You want to see it, or should I just order your favorites?"

"I'd like to see it." I reach for his phone but instead of giving it to me, he comes up beside me and scrolls through the menu.

"How about the fajita platter?" he says.

"It has onions. I hate onions."

He sighs, sounding frustrated. "You order the fajitas almost every time we go there."

"Really?" I say. "Then I guess I must ask for them without onions."

"No, Avery, you don't. You order fajitas as they come, with onions."

That can't be right. I wouldn't order something with an ingredient in it I don't like. Would I?

This keeps happening. I keep finding things out about myself that sound nothing like me. Did I really change that much after getting married? I didn't think I did, but I guess it's possible.

When did it happen? Because I know it wasn't early in our marriage. We've been married for three years, and I remember most of the first one. I was the same Avery I was when I was single. So what changed? When did I become a different version of myself?

CHAPTER TEN

Later that night, when I'm alone in the guest room, I find myself unable to sleep. Spending my days lying around doesn't tire me out, so by the time I go to bed, I can't sleep.

Reaching over to turn on the bedside light, I decide to get up and do a little snooping. I guess it's not snooping in my own house, but that's how it feels. It's like some other woman used to live here and I'm just a guest. The woman I used to be, the one Logan describes, doesn't even sound like me.

According to Logan, I quit my job because of my illness and spent all my time at home. He told me I refused to go out, even for dinner, because of how I looked. Apparently, I kept breaking out in a rash that went up my neck and face, likely caused by my autoimmune disease. The thing is, the old me would go out despite how I looked. I've never been someone who's overly concerned with my appearance. I'm not saying I don't like to look nice, but I'm not glamorous like some women. I've never cared about wearing designer clothes, and I've always worn very little makeup. So I can't imagine telling Logan I couldn't leave the house because of a rash.

I'm starting to wonder if my autoimmune disease was affecting my brain, causing personality changes I wasn't aware of or didn't notice. I'm surprised Logan didn't point them out to me, or maybe he did, and I told him I was fine. But if I became someone who refused to leave the house, wouldn't he try to get me help?

Maybe I misinterpreted what he said. I'm sure I went out, just not as much as I used to. That's probably what he meant.

I go into the bathroom and flip on the light. I walk up to the cabinet and open the top drawer. It's filled with medication bottles. Picking one up, I see it's the painkillers I was given when I left the hospital. I've been slowly weaning myself off them, hoping I'll no longer need them soon. Sorting through the other meds, I see more painkillers, dated last year. I must've had pain related to my autoimmune disease, but it's concerning that it was bad enough for me to need a prescription.

I pick up another bottle and see a drug I don't recognize. I look up the name online on my phone. It's an antidepressant.

When did I start taking drugs for depression? I check the date and see the prescription was filled last summer. Is that why I didn't want to go out? Because I was depressed?

I find another drug I don't recognize. I look up the name and see that it's a drug to treat anxiety. I've never had anxiety, or not that I can remember. But the bottle has my name on it, and most of the pills are gone, so I clearly took them at some point. The date on the bottle indicates it was last fall.

I'm not someone who takes pills. I've always sought out natural remedies, so why do I have all these prescriptions? Was I feeling that bad that I felt I had to resort to pills?

"Avery?" I hear Logan's voice from the other room. "Avery, where are you?" He sounds concerned, almost panicked.

"In here," I say, tossing the meds back in the drawer.

"Are you okay?" he asks.

I turn around and see him standing at the door to the bathroom.

"I'm fine. I just couldn't sleep. Why are you up?"

"I heard a noise and wanted to check on you."

"That's sweet, but I'm okay. You can go back to bed."

"I'll wait for you to go first." He steps aside. "Go ahead."

I wasn't planning to go back to bed. I'm still wide awake, but I know Logan won't leave until I'm safely in the bed.

"Get some rest," he says, pulling the covers over me and kissing my cheek.

"How long are we going to do this?"

"Do what?"

"Sleep in different rooms. I feel weird being in the guest room. I want to sleep with you in our room."

"Not yet," he says, sitting down on the bed. "Your head is still healing. I'd feel terrible if I bumped you in the night and caused more damage."

"You won't." My tone is insistent. "The incision is mostly healed, and it's covered. Come on, Logan. This has gone on long enough."

"I'm sorry, but the answer is no. I wouldn't get any sleep if you were beside me. I'd be too worried I might hurt you."

"Then when? When can we go back to sleeping in the same bed?"

"I don't know. We'll discuss it later, after your next doctor's appointment."

That isn't for another week. I guess I can wait that long, even if it is unnecessary.

Logan checks the clock by the bed. "It's after midnight. Try to sleep." He gets up. "I'll check on you in the morning."

As he walks to the door, I remember the pills I found. I could ask him this later, but I don't want to wait. If I do, I'll be up all night wondering about it.

"Logan?"

He was about to leave but turns back. "Yes?"

"Was I depressed?"

He lets out a sigh. "Avery, it's late."

"I want to talk about it."

"Honey, I need to get to bed," he says, rubbing his face. "I'm exhausted, and I need to be up in a few hours."

"Why? It's Saturday."

He pauses, looking like he forgot what day it is. "Yes, fine, but I still need to get to sleep."

"Would you please answer the question? I need to know why I was taking those pills."

He remains at the door and looks down, then back up at me. "Yes. You were depressed, to the point that you asked for medication."

"That doesn't sound like me. I hate taking pills."

"You were desperate to feel better. Your illness was getting worse. None of your symptoms were improving. The doctors didn't know how to help you. You felt hopeless, like things would never change. Some days, you could barely get out of bed. I didn't know what to do. How to help you. So I took you to see someone, and he prescribed the medication."

"What about the anxiety meds? Did he prescribe those too?"

"Yes. And they helped, at least for a while, then you got bad again."

"Bad, how? What do you mean?"

"You became confused. Said things that weren't true."

"What things?"

"I don't want to get into it. It doesn't matter. It wasn't you saying those things. It was your illness. It was affecting your mental health."

"In what way? What was wrong with me?"

"You were confused. That's all. You were making things up in your head and thinking they're real."

"And you're only telling me this now?" I shove the covers off and get up.

"Avery, go back to bed."

"No." I walk over to Logan, angry that he kept this from me. "Why didn't you tell me I was having mental health issues?"

"Because it's no longer a problem. You're fine now, or it appears that you are. You haven't made any odd comments or accusations."

"Accusations?" I frown. "What are you talking about?"

He leans down to me, gripping my shoulders. "It's over. We're going to leave it in the past."

"I don't want to leave it in the past. I want to know what happened. What I said."

"I'm not getting into this. It's late, and you need your rest." He nods toward the bed. "Go to sleep. I'll see you in the morning."

He turns and leaves, shutting the door behind him.

I return to bed, but there's no way I'm going to sleep, not

after finding out I was having mental issues. It sounds like I was hallucinating or delusional, both of which could've been a side effect of the medications, but it's still concerning.

I need to talk to Mia. She'll tell me what I want to know. She's never lied to me, at least not about anything that matters. If I want the whole story, and not just pieces of it, I need to ask my sister.

CHAPTER ELEVEN

"I'm heading to the store," Logan says, coming up to me on the couch. "You need anything?"

"No, I'm good. Do you have the list?"

He pulls it from his pocket. "Right here." He gives me a kiss. "I'll see you soon."

"You don't need to hurry. I'll be fine."

He smiles. "Are you trying to get rid of me?"

"No, but it'll be nice to have a little time to myself."

"Am I really that hard to be around?"

"Not at all. But I do feel like I'm under a microscope sometimes, like you're watching everything I do."

"It's only because I love you." He gives me another kiss, then finally leaves.

I'm hoping he's gone for at least an hour, but he could be faster than that, which means I need to hurry up and call Mia.

She usually answers right away, so I start to worry when her phone continues to ring. What if she doesn't pick up? This is my only chance to talk to her without Logan listening in. Her phone goes to voicemail. I lean back on the couch, frustrated with myself for not planning ahead. I should've texted her first and told her I was calling.

My phone rings. I pick it up and see Mia's name.

"Oh, thank goodness you called," I say.

"Why? What's wrong?" she asks, sounding panicked. "Is it your health? What happened?"

"Nothing. I'm fine. I just wanted to talk."

"Why do you sound out of breath?"

"Do I?" I pause and notice I'm breathing faster than normal. It's probably because I was so eager to talk to her. "I'm just excited you called. I thought maybe you were out."

"I was. I was doing some shopping. My hands were full, so I couldn't answer the phone, but I'm home now. So what's up?"

"I found something out last night that I wanted to ask you about."

"Yeah, what is it?"

"Was I having mental health issues?"

She's silent a moment, then says, "It wasn't anything serious. I mean, it was serious enough that you saw a doctor, but you always seemed fine to me."

"I didn't seem depressed?"

"Not at all, but it's hard to tell when you talk to someone on the phone. To me, you always made it sound like everything was fine."

"What did Logan tell you? He said he'd been giving you updates about my health."

She sighs. "He wasn't supposed to tell you that. Are you mad at me?"

"No. I understand why you did it. I just wish I'd been the one giving you updates."

"But you wouldn't. You kept saying you were getting better, but I didn't believe you. You wouldn't have quit your job if you were feeling okay."

"So what did Logan tell you?"

"That you were sleeping a lot, not interested in eating or watching TV or really doing much of anything. He said you were feeling hopeless about your health, like it would never get better."

What she's saying matches what Logan said. Why does that surprise me? Why did I think he wasn't telling me the truth?

"Did you know I was on meds for depression?" I ask.

"Yes, which surprised me since you're so against taking pills, but I think you needed them. Before you started taking them, Logan said you wouldn't even get out of bed."

"I don't get it. I've never had issues like that before, so what happened?"

"It's like Logan said, you were feeling like you'd never get better. He was so worried about you, Avery. On one of our calls, he broke down crying. He couldn't bear to see you suffer. You're lucky to have such a caring husband. I've heard a lot of men leave the marriage if their wives become seriously ill, but Logan's become even more dedicated to you. He'd stay home with you every day if he could."

"Yeah, I know. He's been great," I say.

It's true, except for the lack of freedom he gives me. Sometimes I feel like I'm being held prisoner in this house. I know he's just worried about my health, but it's getting to be too much.

"I wish I could find a decent guy," Mia says. "I went out with a guy last night and he showed up with his mom."

I laugh. "You're joking, right?"

"No. I'm serious. He actually brought his mom to the restaurant to meet me. He said if a girl doesn't get his mom's approval, he doesn't date her."

"And? Did you pass the test?"

"Yes, but I told him never to call me again. Are there no good men left? Because all I can find are losers who don't work, have horrible hygiene, or bring their mom to the date. Sometimes, if I'm really *lucky*, all three."

"I'm sorry," I say, trying not to laugh. "That's horrible. I think you're just having a string of bad luck. There *are* good men out there."

"Maybe I should volunteer somewhere. That's how you met Logan, and look how that turned out. He's the perfect husband."

She's being very complimentary to Logan, which makes me wonder if Logan's comments about her not liking him were exaggerated.

"Mia, did you use to have a problem with Logan?"

"No. Why do you ask?"

"He said something about you not liking him because of..." I hesitate, not sure I should bring this up. I'm sure it happened, but probably not to the extent Logan implied. And she's obviously over it, so why bring up the past and reignite old feelings that could make her dislike Logan again?

"Because of what?" she asks.

"Never mind. It doesn't matter."

"What did Logan tell you?"

"Let's not talk about it. It's the past. I know it was just your grief making you say those things."

"My grief? What are you talking about?"

"Your grief over losing John. You wanted to blame someone, so you blamed Logan."

"Blamed him for what?"

"For bringing John the cigarettes. The ones that caused the fire."

"I didn't blame Logan. He bought the cigarettes, but he didn't make John smoke them. And if Logan hadn't bought them, John would've gone out and got them himself."

Am I remembering the story wrong? I could've sworn Logan told me Mia blamed him for the fire. That's not something I'd forget.

"So you were never angry at Logan?"

"I was, but I kept it to myself. I never told him. And I got over it."

"So if it wasn't the cigarettes," I ask, "then why were you angry?"

"Because he wasn't letting you see John. He kept finding excuses for why you couldn't go over there, and when John went to your house, Logan would hurry him to leave."

"How do you know this?"

"John told me. He said whenever he tried to see you, Logan would cut the visit short, like he'd come up with a reason why you two had to leave."

"I don't think that's true. I remember the months before John died. He acted like he was too busy to see me. It wasn't Logan keeping me from John. It was John who didn't have time for me."

"That's not the impression I got, but who knows? I'm sure there's some truth to both their stories, along with some fabrication. It wasn't any secret those two didn't get along."

"Logan and John?"

"Yes. Don't you remember after the wedding? When Logan and John were arguing in the parking lot?"

"They weren't arguing. They were just talking really loud because they'd had too much to drink."

"They were arguing," Mia insists. "I heard them. John told Logan he didn't trust him and Logan got upset. It got so heated that I sent Brad out there to break it up."

"Brad? Your date?"

"Yeah, he was a nice guy," she says, in a wistful tone. "Too bad it didn't work out."

"Why would John tell Logan he didn't trust him?"

"Because he's your big brother," Mia says, like it's obvious. "Big brothers never trust guys with their sister. It's like a rule or something."

"He wasn't that way with anyone *you* dated."

"I'm the oldest. He didn't look out for me the way he did you. And I didn't need him to. If a guy was being a jerk, I told him to get lost. You were more of a pushover."

"I'm not a pushover."

"You can be, especially with a guy you really like. And you really liked Logan, even after a few dates."

"You're saying I'm a pushover with Logan?" I roll my eyes. "Good to know you think so highly of me."

"I didn't mean it as an insult. What I meant is that when you really like a guy, you let things slide to avoid conflict. Like with your wedding. You wanted to get married on the beach, but Logan talked you into having it at a fancy hotel."

"I was fine with either option."

"Maybe, but your dream was the beach. You even made a vision board in college of what your wedding would look like. Do you remember that?"

"Yes, but I was twenty. I didn't get married until I was thirty. People change a lot in ten years. As I got older, I realized a beach would be messy and was weather-dependent. It was more practical to get married at the hotel. We could invite more people, and we didn't have to worry about getting rained on."

"Let's talk about something else. I didn't mean to upset you. Tell me what you and Logan are up to this weekend."

"Nothing. He still doesn't want me leaving the house."

"It's probably for the best. I mean, you do have a hole in your skull. People are going to stare."

"My incision is covered, and I could wear a hat. I really don't care if people stare. I'm not letting that stop me from going out. Logan wouldn't even let me go to the Mexican restaurant down the street last night. We could've been there and home within an hour."

"Sorry, but I'm with Logan on this. I don't think you should be going out yet. If you're bored, why don't you read some magazines? Or binge-watch some shows?"

"I've done all that. Rachel brought me a whole stack of magazines and I've already read them all."

"How's that going? Are you back to feeling like you're friends with her?"

"No," I say flatly. "I'm not sure we ever were."

"You were. Logan used to tell me how you and Rachel were always going shopping. Going out for drinks. Having each other over for a glass of wine. It sounds like you two were really good friends."

"Then why do I feel so uncomfortable around her?"

"Maybe because she's taking care of you? I'm sure it's strange to go from having her be someone you get a drink with to someone who's making sure you don't fall over in your own house."

"Yeah, that's part of it. I feel like she's babysitting me, which is awkward."

"Then don't think of it that way. Just pretend she's coming over to hang out like she did before."

"I would if I remembered that. But I can't. She almost seems like a stranger."

"How much longer will she be coming over?"

"Logan and I haven't talked about it. Every time I bring it up, he says we'll talk about it later. I really don't need her. All she does all day is look at her phone and read magazines."

"But don't you feel better having someone there?"

"No. If something happens, I'll just call for help. I always have my phone on me."

"Yeah, but what if you were unconscious, like last time?"

"That's not going to happen. I'm super careful when I walk, and I make sure not to carry anything. The reality is, I eventually have to be on my own, so why not start now? I feel okay. I'm not having any of the symptoms I had with the autoimmune disease."

"Really? That's strange."

"I know, right? I don't get it. It's like hitting my head fixed my other health problems."

"You've been resting a lot more. Maybe that's helped."

"I don't think so. I rested a lot before and still felt sick, or that's what Logan said." I check the time. "Speaking of Logan, he'll be home soon."

"He left you alone?"

"Just to go to the store. It's only down the street. It's not far."

"I'm still surprised he did it."

"I am too. It's nearly impossible to get him to leave my side. I hardly have a moment to myself. Yesterday, he worked from home and had meetings most of the day, which was great. I could finally get up and do stuff."

"What'd you do?"

"I went through some of my things, trying to see if they'd jog my memory."

"Did it work?"

"No, but I didn't get very far. I went through one of my drawers in the bedroom. It was full of winter sweaters, ones I don't remember wearing. They don't even look like my style. It's weird, but I feel like I don't even know who I used to be."

"What do you mean?"

"Like what I ate. How I dressed. What I did. None of it sounds like me."

"You changed after you got married," Mia admits, "but that's normal. Most people do."

"How, though? Because from what I can remember, I changed a little, but not a lot. I definitely didn't change how I dress."

"You did. I saw pictures. You went from wearing T-shirts and jeans to a more mature look, or I guess sophisticated is a better word. You wore more blouses and sweaters. Skirts. Dresses. Personally, I think you looked great. Very professional and upscale."

"But that's not me. I'm casual, always have been. So why would I dress that way?"

"I don't know. I just assumed you wanted to try a different style."

"Did I tell you that?"

"We didn't talk about it, to be honest." She pauses. "Oh, shoot, someone's at the door."

"I can let you go."

"You don't have to. Let me check who it is."

"Logan will be home soon, so I should go. Let's talk later."

"Okay. Have a fun weekend!"

It won't be fun. I'll be stuck in the house with Logan checking on me every few minutes. I need to find ways to get him out of the house so I can go through more of my things.

Something isn't adding up. The sweaters that aren't my style? That business card for the shelter? Logan saying Mia blamed him for John's death when she didn't?

Why would Logan say that about Mia if it wasn't true? Maybe I heard him wrong. Or maybe I made it up.

What if I'm not getting better? What if my mind is more damaged than I thought? Is there something Logan's not telling me? Is that why he's being so cautious with me?

CHAPTER TWELVE

I'm not sure how much time I have left before Logan gets home, but there's one more thing I need to do before he gets here.

Looking up Harris Row Shelter on my phone, I find their number and call them.

"Harris Row Shelter," a woman answers.

"Hi, I, um..." I don't know what to say. I should've figured it out before I called.

"Hello?" the woman says. "Are you still there? Do you need help?" Her voice is urgent. She probably thinks I'm an abuse victim in need of a place to stay.

"I just had a question."

"About our services?"

"No, about your volunteers. I was wondering if you had a volunteer by the name of Avery Fairmont?"

"I'm sorry, but I don't have a list of the volunteers."

"I see, but do you know anyone named Avery Fairmont? She's in her early thirties, average height, dark hair."

"No. Why are you asking?" she says in a suspicious tone.

"Oh, um, I met her at a charity event last month, but didn't get her number. She mentioned volunteering at the shelter, so I thought you might have her contact information."

"Can't you just look her up online?"

"I did, but her number wasn't listed. I'll just ask someone else who was there that night. Thank you for your time." I end the call.

It sounds like I wasn't volunteering at the shelter, so why did I have the card? And why was I hiding it? Maybe I was planning to volunteer there but didn't want Logan finding out. He made it clear he didn't want me going there because it's in a dangerous part of town. Was I going to go behind his back and do it anyway? That doesn't sound like me. I've always believed couples should be truthful with each other. Logan does too. It's something we talked about early on in our relationship. Yet here I am, calling my sister and then the shelter with no intention of telling Logan.

What does that mean? Do I not trust my husband? But why wouldn't I? Logan loves me. He's taken such good care of me since I got home from the hospital. But it bothers me that he's reluctant to talk about the time before my accident, the years I can't remember. It's possible he wants me to remember on my own, but then why doesn't he just tell me that?

Checking the time, I'm guessing I only have a few minutes before Logan is home. I go into the master bedroom, to our walk-in closet. Logan's side is neatly organized by clothing type and color, starting with his white dress shirts, then blue dress shirts, and so forth. He has several expensive-looking suits and an assortment of silk ties. When I met him, he owned one suit that he bought at a thrift store, and two dress shirts. Now he has a whole closet full. He's definitely upgraded his wardrobe over the years.

On my side of the closet, I see a row of dresses, some skirts, and several suits.

"Why would I ever wear this?" I say, pulling out a red pantsuit that looks like something you'd wear to a corporate job.

Putting the suit back, I sort through the dresses, noticing how they also look like something you'd wear to an office. Why would I buy these? At my old job, I'd wear jeans with a casual shirt. When I quit and was home all day, I was probably wearing sweats. So when did I wear all these office-style dresses and suits?

"Avery?" I hear Logan say. "Avery, where are you?"

I'm walking out of the closet when I see Logan coming into the bedroom.

"What are you doing?"

"Looking through the closet. I was looking for something to wear."

He walks up to me. "You have clothes in the guest room."

"I know, but I wanted to wear something else. And I thought seeing my clothes might bring back some memories."

"And did it?"

"No. In fact, it confused me." I laugh a little. "The suits. The dresses. They're so fancy. Why would I buy clothes like that?"

"You bought them for me, at least at first. Later, you bought them because you liked them."

"Why would I buy them for you?"

"I was moving up in my career. Positioning myself. I was going to high-profile events and meeting important people. I had to look my best and so did you."

"You asked me to buy nicer clothes?" I say, confirming that's what he means.

"Well, yes. I couldn't have you showing up in jeans and a T-shirt, now could I?"

"I guess that makes sense. But why so many? We couldn't possibly have gone to that many events."

"Once you started dressing better, you wanted to keep it up, even if you were just going out to run errands."

"I wore a red pantsuit to run errands?" I laugh. "Are you kidding?"

"Not at all. Look." He gets out his phone and shows me a photo of myself at the farmer's market. I'm wearing a navy dress with a silk scarf and large sunglasses.

"That doesn't even look like me. When was that taken?"

"Last summer, on a day when you were feeling well enough to go out."

I'm not sure who that woman is, but it's not me. I mean, obviously it's me, but not a version of me I recognize. I've never worn scarves, and that dress is ugly and plain.

"I really bought that dress?" I ask.

"Yes, I was with you. We went on a little shopping spree to upgrade your wardrobe." He smiles affectionately, like he's remembering back to that time. "You were reluctant at first, not sure that the clothes were your style, but then you tried them on and were thrilled. You said they made you feel more confident and sophisticated."

Maybe that's when I bought those sweaters in the dresser. Maybe I decided to change my image and get a whole new wardrobe to go with it. Like Logan said, that would've been around the time he was moving up in his career, going to events and networking. It's possible I was being a supportive wife and dressing in a way that would reflect well on Logan.

"Why don't you go back to your room and rest?" Logan says. "I need to put the groceries away."

"I'm not tired. I think I'll stay here and go through more of my things."

I notice his jaw clench and his eyes dart around. Does he not want me in here?

"This isn't up for debate," Logan says, grabbing my arm. "You need to rest."

"I told you, I'm not tired. And I want to look at my things."

"You can do it later, after you've rested."

I yank my arm away from him. "Stop treating me like a child."

"Stop acting like one," he growls, his eyes narrowed.

"Logan, what is going on?" I ask, my pulse racing. "Why are you being like this?"

He grabs me again and pulls on me as if to make me leave my own bedroom.

"Logan, you're hurting me."

"Because you won't listen!" he yells.

The room goes silent, both of us breathing hard. I stare at Logan, shocked that he's treating me this way. What happened to my soft-spoken, loving husband? It's like he snapped and became someone else.

I don't know what to say or how to respond. I'm angry, but also confused.

Logan sighs and lets go of me. "I'm sorry. I shouldn't have yelled."

"No, you shouldn't have."

"I'm just stressed." His eyes rise to mine, and I see the

old Logan again, the kind, caring man I married. "Going back to work. My city council duties. Caring for you. It's all too much. The stress is overwhelming."

My compassion for him takes over, dispersing any anger I felt. "Logan, I know this is difficult for you." I rub his arm. "But part of that is because you're doing too much. You don't have to keep taking care of me, at least not the way you've been doing. I'm capable of making my own meals and taking my meds. I could even try doing some light housework."

"No." He shakes his head. "Absolutely not."

"Then maybe just let me be on my own more. Like this morning, didn't you enjoy going out and doing something instead of sitting here while I sleep?"

"I don't enjoy grocery shopping." He shrugs, but then he smiles a little. "It's more of a chore."

"Yes, but still, you weren't trapped here at home, waiting on me."

"I'm your husband. It's my job to care for you."

"But it's too much, for both of us. I need to do things for myself. It's good for me. The doctor even said it's part of my recovery, getting back to doing regular things."

"It's too soon, Avery. You're not ready."

"Why? I have more energy now, and my strength is coming back."

"I'm not referring to your body. I'm talking about your mind. You're not ready to be left unsupervised when you're still so confused."

"I'm not confused," I say, although I'm finding this whole scenario confusing. "I'm just struggling to remember."

"Which is causing you to become confused. Like with your clothes. You were talking as if they didn't even belong to you."

"Because they don't look like something I would wear."

"But you did. You picked them out."

"Okay," I admit, "but not remembering doesn't mean I can't care for myself."

"I'm worried about you. You keep saying things that don't make sense or that aren't true. That tells me you're not ready to be on your own without someone caring for you."

"What am I saying that doesn't make sense?"

"I don't want to get into it. It'll just upset you."

"Logan, tell me. What is it?"

"You really don't remember? It just happened. This week."

"I don't know what you're talking about."

He takes my hand and brings me over to the bed to sit down. "You accused me of being responsible for your brother's death."

"No, that was Mia." I turn to him. "You told me the story. You said that's why you two weren't getting along."

Logan shakes his head. "I never said that, Avery."

"You did. You said Mia blamed you for John's death because you bought him the cigarettes."

"It wasn't Mia who blamed me. It was you. I was shocked when you said it. John died years ago. I couldn't figure out why you were bringing it up now and then blaming me for it, years later. It shows how damaged your brain is. You're making up things that never happened."

"No, that's not right." I get up and pace the floor. "You're the one who brought up John's death, and you told me that Mia blamed you for it."

"I'm sorry, honey, but that's not what happened. Call Mia if you don't believe me. Ask her if she ever accused me of being involved in John's death."

I already did. And what she told me aligns with what Logan is saying. That it never happened. She didn't blame Logan for John's death. So why did I think she did? Why did I think Logan told me that if he didn't?

He comes over to me and puts his arm around my shoulder. "Let me help you to your room."

This time I agree to go. Maybe he's right and I do need to rest. My mind must be playing tricks on me, making me believe things that aren't true. But I swear Logan told me that story about Mia blaming him for John's death. I can picture him telling me. I can hear his voice in my head as he said the words.

But now I'm wondering... did I imagine it? I must have, because Mia confirmed what Logan's just told me. But what does that mean? Why am I believing things that never happened?

CHAPTER THIRTEEN

I'm unable to rest. I'm too worried that I'm losing my mind. Even with my brain injury, I wouldn't just make up some story and then forget that I said it. Would I?

Maybe what I'm experiencing is due to damage to a part of my brain that can't tell the difference between reality and fiction. I wish it were that easy an explanation, but I have a feeling it's not. So what else could be causing this? And are there other stories I made up and convinced myself were true?

"You're up," Logan says, coming into my room, a big grin on his face. What's *he* so happy about? I'm having a crisis here. He should be as worried as I am.

"I couldn't sleep."

"Can I make you something? Some tea? Maybe a snack?"

"I don't want anything."

Logan walks over to me. "Honey, what's wrong?"

"What you said earlier. That story about John's death. I don't understand it."

"What don't you understand?"

"Why would I make up a story like that, then mix it up and confuse Mia with me?"

Logan sits down on the bed, facing me. "You had a severe head injury. It's normal to mix things up after something like that. Your brain needs more time to heal."

"But what if it heals and I'm still like this? What if I'm still making up stories months from now? What if I never remember who I was before I hit my head?"

"That's not going to happen," he says, his tone gentle. "You have to stay positive, Avery."

"I'm missing two years of our lives. Two years, Logan! That's most of our marriage. That doesn't concern you?"

"No, because it's only temporary. You'll get those memories back. I know you will."

"And what if I don't?"

"Then we'll look forward instead of back. We have our whole lives ahead of us. We can forget about the past."

"I don't want to forget," I almost shout. "I don't even know who I was the past two years. I have a closet filled with clothes that look like they belong to someone else."

"That's not something to be concerned about. A lot of people change their look, especially when they start a new decade. Being in your thirties, you decided it was time to stop looking like a college kid and dress more appropriately for your age."

"So I went out and bought business suits?" I throw my hands up. "I didn't even have a job."

"Honey, I told you, we were going to a lot of upscale events back then. That's what the suits were for."

"What did I do all day after I quit my job? I know I wasn't feeling well, but I'm sure I didn't spend all day in bed."

"You kept things up around the house. Ran errands. Went out with Rachel."

"What about my other friends?"

He pauses, then says, "You don't really have any, other than your work friends, but you lost touch with them when you got sick and had to quit your job."

"I just stopped talking to them?"

"It was more like they stopped talking to you. But to be fair, they weren't close friends."

I should've worked harder to make friends. Logan and I moved to San Francisco three years ago, right after we got married. I didn't want to leave Seattle, but Logan got a job here, so I agreed to move. While he was at work, I got our apartment set up, did some volunteering, and eventually found a job. I made some friends there, but like Logan said, they weren't close friends.

"So I have nobody," I say. "No friends."

"You were starting to get to know some of Rachel's friends. You went out several times with them for girls' night. You should ask her about them. Maybe when you're better, you can all go out again." Logan cups the side of my face and looks into my eyes. "I promise you things will get better. You just need more time."

I nod. "I need to get up. I think I'll take a shower."

"Make sure to use the chair," he says.

"I will."

Logan bought me a shower chair that looks like something an elderly person would use. It was nice of him to do it, but seeing it just reminds me that I'm not like I used to be. I can't even stand in the shower. I mean, I could, but I risk falling if I do.

"Let me know if you decide you want some tea," he

says, that annoying smile on his face again. I'm sure he's hoping it'll cheer me up, but it just makes me mad. I shouldn't be around him right now. I'm in a really bad mood.

When he's gone, I go into the bathroom and close the door. I'm not really going to shower. I just needed some time alone. I turn the water on in case Logan comes back, knowing he'll race in here and check on me if he doesn't hear the shower running.

I lean against the counter and take some deep breaths, hoping it'll lessen the anger I'm feeling about my situation. I shouldn't be reacting this way. I should be grateful I survived. Grateful I have a caring husband. And a nice house. And good insurance to cover my medical bills. Given all that, I shouldn't be upset, yet I am, because I can't remember who I used to be.

Turning toward the counter, I reach down and open the top drawer, the one that has my meds. I take out a bottle of painkillers and get an idea. I shouldn't do it, but I'm desperate to go through more of my things and I know Logan won't allow it if he's around to put a stop to it.

Opening the toilet lid, I dump the pills in the toilet and flush them down. I wait to make sure they're gone, then turn off the shower. I strip off my clothes, wrap a towel around me, and return to the bedroom, the empty pill canister in my hand.

"Logan," I call out.

"Yeah?" he calls back. "What do you need?"

"Can you come in here?"

He appears at the door. "What is it?"

I bring him the empty pill canister. "These are out. Could you go to the pharmacy and get a refill?"

He holds up the pill canister. "You finished these? I thought it was half full."

"You must be thinking of one of my other pills. I only had one of these left, and I just took it."

"Could you wait until tomorrow? I was going to start dinner soon."

"No. I really need it today. My pain is worse at night. I don't want to risk being without my medication."

"Yeah, okay," he says, sounding reluctant to leave. "I'll see if Rachel can come over."

"I don't need Rachel. I'll be fine."

"Avery, I—"

"You were gone this morning, and nothing happened. I promise you I'll be fine."

He nods. "Okay, I'll leave right now. Need anything else while I'm out?"

I smile. "Would you be willing to stop at the bakery?"

"What bakery?"

"The cupcake place. The one by our old apartment. I'd love one of their strawberry cupcakes with buttercream frosting."

"Honey, that place is, like, forty minutes away."

"I know, but I'd really love a special treat." I rest my hands on his chest and look up at him. "Would you please get me one? Or get a whole dozen! All different kinds! Surprise me!"

My enthusiasm makes him smile. "You're really going to make me drive that far for some cupcakes?"

"You're really going to deny a girl cupcakes after she almost died?"

He sighs. "Okay, cupcakes it is. But while I'm gone, I

want you in bed or on the couch. No walking around. No looking in closets. No going outside."

"Got it. I'll curl up on the couch and watch a movie."

"Go get dressed. I'm going to wait until you're settled, and then I'll leave."

He agreed! I'm shocked, but also thrilled. I'll get at least two hours to myself, maybe three if traffic is bad or the pharmacy is slow. I was just going to send him to the pharmacy, but then the cupcake idea popped into my head. I thought for sure he wouldn't agree to go there, given how far it is, but he did!

"Call if you need me," he says when I'm on the couch, a blanket over me and the TV on.

"I will." I give him a big smile. "Thanks for doing this. I'm really looking forward to those cupcakes."

Moments later, he's gone. I get up and look out the window, watching his car go down the road until it's no longer in sight.

I'm finally alone. Now I just need to figure out what to do next.

CHAPTER FOURTEEN

I decide to start in the master bedroom. That's where most of my things are, and I haven't spent much time in there since getting home from the hospital. I'd like to go through the closet again, but I'll save that for later and look around the bathroom first.

Going with the theory that scents evoke memories, I pick up one of my perfume bottles and smell it. I'd spray some in the air, but then Logan might notice the scent and know I was in here. If he even begins to think I didn't follow his order to stay on the couch, he'll never leave me alone again.

The first perfume doesn't bring back any memories of the past two years, but it does bring back memories of my childhood. It smells like a scent my mom wore. I miss my parents. I wish they were still around. And I wish John were still alive. We were really close. I could tell him anything, and he'd always make me feel better. I wish I could say the same for Logan. He can be very judgmental, or he'll dismiss my concerns, saying I'm overreacting. John would never do that.

He was such a great brother. I was thrilled when he moved here just three months after I did. He said he moved for a job, but I think it was more for me. He had a job he loved in Seattle. He had no reason to move other than to be close to his little sister. I'd never tell Mia this, but John and I had a bond that she and I never will. We just don't click the way John and I did. I miss him so much.

I continue sniffing the perfumes with no success, then arrange them as they were on the tray next to the sink.

Logan's colognes are on a shelf above the toilet. I pick one up and sniff it. It's what he was wearing today. It's a musky scent that I don't really like. It doesn't mix well with his skin. The one next to it has a citrusy scent, which surprises me because it doesn't seem like something Logan would choose to wear.

Picking up the last cologne, I take a sniff. My throat constricts and I stumble back against the wall. I drop the bottle, catching it right before it hits the floor. I notice my hands are shaking as I place the bottle back on the shelf. My stomach is churning, feeling like it's about to lose its contents. It must be that cologne. I'm having some kind of reaction to it.

I'm away from it now, but I can still smell it, almost taste it. It's a smoky scent with a hint of cedar. I'm having trouble breathing. My neck feels like there's a band around it, getting tighter by the second. I feel bile rising, burning my throat. Sensing I'm about to be sick, I open the toilet lid just in time.

When my stomach is empty, I rinse out my mouth and splash cold water on my face. I look at myself in the mirror and see sheer terror in my eyes. What is going on? This can't be an allergic reaction. I'm not itching or sneezing or breaking out in hives.

I go into the bedroom and lie down, taking deep breaths, telling myself I'm fine. I don't know what just happened, but I don't have time right now to figure it out. Logan's probably done at the pharmacy and on his way to the bakery, which means I have to hurry up.

Returning to the bathroom, I open up all the drawers. Two of them contain makeup, way more than I need. I'm not someone who wears a lot of makeup. A little blush, some mascara, and that's about it. But the drawers contain tubes of lipstick, eye shadows, powders, blushes, and several containers of foundation and concealer.

When did I start wearing all this? It must've been when I decided to change my wardrobe, which still makes no sense. Even if I was going for a more sophisticated look, as Logan claims, it seems extreme to get rid of all my old clothes and replace them with new.

Taking out the concealers, I count eight of them, all in subtly different shades. Why did I need so many? I consider tossing some of them out, but then Logan would see them in the trash and know I was in here.

I pull out the tray they were stored in so I can put them back and notice something at the bottom of the drawer. It looks like one of those fold-open mirrors. I pick it up and find the little release latch to open it. When I do, something drops out onto the counter. It's a tiny strip of paper with writing on it.

Don't believe him. It's not your fault.

The words are in my handwriting, but why would I write this? What does it mean? And why did I hide it in a mirror?

The paper drops from my hand as I hear a noise coming from the other room. Is it Logan? Why is he home this soon? Did he decide to skip the bakery?

I pick up the tiny piece of paper and shove it in my pocket, then toss the concealers in the tray and put it back in the drawer.

"Hello?" I yell, walking out of the bathroom. "Logan, is that you?"

He doesn't answer, but I hear that noise again, like a tapping sound.

I walk out of the bedroom and hear more tapping, followed by a muffled voice saying, "Anyone in there?"

I think it's coming from the kitchen. I go back there and see Edith standing outside the sliding glass door. She's in her usual gardening clothes—faded jeans and an old sweatshirt—and holding a small basket covered with a dishtowel.

"I'm coming!" I yell, making my way over. I open the slider. "Sorry it took so long. I was in the bathroom."

"You alone?" she asks, looking behind me.

"Yes, Logan went out to run an errand."

"How long's he gone for?" she asks, going past me to the kitchen.

"I'm not sure." I close the slider. "Maybe another hour?"

"I'm surprised. I didn't think he'd trust you to be alone."

"I'm feeling a lot better. I told him he needs to stop worrying so much. I'm not going to fall."

"That's not what I meant," she mutters, setting the basket down on the center island. "I brought you some berries from my garden. Thought they'd help you get better." She takes the dishcloth off the basket, and I see it's filled with an assortment of fresh berries. "Blueberries are supposed to be good for the brain, so I gave you extra of those."

"They look wonderful. Thank you."

"I'll need the basket back. It's my only one. I've been getting rid of things so my son doesn't have to deal with all my junk when I die."

"EDITH, YOU'RE NOT DYING," I say, smiling at her.

"Everyone's dying," she says, looking in one of the cupboards. "You almost died, and you're young."

"Yes, well, that was unexpected."

"Was it?" she asks, glancing back at me.

A chill goes through me. "What do you mean?"

She opens another cupboard. "This will do." She takes out a large ceramic bowl and sets it next to the basket. "I've already washed them, so no need to rinse them off again." She uses her tan, wrinkled hands to transfer the berries from the basket to the bowl.

As I watch her, my mind goes back to what she said, about Logan not trusting me to be alone. If she wasn't referring to my health, then what was she talking about?

"Why wouldn't Logan trust me?" I say.

She coughs, a husky cough that comes from deep within her chest. "What was that? I didn't hear you."

"The comment you made earlier. When you said something about Logan not trusting me to be alone."

"You forgot everything. All his damn rules." She goes to the sink to wash her hands. "With your memory shot, you might wander outside and talk to someone." She huffs. "Heaven forbid if that should happen."

"I'm not sure what you mean." I walk up to her.

"Before you hurt your head." She turns to me, drying her

hands. "He didn't want you leaving the house, not unless he was with you. He didn't even want you going outside."

"That doesn't sound like Logan," I say, although he did just tell me not to go outside.

"He claimed it was because you were sick," Edith says. "Not just your body, but your head. He said you weren't well, mentally, so you couldn't be trusted to leave the house." She walks back over to the berries and plucks one from the bowl, popping it in her mouth. "Personally, I think it was all horseshit. You seemed perfectly sane to me." She takes a strawberry from the bowl. "Try this. Let me know what you think."

Going over to her, I taste the strawberry. "It's delicious. Very sweet."

"It's because of my compost mix. I spent years getting it just right."

"So Logan thought I was crazy?" I ask, wondering if she misinterpreted something he said. I didn't even know they spoke. Logan doesn't like her, so I can't imagine him talking to her.

"He didn't say crazy. It was something more like struggling mentally." She pops another berry in her mouth. "But I knew what he meant."

"But you thought I was fine," I say, confirming her earlier comment.

"For the most part, yes. The only time you seemed off was when he was pumping you with all those happy pills."

"What happy pills? You mean antidepressants?"

"That's what I'm guessing they were. Whenever you took them, you'd have this weird smile on your face and a dead look in your eyes." She glances around. "You got any coffee?"

"No, but I could make some."

"That'd be nice. Black, with two sugars, please."

"When did I start taking the pills?" I ask as I start tinkering with the coffee machine.

"I don't know. Maybe a year or two ago? It was after your brother died. You were pretty depressed after that, not acting like yourself. I offered you some of my homegrown weed, but you didn't want it. You told me you were taking some pills instead." She shakes her head. "I'm telling you, those pills mess a person up. After you started on them, your whole personality changed. You were dressing differently. You changed your hair. You were wearing all this makeup." She points her finger at me. "And then you got sicker. If you ask me, all the problems you were having were because of those happy pills. If you'd gone with the weed like I told you to, none of that would've happened. You'd be the Avery I knew before, back when you moved here."

The pills didn't make me buy all new clothes and wear more makeup. But it's possible they changed my personality. I've heard they can dampen down your emotions, making you feel numb. I could see why I'd want that after John's death. Losing him was so painful, there were days I could barely get out of bed.

"What was I like before?" I ask, raising my voice over the hiss and splutter of the coffee brewing. "When I first moved here?"

I remember that part of my life, but I want to hear how Edith describes me. Then maybe she'll tell me what happened next, during the time I can't remember. Logan's tried to, but I'm not sure I believe him. And I don't know why.

CHAPTER FIFTEEN

"You were more like you are now," Edith says, holding the mug of coffee I've just made her. "Your eyes had some life to them. You weren't so stiff acting. You could actually have a conversation. Those drugs had you acting like a robot." She rolls her eyes as she scoops sugar into her mug. "Just like he wanted."

"Who?"

"Your husband. If you ask me, he wanted you to get hooked on those pills so you wouldn't go back to how you were, or how you are now."

"Why would Logan want that?"

"So you'd do whatever he said. Men like him don't want their women having a mind of their own. They like to be in control. Most all men were like that back in my day. You see less of it now, but there's still plenty of those jerks around." She leans closer, her eyes on mine. "And yes, I meant to include your husband in that."

"Logan's not a jerk," I protest. "You don't know him like I do. I admit he could be friendlier to some of the neighbors, but he's not a jerk. He really cares about people. That's why he's working so hard to build housing for people who are living on the streets. And why he goes to so many charity events to raise money for good causes. It's also why he got a city council seat. His whole life is dedicated to helping people."

She laughs, her head falling back.

"What's so funny?"

"He's really got you fooled, hasn't he?"

"What do you mean?"

"You think he does all that out of the goodness of his heart?"

"Why else would he do it?" I take a sip of my coffee. "It's not like he's in it for the money. City council is a public service job."

"It's also corrupt. You ever meet an honest politician?"

"Logan's honest. We met volunteering. He'd been helping people for years, long before he got into politics."

"Yeah, well, I've been around a while, and let me tell you, a lot of those do-gooders aren't as good as you think. They hide behind their charities, pretending to care when, really, it's all about them. They get off on the praise people give them."

"I'm sure some people are like that, but not Logan."

"If that's what you want to believe." She motions outside. "You want to go sit out back? It's stuffy in here."

"Um, I probably shouldn't. Logan will be home soon."

"What does that have to do with anything?"

"He doesn't want me going outside. I told him I'd stay on the couch and rest."

"It's just like I said. He tells you what to do, like you can't decide for yourself." She takes a drink of her coffee.

"He's worried about me. He doesn't want me getting hurt."

"Yeah, right. He'd rather be the one to—" She shakes her head.

"To *what*? What were you going to say?"

She sets her coffee mug down. "I can't prove anything, but I don't know how else to explain it. I can't imagine you being that clumsy. You walk just fine when I'm around."

"Clumsy? What are you talking about?"

"You kept bumping into walls. Tripping over things and falling down. Or that's what you said when I asked why you had all those bruises."

"What bruises?"

"The ones on your face. On your arms too."

"It's because of my illness. Logan said I'd get dizzy and bump into things."

"That sounds like him," she huffs. "Trying to make you think you did it to yourself."

I cock my head to the side. "Edith, what are you saying?"

She points her finger at me. "I'm saying you shouldn't believe everything your husband tells you. You ever consider he might be lying?"

"Why would he lie? He has no reason to."

"He does if he's got something to hide."

Logan wouldn't hide things from me. Whenever I ask him about the part of our life I can't remember, he answers immediately. He doesn't hesitate, like he would if he were trying to come up with a lie.

"I'm going to shut up now," Edith says. "My son says I need to stay out of other people's business." She looks me up and down. "It's just a shame, you know? You could've done a lot better." She takes her basket and heads to the door. "Enjoy the berries."

She leaves, shutting the door behind her. I like Edith, but I didn't like hearing her say all those bad things about Logan. She doesn't even know him, so I don't know why she was making all those assumptions about him. Maybe she knows he doesn't like her, so her comments are based on the way he treats her.

But some of the things she said do concern me. Like the happy pills. Was it my idea to take them, or did Logan make me? I'm sure he didn't like seeing me so sad after John died, but he could've got me counseling instead of drugs. And what about the bruises? Why would Edith imply that Logan was somehow responsible for them? It's completely untrue. He's never once laid a hand on me and never would.

The sound of the garage door wakes me from my thoughts. Logan's home, and I've barely had time to look at anything, and what I found—the makeup, that strange note—just confused me more.

"I'm home," Logan yells, coming into the house. He stops when he sees me in the kitchen. "What are you doing up?"

"Getting a drink." I take a glass from the cupboard. "How'd you get back so fast?"

"There's a bakery by the pharmacy. I went there instead of the one by our old apartment."

"Oh," I say, unable to hide my disappointment.

"What's wrong?" Logan brings over the sack from the bakery and sets it on the counter. "You wanted cupcakes. I got cupcakes."

"They're not the same. The other place is known for their cupcakes, and their strawberry ones are my favorite."

"And you think you should get whatever you want?" he

says in a harsh tone. "Maybe you should be grateful I got you anything at all."

"I *am* grateful. It was very nice of you." I open the sack and see two small cupcakes with a thin layer of chocolate frosting that's dried out and cracking. The ones at the cupcake place are jumbo-sized and topped with a thick layer of creamy frosting.

"You gonna eat it or just stare at it?" Logan asks.

Why is he acting like this? Did something happen when he went out?

Taking a cupcake from the sack, I peel off the paper and take a bite. It's a plain vanilla cupcake—my least favorite, something I'm sure Logan knows. The cake part is dry and has no flavor, and the frosting tastes stale.

"It's good," I say, wiping the crumbs from my mouth.

"You could do a better job of acting." He leans back against the counter, his arms folded over his chest.

"I'm not acting."

"Yeah, you are. I can tell. You don't like it, do you?"

"It's not as good as the ones at the other place, but it's okay."

"Not as good," he says, sounding disgusted with me. "You're so damn spoiled, Avery. I go and get you what you want, and it's still not enough."

"Logan, why are you so angry?" I set the cupcake down. "You weren't like this when you left. Did something happen?"

"Why don't you tell me?"

"I don't know what you mean."

He points to the bowl of berries. "Would you like to explain?"

"The berries? Edith brought them over. They're from her garden."

"Did we agree that you could invite people over?"

"I didn't invite her. She showed up at the door."

"Why did you let her in? You told me you would stay on the couch. Isn't that what we agreed?"

"Yes, but—"

"But what?" He storms up to me, planting his hands on the counter on either side of me. "We had an agreement, and you broke it. How can I trust you if you can't follow the simplest instructions?"

"Logan, I don't know what's going on here, but I don't like it. It needs to stop. And you need to calm down."

"Calm down?" he yells, slamming his fists on the counter. "I told you no visitors! And then you let that pot-smoking old hag from next door into our house! You know how much I hate that woman!"

"I don't understand why. She's always been nice to us."

"She's a criminal, Avery! She's been in jail!" He storms away, shaking his head. "Sometimes I don't understand how you can be so stupid."

"I'm not stupid for being friends with our neighbor," I say, angry that he'd describe me that way. "If you don't want to interact with her, fine, but that doesn't mean I can't."

"Yes, Avery, it does." He comes over to me and grabs my arm. "We're a couple, and couples make decisions based on mutual agreement. And I did not agree to let that woman anywhere near this house." He tightens his grip on my arm. "She will not be coming over here again. Do you understand?"

"I'm not—"

"Tell me you understand," he says, squeezing my arm so hard it hurts.

"I understand," I mutter.

I don't like giving in, but I don't want to make him even angrier. Something's going on with him, but now isn't the time to ask.

"We're not discussing this again." He lets me go, and his scowl is replaced with a smile. "Why don't you take your cupcake to your room? You can finish it there."

"I'm not hungry."

"I got you the cupcake." He grabs my arm again. "You're going to eat it."

What is his problem? Has he been drinking? Did he not sleep well last night? Neither are excuses for acting this way, but again, I'm not going to try to reason with him when he's like this.

Grabbing a plate from the cupboard, I put the cupcake on it, then go over to the bowl of fruit. I'm about to take a strawberry when Logan snatches up the bowl and brings it to the garbage. I watch in shock as he dumps the fresh berries into the trash, then puts the bowl in the sink.

He comes back over to me, a slight smile on his face. "Go to your room, honey. I'll bring you some tea."

Who is this man? And what's happened to my husband?

I do what he says, not because he told me to, but to get away from him.

CHAPTER SIXTEEN

"Do you need anything before I go?" Logan asks before he leaves for work on Monday morning.

"No, I'm fine." I feel my muscles stiffen as he gives me a hug.

"Then I'll see you tonight." He leans down and whispers in my ear, "Love you."

I don't say it back. I'm still too angry at him for how he treated me over the weekend. After his outburst on Saturday, he calmed down and was back to his old self. In fact, he was sweeter than usual for the rest of the weekend, but he never apologized for acting the way he did. Maybe I should just forget it and move on, but I haven't been able to yet.

"That must be Rachel," Logan says when the doorbell rings. "I'll go let her in."

As he answers the door, I get out of bed and put on my robe. It's after eight. I'm usually dressed by now, but I just haven't had the energy yet today. I haven't slept well since Saturday's incident with Logan. I'm hoping his behavior was just caused by stress from being back at work. He has a very stressful job, plus his city council role, which is a job in itself, and then worrying about his wife. All that stress could make him, or anyone, unable to contain their anger. But where is the anger coming from? I wish he would open up to me and let me know what's bothering him. Maybe talking about it would help.

"Good morning!" Rachel says, appearing at the door to my room as I fasten the ties on my robe. "I got you a coffee." She holds up a paper cup from the coffee place down the street. "It's a mocha latte. Your favorite!"

"Thanks!" I take the drink from her, and as I take a sip, I see the flash of a memory. I'm at the coffee place, sitting along the window, having my drink. "Oh, wow."

Rachel laughs. "Is it that good? Maybe I should've got one for myself."

"No, it's not that." I look at Rachel. "It was a memory. I saw myself sitting in the coffee shop, having a drink."

"Are you sure it was real? I mean, I'm not doubting you. I just know you've had memories you thought were real that weren't."

"I'm pretty sure this one was real," I say, but now that she said that, I'm wondering if I made it up.

"Let's go sit down, and you can tell me all about it!" she says with excitement. She's probably hoping this will lead to me remembering other things, like the friendship we had.

"There's not much to tell," I say once we're seated in the living room. "I just saw myself sitting in the coffee shop by the window, looking out at the street as I sipped my drink."

"Were you with someone?"

"No, it was just me."

"What else do you remember?"

"Nothing. That was it."

"Do you think this is the start of other memories coming back?"

"Maybe, but I'm not getting my hopes up. I've been trying different things I thought might spark a memory, but so far, nothing's worked."

"What have you tried?" She picks up her drink and takes a sip.

I'm not sure I should tell her how I've been going through my things. She might tell Logan, and I don't want him knowing what I've been up to, or what I've found. I still don't know what that note meant, saying I shouldn't trust him. Was it referring to Logan or someone else? And why would I write that down and then hide it?

"I looked through my closet," I say, since Logan already knows this, so it doesn't matter if she tells him.

"And?" She crosses her legs. "What happened?"

"It just made me more confused. I have all these clothes I can't see myself ever wearing."

"You wore them all the time," she says, smiling at me. "Logan helped you pick them out. You're lucky to have a husband who will go shopping with you. Connor wouldn't even go in a store with me." She rolls her eyes.

"Have you talked to him since he moved out?"

"No." She runs her finger over the rim of her cup. "And honestly, I don't miss him. It's kind of nice not having him around."

Her comment makes me think about my own marriage. I don't miss Logan when he's not here. In fact, I look forward to him leaving. Is it just because I want some time to myself, or do I like not having him around?

Seeing how angry he got with me last weekend makes me wonder if we were having problems before my accident.

But Logan would tell me, wouldn't he? It's possible he wouldn't, I guess, if I was the one who was unhappy and he wanted us to stay together. But why would I have been unhappy?

"So how was your weekend?" Rachel asks.

"It was okay." I sip my latte, wanting to tell her more but not sure if I should.

"Did something happen?"

How did she know that? Can she just tell? If so, maybe we were better friends than I thought.

"It wasn't a big deal. Logan and I had a little argument."

"Oh?" Her brows rise. "About what?"

"I shouldn't talk about it. I need to just forget it. I'm sure Logan was just having a bad day."

"Whatever happened is clearly bothering you. I bet it would help if you talked about it."

I hesitate, thinking I should keep this to myself. But if Rachel and I really were good friends and I want to get that friendship back, I need to open up to her, even if doing so feels uncomfortable.

"He went out on Saturday," I say. "To get me more pain pills. I asked if he'd also go to this bakery by our old apartment. It's kind of a drive, but he agreed, knowing how much I love their cupcakes."

"That's sweet of him," she says, smiling. "That totally sounds like Logan."

"But then he got home, and he'd bought me a cupcake from a bakery around here. Or maybe he lied and got it at a gas station or the drugstore. I can't imagine a bakery making a cupcake that bad."

"What do you mean by bad?"

"It had no flavor and was really dried out, like it was

stale. And it was smashed on top, like it'd been dropped on the counter."

Rachel looks at me, her brows furrowed. "I'm sure he didn't lie about where he got it. Maybe when he went there, they only had day-old cupcakes, so he took what he could."

"It's possible, but then why get it for me? If you'd seen this cupcake, it's not something you'd want to eat and definitely not something you'd want to spend money on."

"Men don't pay attention to that stuff. You wanted a cupcake, so he got you one. I'm sure he didn't inspect it like you or I would. He just saw a cupcake and bought it."

"That might be true for most men, but not Logan. He's very meticulous, or he was, and I'm sure that hasn't changed. He would notice if the cupcake was smashed on top and the frosting was dried out."

"What are you saying?" she asks, scrunching up her nose. "That he purposely gave you a cupcake you wouldn't like?"

That's exactly what I'm saying, but I don't know why he'd do that, or why I'd even think that he would.

I'm embarrassed to tell Rachel the truth, so I say, "You're right. He probably didn't even look at it before he bought it."

"So is that what you were arguing about? The cupcake?"

"No. I mean, kind of. He could tell I was disappointed he didn't go to the cupcake place, and then he got mad and said I was being ungrateful."

"I wouldn't take it personally." Rachel shrugs as if to say it's no big deal. "Men don't like disappointing their wives. It's more about them than us. They expect praise if they do something for you, even if they screw it up. They think they should get rewarded for the effort, yet we do stuff for them all the time and they don't even notice. It's completely unfair, but it's just how men are."

"It was more than that." I set my cup down. "It was his reaction to Edith coming over."

"You mean last week?"

"No, she came over on Saturday while Logan was gone. She brought me some berries from her garden. A huge basket full of blueberries, strawberries, and raspberries. I was excited to have them, but then Logan threw them out."

"Why? Because they were from Edith?"

"Yes! Can you believe that? He threw out perfectly good berries that he knew I wanted just because they were from Edith."

"Well, I can't say I'm surprised. He hates Edith."

"But he has no reason to. I know she's a little unusual, but that's what I like about her. I'm not saying Logan has to like her, but he doesn't get to tell me I can't talk to her. And throwing out her berries was just plain wrong."

"Maybe, but I wouldn't let it upset you enough to harm your marriage."

"It was less about the berries and more about Logan's reaction. He was screaming at me, and he grabbed my arm really hard. I've never seen him act that way. He was so angry. He said I'm not to let anyone in the house, as if he's the only one who gets to decide that. And then he threw the berries away, and I was shocked. I didn't know what to say."

"Then what happened?"

"He told me to go to my room, so I did, just to get away from him. I didn't want to be around him."

"Did this go on all weekend?"

"No, just Saturday. After that, he was great. Back to his old self."

"I wouldn't worry about it," Rachel says, setting her coffee down. "It sounds like he was having a bad day. Maybe he's stressed about something at work or at city council. Logan has a lot going on in addition to having his wife almost die. I'm honestly not surprised he lost it. His stress level was probably so high that even the smallest thing, like you complaining about a cupcake, set him off."

"But I wasn't complaining. I just—"

"I'm not saying it was your fault or that what he did was okay. I'm just saying you might want to try to be more understanding and not take it personally. Logan's a great guy. He'd never intentionally upset you. I'm sure he'd just had a long, stressful week and it got the best of him. If I were you, I'd pretend it never happened and move on."

I'd agree with her if I hadn't found that note telling me not to believe him. It had to be referring to Logan. Who else would it be? But why wouldn't I believe him? Was he lying to me? Or cheating on me?

Logan wouldn't do that. Even if he wanted to, he doesn't have time to cheat. After all, he basically has two jobs, along with all the networking events he goes to related to those jobs. Whatever free time he has, he spends with me.

So why am I wondering if I can trust him? Why do I feel like there's something I don't know? A missing piece? Something that would change everything, if only I could figure it out.

PART 2

CHAPTER SEVENTEEN

ONE YEAR AGO

"Why aren't you dressed?" Logan asks, coming up to me in the bedroom.

It's Saturday night, and we're supposed to go to a charity fundraiser event for the homeless. It's being put on by Brickhowser Development, the company where Logan works. It's a ritzy event attended by very wealthy and influential people. Logan's been talking about it for months. I planned to go, but I feel terrible. My head is pounding, my joints are aching, and I'm exhausted. Just showering was enough to wear me out. I haven't done my hair or makeup, and I'm still wearing my robe.

"I can't go," I say. "I don't feel well."

"I'll get you a pill," he says, heading to the bathroom.

"Logan, no. It won't help. I'm staying home."

He stops and turns back to me. "You think attending this event is optional?"

"It is for me," I say, pushing my shoulders back as I attempt to stand my ground. I've spent the past year giving in to his demands, but I've had enough. My health is failing, and if I don't slow down and rest, it's only going to get worse. "Logan, this is your event. It's for your job. You won't even notice if I'm not there."

"I can't show up without my wife. Imagine how that would look. People would think we're having marital problems."

"We ARE having problems. All we do is argue. Maybe it's time we talk about—"

"No!" He storms up to me. "We are not going there. Don't you dare even say it!"

"Logan, I know you're not happy," I say, my voice cracking even though I promised myself I'd be strong. But I wasn't prepared to do this now. I planned to bring it up this weekend, when we had more time. I wish I'd waited, but it's too late now.

"I'd be happy if you shut your damn mouth and got dressed!" Logan shouts.

A year ago, his reaction would've left me speechless. But now? I've come to expect it. Every time Logan doesn't get his way, he explodes with anger. He shouts. Throws things. Breaks things. I've stayed with him, thinking it would get better, but it hasn't.

"I told you," I say. "I don't feel well. I'm exhausted. My muscles ache. My stomach hurts. I haven't eaten all day."

"Good." His eyes move over me. "You need to lose weight. You're getting too thick around the middle."

That's another reason I want to leave him. He's always insulting me. He used to tell me he was kidding, even though I told him his comments were hurtful, but now he's serious with his insults. No matter how much I try to look good for him, it's never enough.

"Do you really think talking to me that way is going to make me do what you want?"

"Apparently not, because you're still not dressed."

"Because I'm not going." I turn away from him.

He grabs my arm and yanks me in front of him. "You're getting dressed and we're going to the event."

"How? I'm in so much pain I can barely stand up."

"You'll take your pills and be fine. Let's go find you a dress." He drags me to our walk-in closet. "I can't believe I have to do this. My wife should be able to dress herself."

"You're right. I should," I say, but I'm not agreeing with him. What I meant is that I should be able to pick out my own clothes. Instead, I have a closet full of items I don't like and don't want to wear.

One day last year, I came home from work and found that all my clothes were gone. I thought we'd been robbed, but no. It was Logan who'd done it. He took everything I had, including my favorite sweatshirt, my treasured rock band T-shirts from college, and a sweater from my mom. It was the last gift she gave me before she died. Logan donated it to the thrift store, along with all my other clothes.

I was beyond furious. We had a huge fight, but I was the only one fighting. Logan acted confused, like he had no idea why I was upset. He said donating my clothes was meant to be a fun surprise. A gift. He was giving me a whole new wardrobe. I should be happy, he said. It was every woman's dream.

It wasn't *my* dream. I liked my clothes. They were comfortable and they fit my style. I've never been someone who buys the latest fashions or wears fancy dresses. I'm a jeans-and-T-shirt type of girl. If I wear a dress, it's a casual sundress with sneakers, not an evening gown. Logan knew this about me, so I couldn't understand why he insisted on giving away all my clothes.

He finally told me when we went shopping the next day. I wanted to go to the mall, but instead he took me to an upscale dress shop. Before we went inside, he said it was time that I looked my age. He explained that my old look was fine for a college kid, but not for someone in their thirties who was married to an executive and future city council member.

That's when I realized the whole thing had nothing to do with me. It wasn't a fun surprise or a gift from a loving husband. It was Logan telling me how to dress. My old look embarrassed him and didn't fit with his new image. He needed to impress people, and that wouldn't happen if his wife showed up to an event wearing a cotton sundress and sneakers.

At first, I was on board with it. I saw his point about needing to look more polished and professional at the ritzy events we were going to. Logan was determined to increase donations for the low-income housing projects he was working on with the city, which meant going to lots of high-end fundraising events and convincing wealthy people to write checks. I believed in the cause, so I was willing to do my part and show up looking my best.

The problem came when Logan expected me to dress up even when I was just going to the store or out running errands. It started when he began his city council term. He was convinced people were watching us wherever we went. A man would look at us in a restaurant, and Logan would immediately assume he was someone from the press and that there would be a story about us online the next day. It was completely ridiculous, and I told him that, which made him angry. He said I wasn't being supportive or taking his new role seriously. I didn't want to argue about it, so I agreed to dress better when I left the house, which to me meant wearing jeans instead of sweats. But to Logan, it meant putting on dress pants with a blouse and a blazer. When he told me that, I thought he was kidding, but the next day, I found more clothes in my closet, all things Logan wanted me to wear.

"Put this on," he says, shoving a red evening gown at me.

"I can't. I'm in too much pain. I can't go." I sink to the floor, my aching legs finally feeling some relief.

"I swear, Avery. If I could do it all again..." His hands ball into fists.

"What?" I look up at him. "You wouldn't marry me?"

He storms out of the closet, cursing under his breath. Moments later, he returns, stopping in front of my slumped-over body.

"Take these." He holds out his hand, and when I look up, I see three of my pain pills on his palm.

"I can't take that many. They're too strong."

"Good. Then you know they'll work."

"The doctor said taking that many could hurt me."

"The same will be true if you don't attend this event."

"What?" I say, not sure what he means.

"Just hurry up and take them! We don't have time for this! We'll be late!"

"I don't want them. They'll keep me up, and I need to sleep."

"Dammit, Avery!" Logan reaches down, yanks open my mouth, and stuffs the pills down my throat. I choke on them and run into the bathroom to spit them out, but they are already too far down my throat.

"Good girl," Logan says, coming up behind me. "See? Don't you feel better now?"

I look up at the mirror and see the smug grin on his face and the darkness in his eyes. This isn't the man I married. This is someone else, someone I don't recognize anymore.

I've spent months making excuses for him, telling myself he was just under a lot of stress and that's why he was acting this way. Or maybe it was me. Maybe I needed to be a better wife. Maybe I wasn't being supportive enough. But in my defense, I never expected to be the wife of a politician or even an executive. When Logan and I were dating, he never once said he wanted to get into politics or run a company. And he didn't seem to care about money or material things. He lived in a run-down studio apartment, drove a rusty old car, and wore faded jeans, stained T-shirts, and cheap sneakers. He was more concerned with saving the world than what kind of car he drove or how much money was in his wallet.

That's the man I fell in love with, but soon after we got married, Logan changed. He convinced himself he could do more good if he looked like the rich donors he was trying to get money from. He spent thousands of dollars on suits and exchanged his rusty car for a brand-new luxury sedan. He insisted we needed a house and talked me into using the inheritance money from my parents to buy it, even though I was perfectly happy in our apartment. The house cost one and a half million, which isn't unusual for a home in this area, but it's more than I wanted to spend. The down payment alone used up most of my inheritance. And I don't even like where we live. It's surrounded by other houses, so I have to drive to go anywhere. In our old neighborhood, I could walk everywhere, which I loved.

If Logan and I divorce, I'm moving back to that neighborhood. I'm not sure how I'll afford it. I've already searched for apartments there, and the rent is more than I can afford on my current salary. I'd have to get a different job, but with all my health problems, I'm barely keeping the job I have now.

It's sad to think that by this time next year, I could be living on my own again. Logan and I were supposed to be together forever. We were the perfect couple.

I want to save my marriage, but I don't know how. Logan wants me to be someone I'm not, and I'm tired of changing myself for him. And then he does things that are completely unacceptable, like shoving those pills down my throat, and I realize this can't continue.

"You need to leave," I tell him, my eyes meeting his in the mirror. "I mean it, Logan. I don't want to be around you right now. Just go."

"I'm not going without my wife." He steps up even closer behind me. "I put the dress on the bed along with some shoes. Go in the bedroom and put them on."

"No," I say through gritted teeth.

"What was that?" he asks, but I know he heard me.

"I said no. I'm not going. And I'm throwing up those pills before they make me sick." I head to the toilet.

Logan grabs me around the waist. He leans down and talks in my ear. "You're going to the event. If you continue to fight me on this, you won't like the outcome."

"What's that supposed to mean?" I say, trying to pull away from him. "You'll send me to bed without supper? Stop treating me like a child. If I don't want to go, that's my decision. You can't order me to go."

"I can, and I will." His arms tighten around my waist and he drags me back to the bedroom.

"Let go of me!" I yell.

He picks me up and throws me down on the bed. My head slams against the headboard hard enough that I see stars. When my vision clears, I see Logan hovering over me, a wicked grin on his face. "Maybe now you'll cooperate."

CHAPTER EIGHTEEN

"Why are you doing this?" I ask, fearful of the man who used to make me feel safe and loved.

"I just want to have a nice evening with my wife. I don't know why you're making this so difficult."

"You hurt me," I say, staring into his eyes. "You hurt me, and you don't even care."

"You hurt yourself. All I did was put you on the bed."

"You *threw* me on the bed!"

He laughs a little. "You used to like that. Remember when we were first married and we—"

"This isn't the same," I say, rubbing the back of my head. "You could've seriously hurt me, Logan."

"You shouldn't have made me angry. It's your own fault for making me react that way." He straightens up, standing beside the bed. "You know, most women would be thrilled to put on a beautiful dress and attend a prestigious event with their husband."

"If you want one of those women, maybe you should go

find one. I know you're not happy with me. Nothing I do is ever good enough for you. So why don't you leave me? Go find someone else?"

"I wanted to," he says, rubbing his jaw. "And I almost did."

"You were with someone else?"

"I thought about it. I didn't actually do it."

"If you want someone else, then why are we still married? Why haven't you asked for a divorce?"

"Because you're sick," he says with disgust. "You just had to get sick." He walks away and paces the floor. "Just when things were going well in my career and I realized you'd never be the wife I needed you to be, I was prepared to let you go. To find someone who aligned with my goals. But then you had to get some mysterious illness and ruin everything."

"What do you mean? What did I ruin?"

"My career. My future." He stops pacing and turns to me. "We were supposed to be a power couple. The media would've loved our story. Meeting as volunteers, young people out to save the world. I get a job that allows me to really make a difference, then get elected to city council, giving me even more power to do good. And my beautiful wife is right there beside me, supporting me in my goal to make sure everyone has access to affordable housing."

I almost laugh. He doesn't care about affordable housing. Logan's desire for power and money overrode his desire to help people years ago. I didn't see it at first, but I do now. He tells a good story about wanting to help the homeless, but it's all an act. A persona he's created to make himself more appealing to the public, specifically voters, who he's hoping will elect him to even higher positions in government.

"But you didn't do that, Avery." He interrupts my thoughts, his tone ice-cold. "You refuse to be the supportive wife. In fact, you've fought me every step of the way."

"Because this isn't what I want. You know that. You know I despise politicians. You used to feel the same way. Or did you just tell me that so I'd go out with you?"

"We share the same goal, Avery. We both want to make the world a better place. The difference is that you want to go about it the hard way and help one person at a time. But money and politics are how real change happens. Think how many people can be helped by one simple policy change or by a billionaire writing a check. Nothing you do even compares to that."

"After-school programs help kids stay out of trouble," I say, offended that he'd insult my job. "They learn skills. Get internships. Some go on to college. These programs can affect their entire future."

"So you change a few lives," he sneers. "I'm changing thousands. Why wouldn't you want that? Why wouldn't you want to help as many people as you can?"

"That's not what you're doing," I say, getting up from the bed. My head is throbbing and I'm feeling nauseous, but I need to stand up and look Logan in the eye when I say this. "You're not out there saving people. You're in a high-rise building, sitting in your corner office, wearing thousand-dollar suits, and making a million a year. You wouldn't go near a homeless person. You claim to care about them, but when you see one on the street, you're repulsed by them."

"If that were true, I wouldn't be devoting my life to helping them."

"You're using them." I step closer to him. "You're using

them to make people think you're kind and compassionate. And you know what, Logan? It disgusts me!"

He slaps me across the face, so hard that I fall to the ground.

I stare up at him in shock, my cheek burning from the force of his blow.

"Get up!" he says, his face red with rage. "We're going to be late."

"I'm not going," I whisper, putting my hand over my cheek. It feels hot, like blood is rushing to it to fix whatever damage he did.

"I said get up!" Logan grabs my arm and yanks me to my feet. "Get dressed, or I'll dress you myself!"

I'm so shocked, I don't know what to say. Logan's never done this. He's yelled at me plenty of times, but never hit me. Before this moment, I wasn't sure about the divorce, but he's just made my decision crystal clear. I am not staying with this man.

"I'm leaving," I say, backing away from him. "I'm leaving this house and leaving you. We're done, Logan." I storm out of the room and head to the hall closet to get a suitcase.

I hear him laughing. I don't know what the hell is so funny. Does he think I won't do it? Does he think I'll forgive him and agree to stay? If he does, then he's delusional. There's no way I'm staying with him after what he's done.

"How are you going to care for yourself?" he asks, watching as I take the suitcase over to the dresser. "You can barely get out of bed most days. I doubt you'll be able to work for much longer."

"I'll figure it out," I say, tossing clothes into the suitcase. "I'd rather live on the streets than be here."

He comes over to me, but I don't look at him. I just keep tossing clothes into the suitcase. They aren't clothes that I want. They're my Logan-approved clothes. I should just leave them here and start fresh.

"Stop it!" Logan shouts. "Stop it right now!"

My drawers are now empty, and I slam them shut. I rise up from the floor, and Logan grabs me, turning me toward him and gripping my shoulders.

"How can you be so ungrateful?" he says. "I've stayed with you! Cared for you! Gone with you to one medical appointment after another! Do you have any idea how lucky you are to have a husband as devoted as me?"

I almost roll my eyes. Does he really believe he's the hero here? The loving husband? After shoving pills into me and slapping me across the face?

"I've got good news for you, Logan," I say, pulling away from him. "You're off the hook. You don't have to do it anymore. I'm giving you your life back. You can go find someone who's healthy." I lean down to my suitcase and drag it across the floor. I don't have the strength to pick it up.

How am I going to do this? How am I going to start a new life on my own when I'm struggling with this disease that even the doctors can't figure out? What if I keep getting worse? What if one day I wake up and find I can't walk? I won't be able to work. I'll have no one to help me.

Maybe I should stay.

No. I can't. I have to get away from him.

"You're not leaving," Logan says, standing at the door to the closet as I yank clothes off the hangers.

I turn and look at him standing there in his tuxedo, every strand of his jet-black hair slicked neatly into place. He looks so different than the scruffy guy who asked me out on a date all those years ago.

"Stop packing." Logan's arms are crossed and there's a smug grin on his face. "You're not leaving."

"Why are you being this way? You should want this! You hate that I'm sick! You should want to get rid of me."

"It's not that simple, Avery. Believe me, if I could divorce you, I would. But they'd destroy me. Everything I've worked for would be gone."

"Who are you talking about? Who would destroy you?"

"The media. The public. The politicians vying for my position on city council. I'd be called a fraud. Be vilified by the press. All the work I've done up to this point would be for nothing."

"You think this would happen because you got divorced? People get divorced all the time. You're not going to be punished for that."

"You're not really that stupid, are you?" he says with a harsh laugh.

"I'm not listening to this," I say, yanking more clothes from the hangers. Maybe I could sell the designer dresses and make some money.

"Think about it, Avery." Logan walks over to me. "Imagine what people would say if I left you."

"They wouldn't say anything. They wouldn't care. Half of marriages end in divorce. People know this." I take another dress off the hanger.

Logan snatches it from me. "You're sick. Don't you know what that means?"

"No." I sigh in frustration. "Why don't you tell me?"

"It means I can't leave you!" he shouts, throwing the dress on the floor. He grabs my arm. "A man in my position does not leave his sick wife! I'm kind. Compassionate. A strong, selfless leader committed to making the world a better place." He leans down, his face inches from mine. "Those are just some of the words used to describe me. They're what got me elected. But do you think I'd still be described that way if I left my wife when she can barely care for herself?"

I see his point, but I'm not staying with him to save his image. He'll just have to deal with whatever happens.

"Nobody needs to know," I say. "We'll keep the divorce quiet. We can just split everything so we don't have to go to court."

"You think that'll work?" he asks, sounding hopeful.

"Yeah, definitely. I'm not going to fight you over anything. We'll make this quick and easy."

"You really believe that's how it would go?"

"Meaning what?"

"When I asked if your little plan would work? I was being sarcastic. There's no such thing as a quiet divorce when you're a public figure. The press is watching my every move, waiting for something like this to happen so they can make me into a villain."

"Then we'll make it clear that this was my decision, not yours. I'll file for divorce and tell everyone I was the one who wanted out of the marriage."

"Nobody would believe you. No woman who's sick and has no family to care for her would rather be alone than with her husband. The only reason you would do that is if you were desperate to get away from me. So again, the press will assume I'm the bad guy and convince the public I did something to make you leave."

I look at Logan. "Then they'd be right."

"You think I'd let that happen? You think I'd let you destroy me like that?"

"I'm not saying I'd tell anyone what you did to me tonight. What I'm saying is that I can't control what the press says about you."

"Which is why you're not leaving." He puts his hand under my chin, tilting my face up to his. "I know we don't always get along, but we'll make this work. We have to."

"No. We don't." I push his hand off me. "I can't do this anymore. I'm tired of you telling me what to do, how to act, what to wear. I've become someone else to please you, but I can't keep doing it. I don't know who I am anymore. I thought we could work on our marriage, but tonight showed me that it can't be saved. You're not the man I married. I can't stay with you. I can't stay in this marriage."

"You can." He cups the side of my face and smiles at me. "And you will." He leans down to kiss me. I try to pull away, but he grabs me and holds me against him. "You're my wife, and you are not going anywhere."

"You can't make me stay." I try to pull away from him, but he's too strong, and I'm too weak to keep fighting. "Please, Logan. Just let me go."

"I can't do that. I've come too far to give up all that I've accomplished."

"You won't have to give it up. I'll tell the press the divorce had nothing to do with you. I'll say I just didn't want to be married anymore."

He chuckles. "That's sweet, Avery. The way your little mind works? It's like a child's." He continues to hold me against his chest, so tight that I can't get a full breath in. "You wonder why I treat you like a child? It's because you act like one, and think like one. You really have no idea how the world works. It must be nice to live in your little fantasyland where things happen the way you imagine."

What is he saying? That I can't divorce him?

He can't force me to stay married to him. He can say whatever he wants, but my mind's made up. I'm getting out of this marriage. I don't know how yet, but it's going to happen.

CHAPTER NINETEEN

"You need to get to your event," I say, hoping the reminder will make him leave. He can't be late. He's scheduled to speak during the opening remarks.

"You mean *we* need to get to the event." He runs his hand down the back of my hair. "Do you need me to help you get dressed?"

"I'm not going," I mutter.

"Not this again," he says with a sigh. "I guess I didn't make myself clear."

"You were very clear. I'm just not agreeing to go."

"It's not a choice. You're going."

"No. I'm not."

"I really don't want to have to do this," he says, continuing to stroke my hair. "She's all you have left."

"Who?" My pulse races, fearing what he's about to say next.

"Your sister."

"What about her?"

"We spoke the other day. She was asking how you're

doing. She really does care about you. She mentioned coming here for a visit."

"Yes, she told me. She said maybe next month."

"It would be a shame if something were to happen to her during her visit. Especially so soon after you lost your brother."

"What are you saying?" I ask, my heart pounding harder.

He grabs a chunk of my hair, pulling it so hard my head is forced back. He gives me that smug grin of his. "You do as I ask and Mia will be fine. You'll still have a sister."

"You're not serious. You wouldn't..." I gulp. "You wouldn't hurt her. I know you wouldn't. You're not that—"

"Aren't I?" He releases my hair and smooths it with his hand, that grin still on his face. "You know, your brother never liked me. He didn't think I was good enough for you. He even had this crazy idea that I was dangerous. That's why he moved here. To keep watch over you. That whole story about moving here for a job was all a lie."

"How do you know that?"

"He told me. The day his shed burned down."

"But you weren't..." My voice drifts off, my thoughts racing as I try to keep up with what he's saying. "You weren't there that day."

His brows rise. "I wasn't?"

"Were you?" I ask hesitantly, not sure I want the answer.

"It's possible I stopped by. I wanted to know what his intentions were. I had my theories, and it turns out I was right."

"About what?"

"John wanted you to leave me. That's why he moved here. To talk you into leaving me."

"No," I say, my voice shaking. "That's not true. He made some comments, but he never told me to leave you."

"But that's what he wanted. He told me himself. The day of the fire. He said you were changing and that it was my fault. He said I was isolating you from your friends and family. That I was trying to control you. It was all lies, but he didn't see it that way. He was determined to get you away from me."

"So what happened?" I ask, tears welling up in my eyes. "What did you do?"

"I left. It was clear that nothing I said would change his mind."

Relief washes over me. For a moment, I thought Logan was going to tell me he had something to do with John's death.

"Oh, but I did do something the day before. When I went over there to look at that table he was building."

"What... what did you do?"

"I soaked some of his rags in paint thinner and left a few packs of cigarettes in the shed, knowing he'd smoke them. Oh, and when I went back the next day, I might've gotten him drunk." Logan chuckles. "A drunk man smoking cigarettes in a shed filled with flammable rags is not a good combination. My guess is he passed out drunk while smoking and lit the place on fire."

"You killed him," I whisper, staring at Logan in disbelief.

"I didn't do it. He did it to himself."

"You set it up so it'd happen." Tears stream down my face. "You wanted him to die. It's your fault he's gone."

"That's just like you, Avery. Blaming me for something I didn't do. I never forced your brother to drink that day. I didn't make him smoke."

"But you knew he would. You knew he was upset about his girlfriend leaving him, and you used that to get him drunk and smoke the cigarettes you brought him. And the rags. That was all your doing. The shed wouldn't have burned like that if you hadn't soaked the rags with paint thinner. Maybe there wouldn't have even been a fire."

"Guess we'll never know, will we?"

"How... how could you..." I'm finding it hard to breathe, and my legs feel like they're about to give out. "How could you do that?" I stumble back to the bed and sit down. "You knew how close I was to John. How much I loved him."

"I did, which is why I knew if anyone could turn you against me, it'd be him. Do you understand now how important our marriage is to me? What lengths I'll go to in order to protect it? We were on a path, Avery. A path to becoming a powerful and influential couple. I couldn't have your brother interfering. Looking back, if I'd known you were going to get sick and ruin everything, I would've just let you go."

"I was never going to be the wife you wanted." My voice trembles, tears continuing to fall. "Even if John had stayed out of it, I was never going to be that woman." I turn away, not wanting to look at Logan, wishing I'd never met him. "I can't believe you did that. I can't believe you killed my brother."

"I didn't kill him," Logan snaps. "Stop saying that. It was his own damn fault. He was being careless."

It's pointless to argue with him. Logan really believes he isn't at fault.

"John was right from the very beginning," I say. "I didn't believe him, but he was right about you."

"You mean all the lies he told you in his effort to convince you not to marry me?"

"They weren't lies. He said I couldn't trust you. He was worried about your temper. Worried you'd hurt me if you got angry." I look at Logan, a surge of anger replacing my shock and sadness. "I stood up for you. I told him you were gentle and kind and would never hurt me or lie to me. I was furious at John for even saying those things about you. We didn't speak for weeks after the wedding. All because of you."

"It was for the best. You didn't need your brother filling your mind with lies."

"But they weren't lies. They were the truth."

"You might believe that, but nobody else does." He grins. "Your brother is gone, and your sister loves me. We've grown rather close the past few months, discussing your illness and all the treatments you've tried. She's always saying how lucky you are to have me as a husband and how she wishes she could find someone as wonderful as me."

I almost gag hearing him say that. He's so full of himself, and the sad thing is, he seems to actually believe he's a good husband and a good person. He justifies everything he does so that he always comes out the hero. It's a sickness. It has to be. No sane person thinks the way he does.

"If you like her, then you'll leave her alone." I go over to him. "Right?"

"That's up to you." He brushes his hand over my bruised cheek. "I don't like having to be this way, but I have to protect myself and the image I've created. I made a vow. A vow to love you in sickness and in health. I can't break that vow and leave you when you're sick. It wouldn't be right."

"You don't care about what's right." I spit out the words. "You only care about how you look and how people see you. But I know the real Logan, and if you don't let me out of this marriage, I'll tell everyone what you're really like."

He lets go of me and takes a step back, laughing to himself. "Are you really going to fight me on this? After everything I've said? What I just told you?"

It takes me a moment to get what he means.

"You wouldn't," I say.

"And yet I did. Once. And I'd do it again if I had to."

"But you don't. Like you said, Mia's on your side. She likes you."

"This isn't about Mia. It's about you. You're the one who decides what happens here. I don't want to see any harm come to Mia, but if you don't cooperate, what choice do I have?"

He's serious. He'd really do it. I never would've believed he's capable of killing someone, but he just admitted he killed John. He may not have lit the fire, but he set the scene, knowing John could die. If he'd do that to my brother, he'd do it to Mia too.

"Okay, fine," I say, desperate to save my sister. "I'll stay."

"That's my good girl." He leans down and kisses my bruised cheek. "Go cover that up. It doesn't look good. And hurry up and get dressed. We're leaving in ten minutes."

That doesn't give me time to do my hair. I'll have to wear it up, which Logan doesn't like, but it's his fault we're running so late. Of course, he'd never admit that. Instead, he'll spend all night telling me my hair looks bad and that I should've started getting ready earlier.

I don't know how I'll get through tonight. The pills Logan shoved down me have helped lessen my physical pain, but my mental pain is indescribable.

Logan killed my brother. And if I don't stay with him, he'll kill my sister. I'm trapped in a horrible marriage. Living with a monster. And I have no idea how to help myself.

CHAPTER TWENTY

"When I started Brickhowser Development, I searched for people who were passionate about our cause," Steve, Logan's boss, says as he begins his opening remarks. Steve is one of the tech billionaires who founded the company. He's only forty and has already created five companies and sold three of them. He's extremely smart except when it comes to seeing my husband for the man he really is rather than the one he pretends to be.

Logan really has him fooled. The same is true for Grant, the man who founded the company with Steve. They're both completely enamored with Logan. In their eyes, Logan's a brilliant businessman with a compassionate heart who's determined to get people off the streets and into safe, clean, affordable housing. And although Logan may be determined to do that, it's because it'll make him look good and earn him a huge bonus, not because he's caring or compassionate.

"When I first met Logan Fairmont," Steve says, "he was a scrappy young guy barely making enough to feed himself. But he didn't care about that. He wasn't trying to climb the corporate ladder like other guys his age. He was out there trying to make a difference. When he wasn't working at his job, he was out volunteering. Spending his free time building homes for the disadvantaged." Steve glances at me and smiles. "It's there that he met a beautiful young woman named Avery, who would later become his wife."

Logan puts his arm around me, knowing people are watching us. I want to pull away, but I don't, fearing what might happen if I do. I have to be on my best behavior, at least until I can find a way out of this. But how would I do that? Would I have to run away and hide? Change my identity? I don't see that happening, especially when my health keeps declining.

"After talking with Logan for just a few minutes," Steve says, "I knew I wanted to hire him. He had the talent, knowledge, and skills to do the job, but more importantly, he had compassion and a true desire to help the less fortunate."

Hearing Steve talk about Logan this way is making me sick to my stomach. I didn't know Steve was going to make Logan part of his speech. I'm not sure Logan did either. On the way here, he said Steve would be talking about the company's expansion and then have Logan describe their latest housing project.

"In just a few short months with us," Steve continues, "Logan proved that he could not only be the lead on projects, but weigh in on strategy as well. It was his idea to combine the apartment complex downtown with a commercial kitchen that would provide jobs to the residents living there as well as meals for those still in need of housing. He is a truly brilliant man, and we're very fortunate to have him." Steve pauses while everyone claps.

Tonight's event is being held in the ballroom of a large

hotel. Tickets cost three thousand dollars apiece and were sold out the day they went on sale. It's great that all that money was raised, but only some of it will go to support the homeless. The rest will go to pay for this event, which I'm sure cost a fortune given the location and the food being served.

"Logan, get up here," Steve says, motioning him to come onstage. "And bring your amazing wife."

Please, no. I don't want to go up there. But I don't have a choice. Logan's gripping my hand, pulling on me to get up. When I do, he keeps hold of my hand as we walk up to the stage.

We stand beside Steve as he continues to talk.

"For those of you who don't know, this is Logan Fairmont, the man I've been talking about, and beside him is his wife, Avery. In addition to being the director of planning and development at Brickhowser, Logan is also currently serving on the city council." Steve laughs. "I honestly don't know how he does it. I asked him if he ever got any sleep. He replied by saying he's willing to give up sleep in exchange for making a difference in people's lives." Steve pats Logan on the back. "This man is truly an inspiration."

Everyone claps. I look over at Logan and see that he's beaming, loving all the attention and praise.

When the crowd quiets down, Steve says, "Before I hand the mic over to Logan, I need to share some news. Logan doesn't know this yet, so it'll be a nice surprise."

I look over at Steve, wondering what he's going to say. Is Logan getting another promotion? He's already as high up as he can go. If he goes any higher, he'll be at Steve's level, running the company. Is that what's happening? Is Steve stepping down and putting Logan in charge?

Logan leans over and talks into the mic. "Can you hurry this up? I'm getting a little nervous."

Steve laughs, causing people in the audience to laugh too.

"Relax," Steve says, gripping Logan's shoulder. "This is a good thing." Steve looks out at the audience. "Grant and I received a letter today saying that someone in our company is going to be awarded the Humanitarian of the Year award. And I can honestly say, we knew who it was before we even got to the name."

No. It can't be. Logan's winning the Humanitarian of the Year award?

"Our very own Logan Fairmont," Steve says. He turns to shake Logan's hand. "Congratulations! This is so very well deserved."

"Thank you," Logan says, pretending to be shocked. Maybe he really is, but it's not because he doesn't think he deserves it. His shock is because he wasn't expecting to find out about it here, onstage, with everyone watching. But now that they are, and he looks out and sees people clapping and rising from their chairs, he's in pure bliss. This is the reason Logan does what he does. It's for moments like this, when all the attention is on him and people are in awe of his greatness.

Watching this is making me sick. I want to get off this stage and go hide somewhere so I don't have to see this.

Logan takes the mic from Steve and waits for the clapping to stop and people to sit down. "I don't know what to say. I'm completely shocked. I'm not sure I deserve this."

"Don't be so modest!" Steve yells from his chair by the stage. "You deserve it more than anyone!"

Logan chuckles. "I think he set the bar too low."

The audience laughs, which is exactly what Logan wanted. He's manipulating them, and they don't even know it.

"Thank you, Steve," Logan says. "And thank you to whoever put my name in the running for such a prestigious award. I never imagined I would even be considered, so this is a huge honor. I'm truly humbled." His voice cracks, and he drops his head. The room goes silent except for a few "awws" coming from some of the women.

Logan has really perfected his acting skills. His performance is excellent. If I didn't know him, I'd genuinely believe he was being sincere.

He clears his throat and looks back at the audience. "I'm supposed to be up here talking about our new housing project, but before I do, let me just say a little more about this award and what it means to me." He smiles at me and puts his arm around my shoulder. "As Steve said earlier, I met my wife, Avery, while volunteering. We were building a house, and she had no idea how to even use a hammer." He pauses as people laugh. "I asked her why she was there if she didn't know how to build anything. And what did you say?" He shoves the mic in my face.

What is he doing? I'm not supposed to talk. This is *his* thing, not mine.

Everyone's waiting for me to say something, so I lean up to the mic and say, "I just wanted to help."

Logan takes the mic back. "She just wanted to help." He pulls me closer and smiles at me. "That's all it took for me to know she was it. The woman I'd marry someday." He turns back to the audience. "Avery and I fell in love for many reasons, but the main one is because we share a commitment to doing good in the world. She doesn't always like that I work so many hours, but she knows I'm only doing it to help give people a better life. It's something that's important to both of us, and it's that shared value that I believe makes our marriage so strong."

He sounds like a politician. Did he practice this speech, or is he just speaking off the top of his head?

"I wasn't going to mention this tonight," Logan says, "but since she's up here and because I know she'd love your well-wishes and support, I'd like to share what my wife has been going through."

No. Do not talk about me. Please keep me out of this.

"My wife, Avery, has been struggling with her health for almost a year now. Some days, she's in so much pain she can barely get out of bed. We've been from one doctor to another, and none of them have been able to offer her any help besides meds to control her pain."

Looking out at the crowd, I see all the sad faces and know why Logan's doing this. He wants their sympathy. He wants them to know he's stuck by me throughout my illness. He wants them to think he's not just a great humanitarian but a great husband. He's using me for his own benefit, and I have no choice but to go along with it.

"It's been devastating for me to watch her go through this. It hurts me so much to see her suffering. I'm sure many of you out there can imagine how horrible it would be to watch the person you love suffer in pain and not be able to do anything about it."

People nod, likely putting themselves in Logan's shoes and thinking how difficult this must be for him. I'm tempted to grab the mic and tell everyone how mere hours ago, he nearly choked me with pain pills and left a bruise on my face. But instead, I remain at his side with his hand cupped around my shoulder.

"As of now, the doctors are calling her condition an autoimmune disease, but they don't have an actual name for it. And they don't have a cure. So we're taking it a day at a time and hoping her condition will improve. We don't know what's going to happen, but the one thing I do know is that I'll always be here for her." He looks at me. "In sickness and in health. When I said that in my wedding vows, I meant it with all my heart. She will not go through this alone. We're in this together." He leans down and kisses me and quietly says, "I love you." But he made sure he was close enough to the mic that people could hear him.

More "awws" come from the women. Then people start clapping.

Logan eats it up, his face beaming with satisfaction at his heart-warming performance.

He looks back at everyone. "Let me help my wife back to her seat, and then we'll continue with the program."

"I can help her," Steve says, jumping up from his seat. Two other men join him, and soon I'm surrounded by three men walking me back to my chair. I don't need their help after all the pain meds Logan shoved into me, but showing I need assistance adds to Logan's tragic story of having a feeble wife who can't get by without him. Everyone just heard a speech about how hard he works at his job and on city council. Add in a sick wife to care for and he's practically a saint.

How did this happen? How did I not see Logan for who he really is? We dated for two years before we got married. That should've been enough time for his true self to come out and reveal what he's really like. Was I just not seeing it? Was I too blinded by love to see the real Logan?

As I watch him onstage, I think back to what happened before we left the house. The violence. The threats. His admission of his role in John's death.

That's the real Logan, but if I told anyone that, they wouldn't believe me. They'd say I was lying. They'd take Logan's side.

Tonight's made me realize that I'm not going to win this battle. It's an unfair game, and it's one that Logan will always win.

CHAPTER TWENTY-ONE

Logan talks for ten minutes about the company's latest housing project, making sure to mention his role in the design along with all the hours he's spent at the construction site. It's a total exaggeration. He sat in on some meetings about the design. That's it. And he's been to the site maybe three times, one of which was the ground breaking, which included a photo shoot of Logan, Steve, and Grant for the media.

Following Logan's speech, a jazz band plays, and dessert is served. There's a silent auction where people can bid on things like box seats at sports games, exotic trips, and rare bottles of wine. I'm bored and tired and would love to go home, but I'm sure we'll be here for at least another hour or two.

Logan's going around the room, stopping at each table, talking to all the potential investors and donors in the hopes they'll throw more money his way. I'm sure it's working. Logan can be very persuasive, and his fake persona of being this kind, compassionate man out to save the world gains people's trust.

As he works the room, I go through one of the gift bags that was just dropped off at the table. A woman is going around and handing them out so people can take them before they leave. It's not an impressive gift bag. Inside is a metal tumbler, a stemless wineglass, some golf tees, and a key chain. All the items have the event's logo printed on them. None of these rich people will use these items. They'll go right into the trash. What a waste.

"Hi, I'm Deloris," a woman says, taking the seat beside me. "Mind if I join you?"

I smile at her. "No, go ahead."

"I just wanted to say how fortunate you are to have a husband like Logan. I could tell from his speech how much he loves you and wants you to get better." She sniffles and laughs a little. "Just talking about it is making me tear up. I've never seen a man so dedicated to his wife's care. I talked to him earlier, and he mentioned he's been to every one of your doctor's appointments."

He hasn't, but I'm not surprised he's telling people he has in his effort to prove once again that he's the best husband ever. He's clearly got this woman fooled. She's older and dripping in diamonds, from her earrings to her necklace to a bracelet and two large rings, one on each hand.

"I'm not sure if he's made it to every appointment," I say, glancing at Logan as he stands by the bar, talking to two older men. "But he goes to them when he can."

"It's amazing he has the time with everything else he's doing. But that just shows how devoted he is to you. Men make time for the important things." She puts her hand over mine. "And you, my dear, are clearly the most important thing in his life. I hope you treasure that and know how rare it is."

"I do," I say with an exaggerated smile. I feel like such a fake putting on this perfect-couple act. I wonder if Logan feels that way too or if being fake just feels natural to him.

"You seem like a lovely young woman," Deloris says, her hand still on mine. "I'd love to get to know you better. What would you think about helping on one of our committees?"

"I'm not sure what you mean."

"A lot of us ladies volunteer on various committees to help plan charity events. I'm currently on five, but you can choose what's best for you. Given your health concerns, you might want to start with just one."

"Oh, I don't think so. I have a job that keeps me busy, and I—"

"What are you lovely ladies talking about?" Logan asks, coming up behind me.

"I'm so happy you could join us," Deloris says, smiling at Logan like he's a celebrity. "I was just telling your wife about all the committees I'm on. I was asking if she'd like to volunteer to serve on one of them. There are so many to choose from, and they all need help."

"She'd love to," Logan says, rubbing my shoulders. He leans down and kisses my cheek. "We were just talking about this, weren't we?"

"Um, I guess I don't remember."

"Sure you do." He laughs and straightens up, his hands still on my shoulders. "Avery loves children," he says to Deloris. "Maybe there's a committee opening on a charity benefitting children?"

"Oh, yes, many!" Deloris says, clapping her hands

together. "I can think of at least three. I can ask Rhonda." She looks around the room. "There she is. She's bidding on something in the auction. I'll grab her when she's done. She's very active in children's charities."

"I'd love to help," I say, "but I really don't have time."

"She means at the moment," Logan says to Deloris. "But she'll have plenty of time when she's done at her job. She's putting in her resignation this week."

I'm what? What is he talking about? I'm not quitting my job.

"That's wonderful!" Deloris says to me. "It'll be so much better for your health to not have all the stress of a job. Volunteer work has its stressful moments, but for the most part it's very enjoyable and rewarding. And the best part is you can work as much or as little as you'd like."

"Sounds perfect," Logan says. "Avery was worried she might be bored being at home all day, so this seems like the perfect solution. She can volunteer a few hours and spend the rest of the day resting. I'll let you two work out the details. I need to go talk to a few more people before they leave." Logan leans down and kisses my cheek. "You doing okay?"

"I'm getting a little tired."

He rubs my arm. "I won't be too much longer. I promise." He kisses me again. "Love you."

I nod and force out a smile.

"He is such a dream," Deloris says, watching Logan walk away. "And so handsome. You really hit the jackpot."

I keep my smile going, hoping it'll hide the rage I feel after Logan just announced to this total stranger that I'm quitting my job. How dare he try to take away the one thing that's mine. The one place where I can get away from him and his control over me. That's why he's doing this. He doesn't like that he can't control me when I'm at work.

Well, it's not happening. I'm not quitting and spending my days volunteering on some committee. It's not that I'm opposed to doing charity work. I actually love it. All through college I volunteered for different charities. But what Deloris is talking about isn't what I consider charity work. It's ladies planning parties. Sure, the parties will raise money, but they're mainly just an excuse for rich people to dress up, eat a fancy meal, and mingle with other rich people.

"I'M NOT QUITTING," I tell Logan on the drive back to our house.

"We can talk about it later," he says, smiling. "Wasn't tonight great? I can't believe I'm getting the humanitarian award. Well, I can. I've certainly earned it. I'm just surprised it's happening this soon. I didn't think it'd happen for a few more years." He comes to a stop as we approach a red light. "The ceremony isn't for a couple of months, but there's a lot of press leading up to it. Steve said a reporter will be calling me next week to set up a photo shoot. I think I'll get a new suit for it and maybe another one for the award ceremony." Logan reaches over to hold my hand. "And we'll get you a new dress. Maybe some new jewelry." He gives my hand a squeeze. "Honey, why aren't you saying anything? Your husband is receiving a major award and you haven't even congratulated me."

"Congratulations," I mutter as the light turns green and he pulls forward.

"You could show more enthusiasm. Do you realize what

this award could do for my career? It could lead to more opportunities. Maybe even a better job."

"You'd leave Brickhowser?" I look at Logan. "I thought you liked it there."

"I do, but there's nowhere for me to go. I'm at the highest position I can be at unless Grant or Steve steps down, and I don't see that happening anytime soon."

"But Grant and Steve have done so much for you. They've been your biggest supporters, and they treat you like family. You'd really ditch them for more money?"

"Money and a better title. Avery, it's business. It has nothing to do with how I feel about those guys. I guarantee if they were in my shoes, they'd do the same thing. How do you think they got so rich? They didn't do it by sticking around at the same company, doing the same job for years."

"Speaking of jobs," I say, "why did you tell that lady I'm quitting? I'm not leaving my job."

"You can't keep working full time in your condition. It's too much. That's probably why you're not getting better. You don't get enough time to rest."

"If you're that concerned about me resting, you shouldn't have made me come with you tonight. It's after midnight. I shouldn't be up this late."

"You can sleep all day tomorrow. I won't be around, so the house will be quiet."

"You're working tomorrow?"

"I'm going golfing with Stan. He invited me to his country club."

"Who's Stan?"

"A guy I met at the event tonight. He said he could get me an invite to join the club, but I don't think it's the right one for us. It's an older crowd, and people with old money.

We need to be at a club with people our age who are making their own wealth, not inheriting it from their parents. People respect that, especially voters. I have a few clubs in mind. We'll have to go check them out."

"I don't want to join a country club. Plus, they cost a fortune. We don't have money for that."

"It's an investment. You need to be around money to make money." He pulls into the driveway, then into the garage.

As soon as he shuts the car off, I get out. "I'm going to bed."

"I'll be in there in a minute," he says, looking at his phone.

I go into the house, needing to get away from him. I can't take one more minute of him telling me how wonderful he is and how everyone loves him. If he'd been like this when I met him, I never would've gone out with him. I definitely wouldn't have married him.

I've been unhappy with Logan for months now. Actually, it's longer than that, but I told myself it was normal and that all couples go through ups and downs. I tried to stay hopeful, but then I got sick, and things between us became worse. I thought for sure Logan would want to leave me and find someone else, someone who isn't sick, but instead, he's determined to stay with me.

"Hey," he says, joining me in bed. "You still up?"

I keep quiet and pretend to be asleep.

"Avery, wake up." He pulls my body against his and kisses me. "The night's not over."

It's over for me. Does he really think I want to do this? I have no interest in being intimate with him. He disgusts me.

How could he even think I'd want him after he admitted what he did to John and threatened to hurt Mia?

He continues to kiss me. I don't kiss him back, but he doesn't care. This is about his pleasure, not mine. I let him do what he wants just to get it over with, then I lie there, wondering how I ended up here. How did I end up married to a man I despise?

CHAPTER TWENTY-TWO

"Hey, it's Rachel," she says when I answer her call. "Mind if I come over?"

Rachel's my neighbor. She moved into the house next door about a month ago. She's renting it, so I'm not sure how long she'll be there. When she was moving in, I went over to say hi, and it led to us becoming friends. She's really the only friend I have other than people at work. Since moving here, I've been meaning to make friends, but it just hasn't happened.

I check the time. It's after three. I thought Logan would be home by now. He went golfing at eight this morning. He can't still be playing, can he? He hasn't bothered to call or text me, so I really have no idea what he's up to or when he'll be home. Of course, if *I* did that, he'd throw a fit, saying he needs to know where I'm at so he doesn't worry. As if he'd actually worry about me.

"You can come over," I say. "It's just me here. Logan's out golfing."

"You should've called me. We could've done something. Maybe we still could. When's he coming home?"

"I don't know, but I don't really feel up to doing anything."

"I'm sorry. Is it really bad today?"

She's referring to my autoimmune disease, but the reason I don't feel like doing anything is because I'm feeling depressed and hopeless after what happened last night.

"I'm just tired," I tell her. "Logan and I didn't get home until after midnight."

"How was the event? Did you have fun? Wait—why don't I just come over and we can talk about it there?"

"Okay, see you in a minute." I shut off the TV and get out of bed. I've spent most of the day lying here, watching TV, hoping it would take my mind off everything that's worrying me. It didn't work, but I drifted off a few times, so I might've gotten an hour or two of sleep.

The doorbell rings as I'm walking to the door. I open it and see Rachel looking gorgeous as always in a casual floral dress and sandals, her hair and makeup done.

"I like your dress," I say, opening the door.

She gasps. "What happened?"

"What do you mean?"

"Your face. Did you fall?"

She's staring at the bruise on my cheek. I forgot it was there. It feels a lot better today, but it looks worse. I didn't even think to cover it up.

"I tripped and bumped into the wall," I tell her, not able to come up with a better excuse. "It looks bad, but it doesn't really hurt."

"I can show you how to cover it up. I'm an expert with

concealer. I had terrible acne as a teen and watched, like, a million makeup videos to learn how to hide it."

"That's okay. It'll go away. It's already starting to fade."

It's not, but I don't want her giving me makeup lessons. And I'm not planning on getting more bruises, so I don't need any concealer skills. Last night had better be the one and only time Logan does something like that.

"I brought wine!" she says, holding up a bottle of red. "I know it's kind of early in the day, but it's the weekend, so I figured we could bend the rules."

"I'll get some glasses," I say, going to the kitchen.

Rachel follows me in there. "So how was the event last night?"

"It was okay. Logan found out he's getting an award for Humanitarian of the Year."

"How exciting! You must be really proud of him."

"Yeah, I guess." I hand her the corkscrew to open the wine.

"You're not happy about it?"

"About what?"

"The award. You don't seem too thrilled that he got it."

"It's not that. I'm just tired. I don't have the energy to get excited."

I wish I could tell her the truth. Or tell Mia. I'm desperate to talk to someone about Logan, but I can't. It's too risky. If he found out, he'd do something to punish me, and he might actually hurt Mia.

"You want any of this?" I say, holding out the gift bag from last night.

Rachel looks in the bag. "I'd take the key chain."

"It's yours. You can take it when you leave."

She pours me some wine. "Let me know what you think."

I take a sip. "It's good."

"I know, right? A guy at the store recommended it. I couldn't believe how good it was, given the price. It really wasn't that expensive."

Rachel's a wine snob. I know nothing about wine. To me, it all tastes pretty much the same.

"Who was the guy?" I ask, smiling at her.

"I don't know. I didn't get his name. It's not what you're thinking. I have no interest in that."

"What? Men?"

"Dating, especially with my ex about to move in. Can you imagine how awkward it'd be to bring a guy home with my ex living there?"

"Wait—what ex? And why's he moving in? Did you tell me about this guy?"

"I thought I did, but maybe not." She takes a drink of her wine. "His name is Connor. He's cute, but really immature despite being almost forty."

"How long did you date him?"

"Let me think." She pauses. "I guess it was about six months before we got married."

"You're married?" I say, shocked that she's never mentioned this.

"Separated. We were together for a year. I knew it wouldn't last, but I married him anyway."

"And now you're going to live together?"

"It's just temporary. I needed help with the rent and he needed a place to stay, so we decided to live together."

"Isn't that going to be awkward? Living with your soon-to-be ex-husband?"

"Maybe, but we'll get used to it." She swirls the wine in her glass.

"You think you two will get back together?"

"No. Definitely not." She points to the other room. "You want to go sit down?"

We take our wine to the living room and sit on the couch.

"How do you and Logan do it?" Rachel asks.

"Do what?"

"Stay married. It's so much work. I honestly don't know how people do it."

I used to think it was easy. When Logan and I were first married, we got along great. I couldn't see us ever having problems. And now? I can't imagine us ever getting along again.

"I think it's different for everyone," I say. "Some people are just better together than others."

"Like you and Logan." She smiles. "I bet you two never fight."

"We do. Everyone does." I gulp down my wine, hoping it'll make me forget last night.

"What could you possibly fight about? Logan seems so sweet and easygoing, like he'd happily go along with whatever you want."

Her comment couldn't be further from the truth. Logan really has her fooled. He's only been around her a few times, but he made sure to turn on the charm. And she ate it up, gazing at him like she had a crush on him. He has that effect. He's good-looking and charismatic, a combination many women love.

"He doesn't give me everything I want," I say. "Like last night, I didn't want to go to that event, but he wouldn't let me stay home."

"But can you blame him? He was receiving an award. It makes sense he'd want his wife there."

"He didn't get the award. The ceremony isn't for a couple of months. He just found out he was chosen for it. Most of last night I didn't even see him. He was off talking to people while I sat at the table."

"The same thing used to happen to me when I was with Connor. He'd make me go to dinner with clients and ignore me the whole night." She shrugs. "But I get it. He was there for work. It's not like we were on a date."

"That's the thing. I knew Logan would be working last night, which is why he should've let me stay home. He knew I wasn't feeling well."

"So maybe he's not perfect," she says in a lighthearted way. "But what man is, right?"

"He wants me to quit my job," I tell her.

"Maybe you should." She turns to me, tucking her leg under her. "Logan makes good money, doesn't he?"

"Yes, but this isn't about money. I like my job. I'm not giving it up to sit at home."

"Is that what he wants? For you to stay home?"

"He wants me to volunteer on committees that organize charity events so I'll make friends with the wives of the wealthy men he wants to do business with."

"And you don't want to?"

"I don't want my life being all about supporting his career. I want my own life. My own career."

I need to change topics before I tell her more than I should. This is really hard. I'm desperate to tell someone what's going on, to get their opinion or advice on what I should do, but I can't. Logan has silenced me with his threats. And since his threats involve Mia, I'm not willing to call his bluff.

CHAPTER TWENTY-THREE

"So what's Connor like?" I ask. "What's he do for work?"

"He sells investments, but he's not very good at it. He's always getting fired for not meeting his sales quota. He claims he's better at it now, but I don't know what that means. As long as he pays the rent, it really doesn't matter."

"He's only paying half, right?"

"No, all of it." She smiles. "It's the price he has to pay to live with me. Did I mention he's still in love with me?"

"That's why he's moving in? Because he thinks you might get back together?"

"I never told him that, but yes, he thinks living in the same house will somehow fix our relationship. But trust me, it's never going to happen."

"Isn't that kind of mean? To get his hopes up like that?"

"I didn't get his hopes up. He did. I told him we're not getting back together. He thinks he can change my mind, and I'm just going to let him think that if it gets me what I want."

"What do you want?"

"Clothes. Jewelry. Purses. I'm using this to my advantage. Connor will buy me whatever I want if he thinks it'll convince me to take him back."

"That seems wrong, doesn't it?" I say, a little surprised by her attitude. "Using him to get stuff?"

"Why is it wrong? Men are always using people to get what they want. Why can't we do the same?"

"I guess I don't think that way. I'm too honest. I'm not good at hiding my intentions."

"You're so sweet," she says, but she says it like she thinks I'm stupid.

I'm not stupid. I just don't like deceiving people. That's what Logan does. He's an expert at it. I don't want to be like him.

"Want some more wine?" Rachel asks, getting up.

She's already heading to the kitchen before I can answer. She returns with the bottle of wine. I really shouldn't have any more. I tend to overshare when I drink, but the wine is really good, and it's making me feel relaxed, which I need after feeling so stressed from last night.

"Can I ask you a hypothetical question?" I say.

"Sure! Go ahead." She refills my glass, along with her own.

"If someone was making you do something you didn't want to do, like by threatening you or blackmailing you, how would you stop it?"

"Let me think." She looks up at the ceiling a moment, then back at me. "First, I'd let them think they're in charge. You never want to challenge someone who thinks they have all the power. It makes them want to control you even more. So you play along and work behind the scenes."

"Doing what?"

She shrugs. "Depends on the situation. Give me an example."

The only one I can think of is my own. I want to tell her, but I can't risk Logan finding out. And I'm not sure I trust Rachel. Now that she told me she lies to her ex to get what she wants, I'm wary of her.

"I can't think of one," I tell her. "Never mind. It was a dumb question. I heard it on a talk show the other day and didn't stick around to hear the answer. I was just curious what you thought."

"What would *you* do?"

"I don't know. Maybe try to go to someone for help?"

"What if you don't have anyone you can trust?"

"There has to be someone. Maybe she could go to the police."

"This is a she?" Rachel shakes her head. "The police won't help. They never believe women. They always take the man's side. I'm assuming the blackmailer in this situation is a man?"

"It could be. But even if it is, I think the woman should go to the police. Cops don't always side with the man."

"They do if the man is convincing. A good liar can get away with a lot."

Logan is an expert liar. If I went to the police and it was my word against Logan's, they'd believe him over me. I'm sure of it. He can get most anyone to take his side. I was hoping the police might be able to help me, but now I'm not so sure. And if I reported Logan to the police, he'd for sure do something to Mia.

The front door opens and Logan walks in, his face tan from a day in the sun. He's still in his golf clothes, a white polo and light-colored pants.

"Rachel," he says, smiling at her, "I didn't know you were coming over."

"I invited myself," she says, smiling back at him. "How was your golf game?"

"Great! Had one of my best rounds. Thank you for asking." He glances at me like I should take a lesson from Rachel and show more interest in the things he does.

"I brought over some wine. I'd offer you some, but we drank it all." Rachel laughs. "But we can open another bottle if you want a glass."

"Thank you, but I'll pass. I need to go clean up." He walks over to me and kisses my forehead. "Hi, honey. How are you feeling today?"

His fake concern for my health is so irritating. If Rachel weren't here, he would've walked right past me, not even saying hello. Or he'd be asking why dinner isn't made.

"I'm okay," I tell him.

He leans down and rubs my back. "Maybe you should rest a little before dinner."

"I'm not sure when that'll be. I didn't make anything."

"I didn't expect you to. I was planning to take you out if you're up for it. I thought we could go to that new seafood restaurant you've been talking about."

"I read about that place," Rachel says. "It sounds amazing, but I heard they're booked up for weeks."

"I know the owner," Logan says. "We met at one of the fundraising events for my campaign. She said she'd get me a table anytime I'd like."

She? Who is this woman, and why am I just now hearing about her? I've brought up that restaurant several times, and Logan never once mentioned knowing the owner.

"Guess there are perks to being a politician," Rachel

says, glancing at me. "You should take advantage of that, Avery."

"What do you think?" Logan says to me. "Are you up for going to dinner?"

"If she's not, I'll go," Rachel says. "I'm dying to try that place."

"I'd invite you," Logan says. "But I'm really looking forward to a night with just my wife. I'm sure you understand."

"Of course." Rachel gets up from the couch. "I'll leave so you two can get ready."

"You don't have to," I say, feeling safer having her here.

Has it really come to this? Do I no longer feel safe being home alone with my own husband?

"I'm going to go change," Logan says. "It was nice seeing you, Rachel."

"You too," she says.

As Logan leaves, I point to Rachel's glass. "You could at least finish your wine before you go."

"I've had enough." She glances at the hall that Logan just went down. "And I think your husband wants to be alone with you."

I don't want to be alone with him. I want to get away from him.

"Have fun!" she says with a wink as she walks to the door.

She thinks Logan wants to be alone with me for romantic reasons. I wasn't even thinking of that. I hope that's not what he wants, because I don't. I never want to do that with him again.

"Honey?" Logan calls out. "Can you come in here a minute?"

He's being polite because he thinks Rachel is still here. I go into the bedroom and find him in the bathroom, searching around in the drawers.

"She's not here," I say. "She left."

"What does that have to do with anything?"

"You can go back to being yourself."

He stops searching and looks over at me. "I don't know what that means."

"It means you can stop pretending we get along. So what do you need? Why'd you call me in here?"

"We're out of soap, or I can't find it."

"It's in here." I open the linen closet and show him.

"Thank you."

"Sure," I mutter.

I turn to leave, but he steps in front of me. "I missed you today."

"Why?"

He laughs. "What kind of question is that? Can't I miss my wife?"

"What's going on? Why are you acting like this?"

"Like what?"

"You don't remember last night? When you threatened to hurt my sister if I didn't stay with you?"

"Avery, I would never say something like that. You must've imagined it. Probably because you took so many of those painkillers."

"I didn't take them. You shoved them down my throat!"

He backs away, confusion on his face. "Honey, are you feeling okay?"

"After last night? No. I'm furious that you did that."

"I didn't. I didn't even touch your pills. You're the one who took them. I watched you do it." He puts his hand on my shoulder. "Why don't you go rest while I get ready? Then I'll take you out for a nice dinner."

"Really, Logan? You're just going to pretend last night never happened?"

"Last night was great." He kisses me. "I had a wonderful time. Go get some rest. We'll leave at six." He starts undressing, so I leave and go to the bedroom.

He's denying it, trying to make me believe nothing happened. And what's with the nice-husband act? He must want something, but what?

It makes me think of what Rachel said, about people lying to get what they want. Hiding their true intentions.

Maybe I should do that with Logan. I could play along and do what he says until I figure out how to get away from him. It would be better than trying to fight him, which, like Rachel said, will only make him want to control me more.

This isn't who I am. I've always believed in being truthful. But I can't be that person right now. If I want to survive this, I need to throw Logan off. Make him think I'm committed to him. And hope that he'll believe me.

CHAPTER TWENTY-FOUR

"You really don't have to do that," Maureen says as I organize the files. "I'll have one of the volunteers work on it."

"Why wouldn't I do it?" I say, stuffing one of the files back into the cabinet. "It's part of my job, and I don't have anything else to do right now."

She doesn't say anything. I look up and see her biting her lip. It's a nervous tic she has that shows up when she has to have an uncomfortable conversation, like with a volunteer who isn't working out.

"What's wrong?" I ask.

She hesitates, then says, "It's just that I... I can't have the files getting mixed up."

"That's why I'm organizing them. The file cabinet is a mess. The volunteers just stuff files in there without considering where they need to go. We should probably talk to them about that." I take out another file and sort through it.

"Avery, can you stop for a moment?" Maureen says.

"Why?" I look over at her. "Do you want me to organize them a different way? Because I was thinking—"

"This isn't about the files. Well, it is, but it's also about... other things."

"What do you mean?"

"I'm concerned. That's all."

"Concerned about what?"

"About you, and your health." She looks down, then back up at me. "I think we both know you're no longer able to perform here at the level that's needed."

"Wait—what?" I shove my chair back and stand up. "What do you mean? Did I do something wrong?"

Maureen hired me and has been my boss since my first day here. She's always complimented my work and told me how grateful she is to have me as an employee, so hearing her say this is a complete surprise.

"It's not that you did anything wrong, but I'm worried mistakes could be made going forward."

"What kind of mistakes?"

"It could be anything," she says with a shrug.

"You can't give me an example?"

She sighs. "What I'm trying to say is that I don't think this job is right for you anymore. In fact, I think it would be best if you didn't work at all right now and gave yourself time to rest and deal with this illness you've been struggling with."

"You're firing me because I haven't been feeling well?" I ask, thinking that can't be legal. Can it? She can't fire me for being sick.

"Avery, please don't be angry. I hope you'd agree that I'm not only your boss but your friend. And as your friend, I can see that this job has become too much for you. Just last week, I found you napping in the break room."

"It was my break," I point out. "I'm allowed to do what I want on my break, aren't I?"

"Well, yes, but you were clearly exhausted. Maybe you don't see it, but I've watched you, Avery, and I can tell you're struggling to make it through the day."

"But I'm still doing it. And if I'm getting my work done, I don't know why you'd fire me."

She sits on the chair across from me, looking down at her hands as they rest in her lap. "I spoke with your husband. And he agreed that this job has become too much for you."

My muscles tense, and I feel a heat building inside me. How dare Logan go behind my back and talk to Maureen! And then he doesn't even tell me?

"When did you speak to him?" I ask, trying to remain calm.

"Yesterday. He asked if we could meet. Since it was Sunday, I suggested we wait and talk today instead, but he insisted he needed to talk to me right away. He sounded very concerned."

So that's where he went. Logan said he had to run an errand yesterday, but he didn't tell me what the errand was, and I didn't care enough to ask. I was relieved to have him out of the house. I had no idea he was going to talk to my boss.

"And what did my husband have to say?" I ask, my hands forming fists as I try to contain my anger.

"He expressed his concerns." She looks at me, a sad smile on her face. "He really loves you, Avery. You should've heard all the wonderful things he said about you. He knows how much this job means to you and knows you would never leave here of your own accord, which is why he felt he had to intervene."

"Logan never should've done that. He should've talked to me before coming to you."

"He told me you'd say that. He knew you wouldn't agree with this decision, but after speaking with him, I think it's for the best that you take some time off to get better."

"Then I'll take a day or two off, but I'm not quitting. I don't need to. Yes, there are days when I don't feel great, but I can still do my job."

"Avery, please." Maureen reaches across the desk and puts her hand over mine. "Don't make this harder than it needs to be. This isn't the end of your career. You're just taking a little break."

"But I don't need a break!" I yank my hand from hers. "Don't you see what's happening here?"

She starts biting her lip again as she sees how angry I am. I'm usually able to hide it, but I'm so angry right now that I can't.

"This isn't about me. It's about Logan," I say to Maureen. "He wants me to quit my job. We had a fight about it last weekend. I refused to quit, so now he's gone behind my back and made up some story about me not being able to work."

"Avery, that is not what happened. Logan didn't want to do this. If you saw him when he was here yesterday, you'd know how torn he felt even discussing this with me. He knows you love it here, and he wishes you could continue, but he doesn't want this job compromising your health."

"It's not," I insist. "Logan is the one who's compromising my health."

"I don't understand," she says, looking confused. "How is Logan—"

"It doesn't matter," I say, knowing I can't tell her the truth. Even if I tried, she'd never believe me. Logan's got her under his spell, believing whatever he says. "The point is that Logan isn't making this decision. I'm perfectly capable of doing this job. And given how long I've worked for you, I would hope you'd consider what *I* want over whatever my husband is telling you is right for me."

Her sad smile returns. "I'm not sure you're able to make that decision."

"What are you talking about? Of course I'm able to."

"Logan told me how confused you've been." She pauses. "And, well... paranoid."

"Paranoid? I'm not—"

"He told me what you accused him of," she says in a solemn tone. "In regard to your brother's death."

I wait for her to continue, wanting to know what Logan said.

"He wasn't even there the day John died," Maureen says. "Isn't that what you told me?"

"Yes, but I found out that it wasn't true. Logan admitted to me that he went to see John that day, and he—"

"Soaked rags in paint thinner and spread them around the shed?" she says, her brows raised.

My jaw drops. I can't believe he told her that.

"Why would you make up a story like that about your husband?" Maureen says. "He's done so much for you, caring for you as you've struggled with your health. The fact that you even came up with a story like that is proof that your mind is being affected by your illness. You're imagining things that aren't true. I know it's not your fault, and I really do hope you get better, but I can't have someone working here who's struggling to tell the difference between what's real and what's not."

"Maureen, he's lying. I didn't say those things! Logan did. He's the one who told me about the paint rags."

"He told me you'd say that. He said you'd turn it around

on him. He thinks it's part of your confusion. You say something, then accuse someone else of saying it. He said you've been doing it for weeks. He thought it might be because of your medication, but he said you're like this even when you're not taking it."

I laugh, not because it's funny, but because I can't believe she's taking Logan seriously. How can she not see through his lies? Maureen knows me. She sees me every day at work. If I was losing my mind, she would've noticed. She wouldn't need my husband to tell her.

"What's so funny?" she asks.

"This!" I throw my hands up. "This entire conversation. Do you even hear what you're saying? You're acting like we just met. Like you don't even know me. Maureen, you know I wouldn't make up a story like that."

"I do, which is why this is so concerning."

"No, you're not getting it! Logan lied! That story he told you was his! I didn't know anything about the rags. He—"

"I'm sorry, Avery, but we're done here." She quickly gets up, seeming nervous, almost like she's afraid of me. "We don't need to keep discussing this. Maybe when you're feeling better, you could come back as an employee, but as of now, your work here is done." She walks to the door. "Please pack up your things." She gives me a half-smile. "And I really do hope you get better."

When she's gone, I get out my phone and call Logan. He doesn't answer. I call again, and he still doesn't answer. He's avoiding me. He knows why I'm calling, and now he's refusing to talk to me.

I send him a text.

> You're not getting away with this.

But then I realize he already did get away with it. Maureen's not giving me back my job. Logan's convinced her I'm not capable of working here.

How does he do it? How does he convince people to believe whatever he says? Is it his tone? His appearance? His conviction?

Going into the storage room, I find an empty box and bring it to my desk. I don't have much, but the few things I do have, I toss into the box. Then I take one last look at my office, still not believing this is happening.

As I head to the door to exit the building, I consider stopping to say goodbye to Maureen, but then decide not to. I thought we were friends, but a friend would've believed me. A friend wouldn't take my husband's side over mine.

Logan may have gotten what he wanted, but I'm not giving up. I can't let him win. I'm still going to fight to get out of this horrible marriage.

CHAPTER TWENTY-FIVE

I've been calling Logan since I got home, but he refuses to answer. I don't know if it's the stress of losing my job or my anger at Logan, but I'm feeling worse than usual today. My joints ache, my head is pounding, and I have no energy. I've spent the past few hours lying in bed, waiting for Logan to get home. I haven't figured out what to say when he does. I want to yell at him and tell him to get my job back, but I know he'd never do that.

Just after six, I hear the garage door open and the sound of Logan walking in.

"Avery?" he calls out. "Honey, where are you?"

Honey? Is that how he's going to play this? Pretend to be the caring husband who was worried about his sick wife, so he went behind her back and got her fired?

"There you are," Logan says, coming into the bedroom with a huge bouquet of flowers. "Sorry I'm late, but I wanted to stop and get you these." He holds up the flowers, a big smile on his face.

"What are they for?" I ask, sitting up and leaning against the headboard. "To congratulate yourself for getting your way?"

He walks over to me and sits down on the bed. "Honey, don't be that way. You know I only did it because I love you and want you to get better."

"That's love to you?" I huff. "Getting me fired? Telling my boss lies about me so she thinks I'm crazy?"

"You aren't crazy. You're ill. That's different. But you're going to get better. Now that you're no longer working, you can put all your energy toward getting your health back."

"Like you care about my health," I say, rolling my eyes.

"Of course I do. Why would you even say that?"

"What you did had nothing to do with my health. You didn't want me working. That's why you did this. You want me to be like one of those wives at the event last weekend, spending my days going to afternoon tea and serving on committees and then coming home and having dinner waiting for you."

"What's wrong with that? A lot of women would like that lifestyle."

"I'm not one of those women. And honestly, I doubt the women who live that way are happy. The ones I met last Saturday night didn't seem like they were."

"That's just your perception. You're very negative toward people with money, which is odd, because you didn't exactly grow up poor."

"Forget about them. We're talking about me and what you did to me. Do you know how humiliated I was having to listen to Maureen talk to me like that? Like I'm too confused to even know what I'm saying? Why would you do that to me? Do you really hate me that much?"

"I don't hate you at all, Avery." He sets the flowers down. "I did it because I love you. Because I want you to get better."

"You're such a liar." I lie down, turning away from him. "Just go. I can't be around you right now."

"Have you had dinner? I could take you out."

He's acting like nothing happened, like I could just go have dinner with him and act as if everything's fine.

"I'm not hungry. Would you please just leave me alone?"

"Avery, come on." He rubs my arm. "You need to eat."

"I said I'm not hungry. I don't feel well. I just want to sleep."

"You're very warm. Do you have a fever?"

I think I actually do, but I keep quiet. I'm not answering him.

"You have a fever, Avery. And you can't get out of bed. Do you see why I was forced to make you stop working?"

I want to yell at him and tell him what he did was wrong, but it wouldn't make a difference. He doesn't care what I want or what's important to me. I'm just here to serve him and do whatever will make him look good and help him in his career.

He finally leaves, and I fall asleep. I wake up later and hear him talking to someone.

"She wouldn't tell me, but you know how she is. She doesn't want to worry anyone. But I'm her husband. Of course I'm going to worry." He pauses. "Yes, I'll do that. We'll go first thing tomorrow morning."

He must be on the phone because I don't hear anyone else's voice.

"I'm glad you were able to talk," he says. "I feel so alone sometimes, trying to care for her but not sure if what I'm doing is right." He listens, then softly laughs. "Yes, she is stubborn. And thank you for the compliment. That's very kind of you to say. I'll keep you updated on how she's doing. Goodbye, Mia."

Mia? He's talking to Mia?

I shove the covers off me and get up just as Logan opens the door.

"What are you doing?" he asks.

"Why were you talking to Mia?"

"Because she's your sister. She cares about you. I called to let her know how you're doing."

I storm over to him. "Do *not* talk to her. I mean it, Logan. Just leave her alone."

"And how would that look?" he says, putting his hand on my shoulder. "For me to not speak to my own sister-in-law?"

"Don't touch me," I say, backing away from him. "Why are you doing this? Why are you bringing my sister into this?"

"I'm not. Mia is fine. Actually, she's great. She went on a date last night. Her job is going well. And she's thinking of coming here in the fall."

"No." I shake my head. "She's not coming. I don't want to see her."

"She's your sister. Of course you want to see her. I do too. I told her we'd love to have her and that she could stay at the house."

My heart's pounding as I imagine all the terrible things he might do to her. "Logan, please stop this. Please don't—"

"Relax." He steps up to me and forces me into his arms. "You worry too much. It's not good for your health. Speaking of that, Mia and I agreed you should see your doctor tomorrow. We're concerned about this fever you're having. I'll cancel my meetings tomorrow and take you."

I don't tell him no because I probably should see the doctor given how awful I'm feeling.

What if this is Logan's doing? What if he's the reason I'm sick? What if he's somehow poisoning me? But why would he do that? He doesn't want a sick wife. If anything, he'd rather see me dead than sick, and if he wanted to kill me, he would've done it by now.

As I'm having these thoughts, I wonder if I really am paranoid. Logan wouldn't kill me. Or maybe he would. He killed my brother, or at least created a scenario that would almost certainly lead to his death. It's possible he'd do the same to me. But the cops always suspect the husband first, which means Logan would be in the press as a possible suspect in my death. Even if he wasn't found guilty, his reputation would be tarnished, which could cause irreversible harm to his career.

"Let's go to the kitchen," Logan says, releasing his hold on me. "I'll make you some tea."

I don't understand him. One minute he's destroying my life, and the next he's making me tea. Is this some kind of game he's playing? Is his aim to keep me guessing so I never know what to expect next?

"It's your favorite," Logan says, setting a cup of honey-chamomile tea in front of me. "Are you hungry? I could make you something."

"You don't cook."

"I can make toast." He smiles. "I'm actually really good at it."

He almost makes me laugh. That's something the old

Logan would say. He does this sometimes, and it confuses me. I see glimpses of the man I fell in love with, but then he turns on me and becomes someone else.

"Toast sounds good."

"Coming right up." He gets the bread out and puts two slices in the toaster, then comes over to the table and sits across from me. "I met the new neighbor. We're going golfing tomorrow after work unless you need me to stay home with you."

"What new neighbor?"

"Connor. Rachel's husband."

"He's her ex-husband, or he will be soon."

"He called her his wife, but anyway, I thought I'd take him golfing. You spend so much time with Rachel that I felt like I should get to know her husband. Maybe we could all go out sometime."

"Why would we go out?"

"Because they're our neighbors. I don't get what you're asking."

"Every time I've suggested we go out with another couple, you refuse. Like Maureen and her husband. Or Sara and Jake. You didn't even want them coming here for dinner."

"Who's Sara and Jake?"

"The people who used to live two houses down."

"You mean the plumber?" Logan shakes his head. "I didn't like that guy."

"Why? Because he was a plumber?"

"Because I didn't like him." The toast pops up, and Logan gets up from the table. "I don't have to like someone just because they live on our street."

Logan puts the toast on a plate, then gets out the peanut

butter and spreads a thin layer on top, just the way I like it. He takes a banana from the bowl, peels it, and cuts it into thick slices, laying them next to the toast.

Watching him, I once again feel like the old Logan is back. The Logan who knew what I liked and wanted to make me happy. What happened to that Logan, and how do I get him back?

"Dinner is served," he says, setting the plate in front of me. "How'd I do?"

"Good. I thought I was just getting plain toast."

"You hate plain toast. You like it the way I made it. Just a thin layer of peanut butter and a side of banana." He sits back down across from me. "How is it?"

I bite into the toast. "It's okay."

Actually, it's really good. It's got the perfect amount of peanut butter.

"Do you feel any better after getting some sleep?"

"Not really. I think I'll go back to bed after this."

"I spoke with Deloris. She called while you were resting."

"Deloris?"

"The woman you met at the event last weekend. She talked to you about volunteering for a committee."

"Oh. Yeah, I know who you mean. What did you tell her?"

"I said you weren't feeling well and that you'd call her back. We talked for several minutes. She listed off a few committees she thought would be a good fit for you."

"Logan, I don't want to be on a committee. If I'm not capable of working, I can't volunteer."

"It's not a full-time position. It's only a few hours a week, and I already told her you'd do it. You'll call her tomorrow and she'll give you the details." He says it like I don't have a choice.

I'm too tired to argue, so I say nothing and finish my dinner while Logan looks at messages on his phone.

"We have an appointment at eight," he says as I'm drinking my tea. "It's the earliest I could get."

"A doctor's appointment?"

"Yes, although I'm sure it'll be a waste of time."

"Then don't go. I don't need you there."

"I'm your husband. I'm expected to be there."

"So that's why you're going? Because people expect you to?"

He sets down his phone. "What do you think is wrong with you?"

"I have an autoimmune disease."

"The doctors labeled it that. They don't really know what it is, which makes me think..." He rubs his hand back and forth over his jaw.

"What? What were you going to say?"

"That maybe you're not actually sick."

I stare at him, not believing what I'm hearing.

"You think I'm pretending? You really believe that?"

"I don't know what to believe. It just doesn't make sense to me that you've seen countless doctors and none of them can figure out what's wrong with you."

"Yeah, so imagine how I feel. I can't get a diagnosis. I can't get treatment. And now my own husband is accusing me of making it up." I shove back from the table. "I'm going to bed."

I go to my room and shut the door, furious with Logan. He thinks I'm faking my illness? Is he serious? Does he really think I'd try to fool everyone into thinking I'm sick? Logan's crazy if he really believes that. I mean, why would I do that?

This illness has ruined my life. I've lost my job. I rarely go out. I'm always going to medical appointments. I'm taking drugs that don't seem to do anything. Why would I purposely choose to have this as my life?

CHAPTER TWENTY-SIX

"Hello?" Mia says, answering my call.

"Hey, it's me."

"Avery?" She says it like she just woke up, and I realize I forgot the time difference.

"Sorry! I forgot it's the middle of the night there. I'll call you tomorrow."

"I'm already up. What's going on? Are you okay? Logan said you weren't doing well."

"About that. I don't want you talking to him."

"Why not?"

"Because I don't like you two talking about me when I'm not around. Promise me you won't do it anymore."

"I can't talk to your husband? Avery, what's going on?"

"Nothing. I'd just rather have you talk to me than to Logan."

"Why? Did you two have a fight? Or is it something more serious? You aren't divorcing him, are you?"

"No, but we are having problems, so I'd really like it if you didn't talk to him."

"What kind of problems?"

"I don't want to get into it. Just promise me you'll stop calling him."

"He's usually the one who calls. What am I supposed to do? Not pick up?"

"Yes. I'll tell him you're busy and don't have time to talk."

"Something doesn't seem right about this. You're not telling me the whole story, are you? What's really going on?"

"Can you just stop talking to him without asking all these questions?"

"No, because it doesn't make sense. You used to want me to talk to him, and now you don't? What changed?"

"I told you, we're having issues."

"What kind of issues?"

I should've known Mia would push me on this. She won't agree to do something without knowing why. She's always been that way, and it's so annoying.

"He made me quit my job today," I say, deciding not to tell her I was let go.

"Yeah, he told me."

"He did?"

"Yes, and I agreed it was the right thing to do."

"You agreed with him?" I'm so shocked I almost drop the phone. "Why would you do that?"

"Because I want you to get better. That's not going to happen if you're working a full-time job."

Logan convinced her to think that way. He talked to her behind my back and got her on his side. Once again, I lose and he wins. He turned my own sister against me, the same sister he threatened to harm if I didn't do what he says. I wish I could tell Mia that, but if I did, she'd call Logan and ask if it was true. He'd tell her it wasn't, and then convince her I'd made it all up.

"I didn't need to quit," I say. "But Logan wouldn't let it go, and I was tired of fighting about it. So now I'm without a job and have nothing to do all day."

"He said you volunteered for a committee. Some charity thing."

He told her that too? How long did he talk to her?

"I didn't volunteer. That was Logan's idea, but I don't want to do it."

"Why not? You love volunteering. And you could just do it a few hours a week."

She sounds like Logan. Did he tell her to say that?

"I like doing actual work, like volunteering to collect clothing donations, not sitting on a committee, planning parties."

"I think it sounds fun, and you'd get to meet people. I don't see the problem here."

"Okay, well, I should go."

"Come on, Avery. Don't be mad at me. Are you mad because I agreed with Logan?"

"Yes. You're my sister. You're supposed to take my side."

"Not when you're doing something that isn't good for you. And I really think working all those hours was too much for you."

"How would you know? You're not here."

"No, but Logan is, and I believe him when he tells me how you're doing."

"Just ask me. You don't have to talk to Logan."

"You'll lie and say you're fine so that I don't worry. That's why I can't agree to stop talking to him. I'm sorry, Avery, but that's just how it's going to be."

I'm so angry I want to scream. I need to end this call before my temper gets the better of me.

"I need to go," I say. "We'll talk later."

I end the call, not waiting for her to say goodbye. I really thought she'd respect my wishes and agree not to talk to Logan, but I should've known it was too late for that. Logan's built a relationship with her during these secret calls they've been having, and now she trusts him more than me.

Logan knocks on the door, then comes in. "I heard you talking. Did you call Mia?"

"Yes." I stare at my husband. "It sounds like you two have been talking a lot."

"We have." His smug grin appears. "It's been nice getting to know my sister-in-law better. I'm finding we have a lot in common."

"Like what?"

"Our concern for you. Wanting what's best for your health."

"I don't need you, or Mia, making decisions for me. And I don't want you talking to her anymore."

"Does she agree with you? That we should no longer talk?"

"I think you already know the answer to that."

He walks over to me. "I'm sorry that it upsets you that your sister likes me. I would think you'd want us to get along. After all, she and I are the only family you have left."

"I'm going to sleep in the guest room tonight," I say, getting up.

Logan steps in front of me. "You'll sleep here. We're husband and wife. We don't sleep in separate rooms."

It's another fight I won't win. Knowing Logan, he'd tie me to the bed just to get his way.

"You need to cover this better," he says, running his hand over my bruised cheek. "Rachel gave me some concealer to try. I left it in the bathroom."

"You talked to Rachel?" I honestly feel like my head might explode right now, knowing the number of people Logan is talking to about me without even telling me.

"When I was over there to see Connor. She mentioned the bruise and then gave me the concealer and asked me to bring it to you."

"You're not upset that she saw it?"

"Why would I be upset?"

"She knows you hit me," I lie, just to see how he'll respond.

"I never hit you." He gazes at the bruise, running his hand over it again. "You ran into the wall. Isn't that what you told Rachel?"

She told him what I said. And now, if I went to the police and told them Logan hit me, my story wouldn't add up. Why didn't I just tell Rachel the truth?

Logan leans down to my face. "No one will ever believe you. Just stop fighting, Avery. It's not worth it."

But it is to me. I want my life back. A life where my husband isn't controlling what I do and say, or how people see me. Is it possible to get that life back? Or is it too late? Is it pointless to even try?

CHAPTER TWENTY-SEVEN

"We're thrilled to have you join us," Deloris says as she leads me into the private dining room.

It's Wednesday, and the committee I'm now part of is meeting at a very nice restaurant inside an even nicer hotel. Yesterday, after my medical appointment, Logan made me call Deloris and volunteer for this committee. He said one is enough for now and that he'd see how I do before making me volunteer for even more committees.

I feel like I'm his employee and he's monitoring me, evaluating my performance. The whole reason he's making me do this is so that we fit in with these people and work our way into their social circle. Logan is doing his part, golfing with the men, having drinks with them, and for my part I have to attend these committee meetings.

Logan is so worried about me not living up to expectations that he told me what to say and how to act. He also picked out my outfit, a navy-blue dress with a patterned scarf tied around my neck. I told him I look like a flight attendant, but he said the dress was perfect for a midday lunch meeting.

"Attention, everyone," Deloris says, quieting the chatter in the room. "I'd like to introduce you to our newest member, Mrs. Logan Fairmont."

"It's Avery," I say, annoyed that she used Logan's name instead of mine.

"The city has just named her husband Humanitarian of the Year," Deloris says proudly.

The women in the room smile at me, some looking envious and others impressed that I married a man worthy of such a prestigious award. I get the feeling these women base their success on their husbands' accomplishments rather than their own, which I guess makes sense if their lives are devoted to supporting their husbands' careers.

"As some of you know," Deloris says, "Avery is currently dealing with some health issues that limit what she can do. She may not be able to attend every meeting or help out as much as we'd like with events. Please keep that in mind before assigning her tasks." Deloris smiles at me. "Would you like to say a few words?"

"I'd just like to thank everyone for welcoming me." I smile at the group of women. "I look forward to serving on the committee and doing what I can to make a difference in children's lives."

I sound like a beauty pageant contestant, but it's what they want to hear. Logan coached me on this before he left this morning, saying first impressions are everything and that my introduction needed to be brief but impactful. I considered ignoring his advice and saying what I want, but I was too tired to come up with anything else.

I haven't been sleeping much since Logan confessed his part in John's death. I keep going over it in my head, not wanting to believe Logan would do that. John never liked

Logan and didn't like that I was with him, but that's not a reason for Logan to kill him.

"Anything else?" Deloris asks, and I notice everyone staring at me. I must've spaced out for a moment.

"Um, no, that was it," I say.

"Then, everyone, take your seats and we'll get started," Deloris says.

The meeting begins with a recap of the last meeting. I'm already bored and finding my mind wandering. I'm so tired that it's hard to stay focused. The doctor gave me pills to sleep, but I tried them and they didn't do anything. I almost think they made me more awake.

My doctor's appointment yesterday was a waste of time, as Logan predicted. They did blood work, like they always do, and I had a short exam, then the doctor sat us down and said what he's told us many times before. That my immune system isn't working right and my body is attacking itself, which is causing all my symptoms. They don't know why or how to fix it, so I just have to try to live with it. I left feeling hopeless, which is how I always feel after those appointments, but now I feel even more hopeless because I'm being held hostage by Logan.

Even if I was able to leave him, how would I survive on my own? I need someone around in case something happens to me, like if I pass out or get dizzy and fall. I've experienced both those scenarios, but Logan was home to help me. What would happen if I lived alone?

"Do you have any ideas, Avery?"

I hear my name and wake from my thoughts. "I'm sorry, what did you say?"

The woman next to me answers, "The carnival. I was asking if you had any ideas to add."

Carnival? When were they talking about a carnival? I really need to pay better attention.

"I don't," I tell her, "have any ideas, but I'll get back to you if I do."

She gives me a polite smile, then looks around the table. "Anyone else?"

"I think having some animals there would be fun," a woman seated next to Deloris says. She's the only woman here who looks close to my age. Everyone else is at least twenty years older than me.

"We can't have animals," the woman next to me says. "That's too much of a liability."

"I was thinking stuffed animals, like stuffed tigers and elephants. We could use them as decorations and then give them away as prizes at the end of the night."

"I think the children would love that," Deloris says. "Excellent idea, Paige! Perhaps you and Avery could work on this together."

"Sure." Paige smiles at me across the table. "Are you good with that, Avery?"

"Yes, I could help," I say, not sure what I'm agreeing to.

The meeting continues, and I force myself to pay attention. I find out we're planning a carnival for children who are living in shelters. I'm pleasantly surprised that we're actually organizing an event that's not another ritzy fundraiser catering to the rich. Maybe being on this committee won't be so bad after all.

When the meeting ends, lunch is served, and Paige switches places with the woman next to me so we can discuss the task we've been assigned.

"I hope you don't mind that they volunteered you to work on this," Paige says as she puts her napkin on her lap.

"I don't mind. It sounds fun. I didn't know this group did actual events for the kids. I thought they just raised money."

"They used to only raise money," she says, lowering her voice. "But I talked them into doing more. It seems silly to say we're helping kids, but then all we do is plan parties for ourselves. I know the parties raise money, but they also cost a lot. Half the money we raise goes to pay for the event."

"I feel the same way," I say, pleased that someone else here thinks the way I do. Maybe Paige and I could be friends. We're close in age, and she doesn't seem uptight and snooty like the other women here. She's not even dressed up, or at least not compared to the rest of us. She's wearing a casual white cotton skirt and a fuzzy pink sweater. Logan would not approve.

"Do you have any kids?" she asks, her face lighting up, like she's hoping that's another thing we have in common.

"No kids," I tell her, picking up my fork. Our lunch is a tiny scoop of chicken salad served with a small roll and some berries. It's more like a snack than lunch, but I don't have much of an appetite, so it's plenty for me.

"I have two," Paige says as she butters her roll. "A boy and a girl. That's one of the reasons they asked me to be on the committee. They wanted a young mom to represent the moms we help. Well, we help the kids, but the moms are part of it. They're the ones getting the kids to the events. Most of them are single moms, like me."

"You're not married?" I ask, surprised she'd be allowed on the committee without a husband.

"I'm divorced. It's a long story, but basically, I ended up in a shelter years ago with my kids, and that's when I met Deloris. She was at the shelter, giving out women's suits that had been donated. I was applying for a job that week and needed a suit, so it was great timing." She smiles. "And I got the job! Executive assistant at a law firm. The suit definitely helped. I looked the part, and they hired me on the spot."

Paige was in a shelter? And now she's here? I really want to ask more about her background, but I'm not sure if I should. Maybe she doesn't like talking about it, although she's the one who brought it up.

"Can I ask what happened?" I quietly say, not wanting the other women to hear. But they're engrossed in their own conversations, so I doubt they're listening to mine.

"You mean with the job?"

"No, how you ended up in the shelter. If you don't want to tell me, that's fine. I was just curious."

"I don't mind. It's not a secret. Everyone here knows my story. I even spoke at one of our events." She sets her fork down. "My ex was abusive. He'd get drunk and lose control. It got to the point that I thought he might kill me. I didn't want my kids being without a mom, so one night when he was out at the bar, I packed a suitcase, took the kids, and went to the shelter."

"What happened when your husband found out?"

"I don't know. I wasn't there when they told him we were gone. I'm sure he wanted to kill me, but he couldn't because they locked him away."

"He went to jail?"

She nods. "The cops arrested him that night. Turns out he killed a guy a few days prior to that. Apparently, he was driving drunk and hit a guy, then drove off. The cops tracked him down and arrested him. It was all caught on a street camera, so Jerry couldn't try to say he didn't do it."

"And he never told you this happened? That he hit a guy?"

"No, I had no idea. And then I found out he'd racked up all this debt and hadn't been paying the mortgage, so I lost the house and had to stay in the shelter." She picks up her purse and takes something out. It's a business card, and she hands it to me. "This is the shelter. They're always looking for volunteers, if you're interested."

The card reads *Harris Row Shelter*. I've never heard of it, but I recognize the address. It's in a part of town that's always on the news because of all the murders and other violent crimes that happen in that area.

"Thanks," I tell her, tucking the card in my purse. "I'll look into it."

I'm just being polite. I'm not volunteering there. It's too dangerous. I can't believe Paige lived there with her kids. She must've been desperate to get away from her husband.

Will that be me someday? Will I be at a point where I'm so desperate to get away from Logan that I'd rather be anywhere else than home with him?

"So what about you?" Paige asks, smiling at me as she dabs her napkin on her mouth. "What's your story?"

"It's not that exciting," I say, picking at my chicken salad. It's not very good, so I haven't eaten much of it. "I'm originally from Seattle. I moved here for my husband's job."

"The amazing Logan Fairmont," she says with a laugh. "I'm kidding. He sounds great. It's just people are making such a big deal over him, like he's a celebrity or something."

"I know, right?" I say, keeping my voice down. "I don't get why people are making such a fuss over him. And I'm his wife."

She smiles. "I like you, Avery. I wasn't sure what to expect from Logan Fairmont's wife, but you surprised me. You're not at all like I thought you'd be."

"Which was what?"

She shrugs. "I don't know. Fake, I guess? But you don't seem that way at all."

I feel like a fake, pretending everything's fine when I'm trapped in my marriage by a psychopath who has everyone fooled into thinking he's wonderful. I must be a good actress if no one can tell how miserable I am.

"Do you work?" Paige asks.

"I did, but Logan made me—" I stop, realizing I almost said something bad about Logan. If that got back to him, he'd do something to punish me. "I quit. This week, actually. Monday was my last day."

"You mean your husband told you to," she says, tearing off a piece of her roll. "It's okay to admit it. All the women here quit their jobs because of their husbands. I don't think it's right, but it's not my place to judge. People can do what they want." She pops the roll in her mouth.

"I'm having some health issues," I say, not wanting her to think Logan is the reason I'm no longer working. "I'm taking time off to get better."

"Really, you don't need to explain. No judgment here." She picks up her iced tea and takes a drink.

"Are you still working at the law firm?"

"Yes, but now I'm a paralegal," she says with pride in her voice. "I went back to school. Got my degree. It was a lot of work, but it paid off. I'm able to support myself and my kids."

"That's awesome," I say. "You think you'll ever get married again?"

"No. Never. After what I went through, I won't even date a man."

"Did he really try to... kill you?"

"No, but he threatened to, usually when he was drunk." She leans closer, keeping her voice down. "I used to hide things around the house. Notes. Pictures. Evidence, in case he actually did kill me. I wanted to make sure the cops locked him away."

"Pictures of what?"

"Where he hit me. And I'd write notes telling whoever found them that Jerry did it. That he's the one who killed me. I'd write one every time he threatened to do it and include the date. The problem is, I hid them so well I couldn't find them later. I found, like, two, but I hid at least ten. Maybe Jerry found them and threw them out. Who knows?"

Her story has me thinking of my own. Should I be doing that? Hiding photos and notes around the house in case Logan kills me? But he's not going to kill me. I've been over this a million times in my head and decided he'd never do it. He wouldn't risk being named a suspect and having everything he's worked for being taken away.

"We should probably get together soon to talk about the carnival," Paige says as dessert is served. "Maybe we could meet for coffee."

"Um, yeah. Maybe this weekend. I'll have to check my schedule."

"Great!" She pushes her chair back and gets up. "I have to get back to work, but I'll give you a call and we'll set up a time to meet."

"Sounds good."

"I'll see you later!" She waves at the women at the table. "Thanks, ladies! It was good seeing you all!"

They tell her goodbye as she leaves. I'm disappointed she had to go. I liked her. She was easy to talk to. And I liked hearing her story, especially the part about making sure her husband would go to prison if he ever harmed her.

I'm going to do the same. I'm going to hide evidence just in case something happens. I really don't think it will, but if it did, I want to make sure Logan pays. He got away with killing John, but he won't get away with killing me.

I finally feel a sliver of hope. A tiny bit of control. And it's all thanks to Logan for making me come here today.

CHAPTER TWENTY-EIGHT

"Have a good day," Logan says, giving me a kiss. His cologne engulfs me, a woodsy scent with a hint of cedar. Every time I smell it, I feel sick, knowing it means Logan is near. "Don't forget dinner tonight with the Fieldstones."

"I won't." I smile at him. "I'll make sure I'm ready to go when you get home."

"Good," he says with a triumphant grin. He's proud of himself for what he's done to me. Making me into the obedient wife. One he can show off and not worry about embarrassing him.

It's been almost a year since Logan slapped me that night. Nearly a year of pure hell. But I've survived it, and I've convinced Logan he's broken me to the point that I've given up fighting and accepted that my sole purpose is to be the wife of Logan Fairmont. Everything I do and say is meant to support him, praise him, and make sure everyone thinks he's wonderful.

Logan actually believes that, which surprises me because I thought for sure he'd know that I'm putting on an act. It started the day I met Paige. On the way home from the committee meeting, I stopped at the store and bought one of those instant print cameras. I took a picture of my bruised cheek, printed it, dated it, and hid it at the back of my lingerie drawer, a place where Logan would never look.

Then I wrote a note that read:

He hit me across the face. He told me he soaked rags in paint thinner and put them in John's shed.

The note continued to describe the scene Logan created that led to the death of my brother. Logan didn't actually kill him, so I doubt he'd get charged with a crime, but I at least wanted people to know Logan's intentions.

Next, I wrote down the threats Logan made against Mia that night and how he shoved those pills down my throat. The note was so long that it took up a whole sheet of paper. I folded it up into a tiny square and hid it in the jewelry box John gave me as a wedding gift.

I've written several notes since then, detailing Logan's threats along with what he's done to me. The worst was when he broke my arm during a weekend trip to Napa. Logan told everyone he was taking me there to celebrate the anniversary of our first date, reinforcing his image of being a thoughtful and romantic husband. I didn't want to go, but Logan made me. We were alone in a vineyard when we got into an argument. Logan threw me to the ground and I landed on my arm, breaking it in two places.

Then there was the daily abuse, like Logan slapping my face when I said things he didn't like. Or if I tried to walk away during a fight, he'd grab me and force me to listen to him, holding me tight enough to leave bruises behind. I took photos every time and hid them.

After a few months of this, I decided to let Logan think that he'd won. I played the obedient wife and did what I was told. Logan was thrilled that I was finally being the wife he wanted, and as a way to reward me, he stopped the abuse, or at least the physical part. The emotional abuse continued, but it was not as intense as before.

Now, I'm such a good wife that Logan has nothing to yell at me about except when I'm not feeling well. I try to hide when I'm having a bad day, but sometimes I feel so awful that I can't. Logan hates that I'm sick and keeps accusing me of faking it, even though my blood work proves that my body isn't working like it should.

The past few months, my symptoms have been getting worse. I have excruciating headaches almost daily. I struggle to eat and have lost a lot of weight. And one day last month I got dizzy and blacked out. The doctors can't explain why this is happening or how to fix it. They continue to blame it on an autoimmune condition.

Logan just left for work, and I watch his car drive away. When it's out of sight, I take a deep breath and prepare myself for the day. The day I've been waiting for.

This is it. I'm finally leaving Logan. I'm going to gather up all the notes and photos, pack a bag, and go to my new home, the Harris Row Shelter. I went there a few weeks ago, pretending I wanted to volunteer. The lady in charge gave me a tour of the place, and while we walked around, I asked her all my questions, like how secure it was and if a resident could hide there and not be found by their spouse. The lady probably wondered why I was asking that stuff, but I didn't care. I needed answers.

My phone rings. It's Rachel. I haven't told her what Logan has done to me or that I'm leaving him. I haven't told anyone. It's been hard to keep it a secret, especially from Rachel since I see her almost every day and tend to have a few glasses of wine when I'm with her, but I've managed to not say anything.

"Hey," I say, answering the call. "I have a ton of stuff to do today, so I can't really talk."

"Oh," she says, sounding disappointed. "I was going to ask if you wanted to go shopping with me. I need a dress for this weekend, and I was hoping you'd help me find one."

Rachel's cousin is getting married this weekend. She's going by herself, which makes me think there's nothing going on with her and Connor. Logan is convinced they're a couple, but Rachel keeps insisting they're not. When we go out with them, they're not at all affectionate with each other. In fact, all they seem to do is fight, but Connor has no plans to move out, so maybe there's still a chance they'll get back together.

"I can't today," I tell her. "But I'm sure you'll find something fabulous."

"Oh please," she implores. "I hate shopping alone. I'll buy you lunch when we're done."

"Sorry, but I can't. I have too much to do."

She sighs. "Okay, but if I get a dress that looks horrible on me, I'm blaming you."

"That's not going to happen." I try to laugh and keep the tone light. "Nothing looks horrible on you. You look great in anything."

"Aww, you're so sweet."

"I gotta go. We'll talk later."

"Okay. Bye!"

As I end the call, I hear someone yell, "Hello?" It's followed by knocking.

I'm in the kitchen and look over at the sliding door. Edith is peering through the glass.

She knocks again. "Anyone home?"

What does she want? I like Edith, but I don't have time for her today. I turn to sneak out of the kitchen, but she catches me.

"Hey! Avery! You gonna let me in?"

I sigh and walk over to the slider, unlocking it and opening the door. "Hi, Edith. I'm kind of busy so—"

"I won't stay," she says, coming into the house, her dirt-covered boots leaving a trail all over the floor. "Just wanted to give you these." She shoves a paper sack at me.

I take it and open it up. "Tomatoes?"

"From my garden." She walks past me to the cupboard next to the sink. "I got way too many, and I remember you saying you like tomatoes, so there you go. Enjoy." She takes a mug from the cupboard and brings it to the coffee maker, filling it with what's left of the coffee.

"Edith, you can just take that to go," I tell her. "I've got a lot to do. I really don't have time to—"

"What is it you gotta do?" she asks, scooping sugar into her coffee. "You don't work. You never go anywhere. That husband of yours has turned you into a prisoner in your own house."

How does she know that? Has she been watching us? Did she overhear something?

"I had an aunt like you," Edith says, taking her coffee to the table and sitting down. "Stayed at home all day, waiting for her husband to come home. Made his meals. Did his laundry." She looks over at me. "Why do you do all that for him? You know women don't have to be like that anymore. Times have changed. Get out of this house and do something for yourself. Let the jerk fix his own dinner."

"I go out. You just don't see me leave."

"Oh, yeah? Where do you go? To pick up his dry cleaning? Buy him groceries?" She huffs. "If I were you, I'd leave him. You're too good for him."

Edith might be the one and only person who doesn't like Logan. Well, other than me. She's never liked him, and he's never liked her. He's always telling me to stay away from her, but every time I go in the backyard, she sees me and comes over to talk.

"Why don't you like Logan?" I ask, joining her at the table.

"He's a pompous prick who thinks he's better than everyone. I don't know why you ever married him."

"He wasn't always like that."

"So you admit it," she says with a laugh. "You admit he's a jerk."

"I didn't say that."

"But you know it, and if you know it, then why are you still with him?" She sips her coffee.

"No marriage is perfect."

"No, but it shouldn't make you miserable."

"I'm not."

"You sure look like you are. I see you when you got the curtains open. Walking around this kitchen, looking like you hate your life. And then the jerk comes home and you're all smiles. I don't know how you do it. I can't pretend to be something I'm not. And you shouldn't either."

She's right. I'm miserable but pretending to be happy.

Pretending to be someone else. But it's what I had to do to make it to today, the day I'm finally getting away from him.

"You know, it's bad for your health to be miserable all the time," Edith says. "That's probably why you're sick."

"Maybe we could talk later," I say, getting up from the table. "I have stuff to do, and I really need to start now."

"Yeah, fine, I'm going." Edith finishes her coffee and brings the mug to the sink, rinsing it out and putting it in the dishwasher.

"Thank you for the tomatoes," I say as I open the slider door.

"Let me know what you think of them," she says, meeting me at the door. "It's a new kind I'm trying. They're a little sweet, kind of like a cherry tomato."

"Okay, I'll let you know," I say, hoping she doesn't go on to tell me about the many varieties of tomato plants. She can talk about gardening for hours.

"Get out of the house today," she says as she leaves. "Go do something for yourself."

"I will," I tell her before closing the slider door. "I promise."

It's odd she'd tell me to do something for myself on the very day I plan to do just that. It's almost like she knows what I'm up to. She doesn't, of course. It was just a coincidence, but I'm taking it as a sign that I'm doing the right thing. It's risky and might not work out, but I have to try.

Just before noon, I grab the laundry basket and bring it to the bedroom. I toss my clothes in it, the ones I'll be wearing in my new life. Jeans, T-shirts, hoodies. All the things Logan wouldn't let me wear in public and didn't even want in my wardrobe. I convinced him I needed jeans and T-shirts for cleaning around the house, which is the only reason he let me keep them.

As I'm leaving the bedroom with the laundry basket, I hear a noise. It sounded like a door closing.

"Hello?" I call out. "Is anyone there?"

The house is silent. I must be hearing things. It's been happening all morning. I'm so on edge, worrying Logan's going to catch me, that I keep thinking I hear him coming home. But I checked his schedule, and he has meetings all day.

I continue down the hall to the kitchen, stopping when I hear a noise again.

"Hello?" I pause to listen but don't hear anything. "Is someone here?"

Again, nothing. Not a sound.

I take a step forward and feel something hard slam against the back of my head. The laundry basket drops from my hands and my vision blurs. Confused and disoriented, I stumble back, hitting the center island and falling heavily to the floor. My vision goes dark, and I feel myself drifting out of consciousness.

PART 3

CHAPTER TWENTY-NINE

PRESENT DAY

"Your recovery is coming along better than I expected," Dr. Heron, my neurologist, says as Logan and I sit in his office. We're here to get the results of my most recent blood work and brain scans.

"What does that mean?" Logan asks.

"The incision is healed, the scans show no swelling on the brain, and the blood work looks good."

Logan looks at me, then back at the doctor. "I don't understand. You're saying Avery's blood work is normal?"

"There are a few values that are out of the normal range, but it's nothing to be concerned about."

"What about her autoimmune disease? It couldn't have just gone away, could it?"

"It's unusual but not impossible." Dr. Heron glances up at his computer screen and clicks on the keyboard. "I can't explain it, but whatever was causing your autoimmune condition, Avery, doesn't seem to be an issue anymore."

"How could that be?" Logan asks. "She's been sick for years."

"It's hard to say. It's possible the trauma to the brain caused Avery's immune system to redirect its focus to healing rather than attacking her as it had done in the past."

"Have you ever seen that happen before?" I ask.

"I haven't, but that doesn't mean it isn't possible. Your blood work has been gradually improving since your head injury, which tells me the two are related. Or there's another theory, but it's far less likely."

"What is it?" I ask. "What's the other theory?"

He leans back in his chair. "Sometimes when a person is under a great deal of stress, their body responds by getting sick in an attempt to get them to slow down and take better care of themselves."

"I wasn't stressed. I mean, I don't think I was. Obviously, I can't remember, but I don't know why I'd be stressed. I didn't have a job."

"Your illness was causing you stress," Logan says. "You were upset that you weren't getting better."

"But what started it? I don't remember being stressed when I first started having symptoms."

"Honey, your brother died," Logan says, reaching over to hold my hand. "Don't you remember how awful that was for you? The stress it caused you?"

"I remember John's death, but my symptoms started later." I look over at Dr. Heron. "I guess I don't understand what you're saying. What does this have to do with me getting better?"

"I was getting to that." He leans forward, resting his hands on his desk. "With your memory loss, you don't remember whatever it was that caused you to feel a high enough level of stress that your body reacted physically, causing your symptoms. Without those memories, your body healed itself of the condition and the symptoms that went along with it."

"So if I remember whatever caused it, the symptoms will come back?"

"It's possible, but again, it's just a theory. Autoimmune disorders can be very complex."

"Well, I can assure you," Logan says to the doctor, "I did everything I could to make sure her stress level was as low as possible. That's why I insisted she quit her job and why I—"

"Wait, you told me to quit?" I say. "I thought you said it was my decision."

"It was," he says, rubbing my hand. "What I meant is that I supported your decision to leave. You didn't think I'd be okay with you not working, which was completely untrue. I wanted you to stay home and get better." He smiles at me, but it doesn't seem sincere. I feel like he's only doing it because the doctor is watching us.

Why do I keep feeling this way? Like people are lying to me, specifically Logan? Is it because I found that note telling me not to believe him? Or is it the other stuff? Like the foods he claimed I liked when I'm almost certain that I didn't. But why would Logan tell me something that wasn't true?

I wish I knew what was going on. Are any of the memories I'm having real, or is my mind making them up?

"Do you have anything else to tell us?" Logan asks the doctor. "I don't mean to rush you, but I have a city council meeting in an hour."

"Go," I say, smiling at him. "Go to your meeting. I can take a ride service home."

"Honey, no, I'll take you home, but we need to leave soon if I'm going to make it to the meeting on time."

"That's really all I had for today," Dr. Heron says. "Unless you have any other questions."

"I do," I blurt out. "I have some questions."

"Go ahead."

"It may take a few minutes." I turn to Logan. "Go to your meeting. You don't need to stay."

"No, it's fine. I can be late. Go ahead and ask your questions."

I need him to leave. I don't want him hearing this, and what's concerning is, I'm not sure why. I should want my husband here, but I don't.

"I don't know how long it'll take," I say. "And traffic could be bad at this time of day. You should really go now if you want to make the city council meeting."

He checks his watch and lets out a sigh. "I suppose you're right. I wasn't considering the traffic. But I hate to just leave you here."

"I'll be fine. Go now, or you're going to be late."

"Text me when you're home. I'll call Rachel and tell her to come over and check on you."

I don't need Rachel to come over, but I know Logan will insist on it, so I let it go.

"Dr. Heron, thank you for your time today," Logan says, shaking his hand.

"It's my pleasure." He smiles at Logan. "I'm always happy to share good news."

"I'll see you tonight," Logan says, leaning down to give me a kiss.

When he's gone, Dr. Heron looks at me and asks, "So what other questions do you have?"

"It's about my memory loss. I keep having the feeling

that I'm remembering something, but then I'm not sure if the memory is real."

"Why don't you think it's real?"

"Because when I ask Logan about it, he says it never happened or that it isn't true. Like I had a memory of making salmon for dinner. I saw myself in the kitchen making it. It seemed so real, but then Logan said I've never once made salmon the whole time he's known me."

"And you're sure the memory wasn't from earlier, before you met your husband?"

"No, it was recent. The memory was at our house, in our kitchen. And there's other stuff. Other memories I've had that seem real, but I might be making them up. Is that even possible? That I'd make up memories that didn't happen?"

"Yes. In fact, it can be quite common in people who've had a traumatic brain injury. Sometimes you might experience something that feels familiar but can't access the memory of it, so your brain creates one. Other times, you may be so desperate to get your memory back that your mind comes up with false memories."

I sigh. "So none of it's real. Whatever I thought I remembered was made up?"

"I'm not saying that. I'm simply saying it's possible." He looks over at his computer monitor. "Actually, when I look at your scans, I'm surprised you haven't had more of your memories restored by now."

"Really?" I lean forward to look at the monitor, but I can't tell what it's showing. It just looks like the outline of a skull with different colored sections. "Then maybe the memories are real?"

"I thought your husband confirmed that they didn't actually happen."

"I haven't told him everything I've remembered."

"Then I'd suggest starting there. Ask your husband if the things you're remembering actually happened."

I would, except that I don't trust he'd tell me the truth. But why wouldn't he? Logan wants me to get better.

"Your case is rather unusual," Dr. Heron says.

"What do you mean?"

"Generally, with a traumatic brain injury, patients have trouble remembering things in the present, meaning you forget where you put your keys, or you make an appointment and then forget to go, or you go on a walk and forget how to get home. That's very common after a brain injury, yet you don't seem to struggle with that."

"No, I don't have a problem remembering that stuff."

"Which makes me curious as to why you're struggling to remember the past, specifically the past two years."

"I thought you said it was normal for people with traumatic brain injuries to forget the past."

"It is, but it's usually accompanied by memory loss in the present, too. Forgetting an appointment. Not remembering how to get home. I would've expected you'd be experiencing those lapses in memory, but you're not, which is unusual."

"Why would that be? Why would I only have problems remembering the past but not the present?"

"I have an idea, but I could be way off. I only bring it up because I noticed you seemed uncomfortable around your husband."

"I wasn't uncomfortable," I say, but it's a lie. I've felt uncomfortable around Logan since I woke up in the hospital and saw him by my bed. I told myself it wasn't him making me uncomfortable but my situation. Not being able to remember hitting my head or the two years before that was unsettling and scary.

"When he held your hand," Dr. Heron says, his voice steady, "you flinched, like you didn't want him touching you."

I flinched? I didn't think I flinched, but I doubt the doctor would lie about that.

"Were you and your husband having problems?" Dr. Heron asks. "Before your injury?"

"I don't think so, but I can't remember, so it's hard to say. Why do you ask?"

"There's something called dissociative amnesia. It's a type of memory loss that happens after a distressing event. It could be a single event, like witnessing a violent crime, or it could be something that went on for months or even years. For example, children who have suffered abuse throughout their childhood may grow up to find that they have no memory of it. Their brain has blocked it out as a way to protect them from the pain and trauma of what happened. It's not that they've forgotten. The memories are there. They just can't access them."

"What does this have to do with me?"

"I'm wondering if perhaps something happened to you that your mind is choosing not to remember. Something that caused you significant pain that your mind is trying to protect you from."

I pause to think. "Maybe my brother dying? That was very hard on me. John and I were really close. He was my best friend. I was closer to him than anyone else, even Logan."

"Were you there when he died?"

"No, he died in a fire in the shed behind his house. But

that can't be the cause of my memory loss. I remember when John died. I didn't block it out."

"It may have happened *after* his death. Perhaps the months that followed, having to live without him, were so painful that you blocked them out."

"But it's not just months. I can't remember the past two years."

"It's possible your brother's death affected you for that long. Your medical history shows you'd been taking meds for anxiety and depression. Have you asked your husband what led you to take them?"

"He said it was because I was so upset about losing John."

"Did you go to counseling?"

"I don't think so. Logan didn't mention it."

"It's odd you wouldn't seek counseling if you were that distraught over losing your brother, but I understand not everyone's comfortable talking about such personal matters as grief and family relationships with a stranger."

"So do you think that's what's wrong with me? That my brain just blocked out the part of my past that it didn't want to remember?"

"I think it's definitely possible."

"But why now? If this doesn't have to do with my brain injury, why didn't I have the memory loss before it happened?"

"Your brain injury may have been the catalyst to hide those memories away. The stress caused by those memories would only make your recovery more difficult, so your brain may have blocked them as a way to help you get better faster."

"Will the memories come back?"

"They can, but many times they don't. It really depends on the person. You may experience flashbacks. If you do, I'd pay attention and not dismiss them as being memories that you've made up."

As he talks, I'm feeling more hopeful. Maybe the memories I thought were real actually happened after all, which means I'm not losing my mind. I'm just accessing memories that my mind has blocked.

"You may also have triggers," Dr. Heron says. "The triggers are often emotions linked to the memory. You feel them without knowing why. For example, you suddenly feel very anxious when you're at a certain location or are around a person who's somehow linked to that memory. You can't explain why you're having such a strong reaction. It doesn't make sense. That's usually because whatever memory it's triggering is blocked."

He just described exactly what I've been going through since getting home from the hospital. The feelings I've had that didn't make sense, like feeling sick to my stomach when I smelled Logan's cologne that was on the shelf in our bathroom. Or feeling like I can't trust that what Logan is telling me is true. Feeling uncomfortable when he touches me.

But all of that has to do with Logan, not my brother. Does that mean this isn't about John? Did something happen between Logan and me? Something so bad that my mind doesn't want to remember it?

CHAPTER THIRTY

When I'm back at the house, I go to the bedroom and text Logan, telling him I'm home and that I don't need Rachel to come over. But as soon as I hit send, I hear her at the door.

"Avery?" She knocks, then rings the bell. "Avery, it's me. Rachel."

How did she know to come over? Even if Logan told her to, he didn't know when I'd be home. I just texted him.

"Avery?" Rachel knocks again.

Maybe if I ignore her, she'll go back to her house. Or I could text her and tell her I'm about to take a nap. I get my phone out to do that and hear the front door open.

"There you are," Rachel says, appearing at the door to my room, a big smile on her face. "Why didn't you answer the door?"

"I was taking a nap," I say, standing by the bed, which is made, the comforter smoothed out, pillows in place. It's obvious I wasn't napping, but maybe she won't notice. "How'd you get in? I could've sworn I locked the door."

"I have a key." She holds it up.

"Where'd you get that?"

"Logan gave it to me in case you didn't answer the door and I needed to get in to make sure you're okay."

"Did Logan tell you to come over?"

"Yes, he called me on the way to his city council meeting. He told me you'd be getting a ride home and to watch for the car so I'd know when to come over."

Why does he insist on having someone here all the time? I don't need a babysitter. Logan heard Dr. Heron say how well I'm doing. That should be enough to convince him I can be home by myself now.

I'm glad Logan didn't hear the other part of the conversation, when Dr. Heron explained how I might have dissociative amnesia. If Logan is the cause of that amnesia, I don't want him knowing about it. Because if Logan did something that terrible that my mind has blocked it out, it means I can't trust him. And I don't. I haven't for weeks, but I didn't know why. Now I'm thinking it's related to whatever happened over the past two years, the memories I've apparently blocked.

If Logan really did something awful, he'd want to hide it from me. Any flashbacks I had of the past, memories I think I had, he'd deny, to make me think I made it all up. Even things like the foods I enjoy. Telling me I love ham salad or fajitas with onions? Was he telling me that to confuse me about who I really am? To make me think my memory loss is worse than it actually is?

Why would he do that? What did he do that was so awful that he's determined to keep it hidden from me, even if that means making me think I'm crazy?

"Have you had lunch?" Rachel asks. "Because I was

thinking we could order Chinese. I've been craving it, and their delivery is fast."

"Why don't we go out? It's a nice day. Maybe we could eat outside."

"I would, but we need to stay here. We could order lunch and take it out to the patio." She rolls her eyes. "Except Edith is out back, working in her garden. She'll want to join us if she sees us."

"Why can't we leave?"

"Logan doesn't want you going out." She tucks her key into the pocket of her billowing floral skirt and gets out her phone. "If you don't want Chinese, we could try something else. There's a new sandwich place close to here. Does that sound good?"

I walk up to her. "We're friends, right?"

She lowers her phone, eyeing me with concern. "Of course we're friends. Why are you asking?"

"Because you're acting like you're better friends with my husband than with me."

She smiles. "Come on, Avery. You know that's not true. I barely know Logan."

"But how do I know that?" I ask. "Maybe you two became friends, and I just don't remember."

"Well, yes, Logan and I are friends, but that's because you and I are friends, and because he's friends with Connor. It's not the same kind of friendship I have with you."

"Then why are you always taking his side?"

"I'm not. What are you talking about?"

"If we were good friends, you'd listen to me and forget what Logan says. Like right now, I want to go to lunch, but you won't. Because of Logan."

"That's because I care about your health. It has nothing to do with Logan."

"I just got back from seeing the doctor. He said I'm doing great, better than he expected. Logan was there. He heard the doctor say that I'm fine."

"I'd just feel better if we stayed here," she says, straining to keep her smile going. "That's all."

I always feel like she's pretending to be happy when she's not. Despite what she says, I know she doesn't like coming here day after day, flipping through magazines and making me lunch. So why is she doing it?

She holds up her phone. "I need to make a call. I'll be back in a minute. While I'm gone, think about what you want for lunch." She hurries out of the bedroom, and I hear the front door open and close.

Going into the living room, I look out the front window and see Rachel on her phone, pacing back and forth on the sidewalk that goes between our houses. Why did she go outside to make the call? Who is she talking to? Is it Logan? Is she calling to ask him if she's allowed to take me somewhere?

She can't be calling Logan. He's in the city council meeting. He wouldn't leave it to talk to Rachel.

She ends the call and walks back toward the house, shaking her head like she's angry or annoyed. She comes inside, stopping suddenly when she sees me.

"What are you doing?" she asks.

"Just looking out the window. Who were you talking to?"

"Connor. He said he might come over later, and I wanted to ask him what time." Her smile appears. "I was thinking about what you said, and you're right. I shouldn't be listening to Logan. If you really want to go to lunch, let's do it."

"Why the sudden change of heart?" I ask, wondering if I was right and it was Logan on the phone.

"I feel better about taking you out now that you told me what the doctor said. If you're really doing better, then what's the harm in going out?"

"Are you sure you don't want to check with Logan? Make sure he approves?"

She laughs. "Okay, you've made your point. Do you know where you want to go?"

I pick a restaurant that's in the neighborhood where Logan and I lived when we first moved here. It's a long drive from where we live now, so I'm surprised when Rachel agrees to go there.

"Our old apartment was close to here," I say to Rachel as we're leaving the restaurant. "Would you mind driving by it?"

"We should probably get home. Maybe we could do it some other time."

"Come on. It's really close. It won't take long."

"Okay, fine. Tell me where to go."

She sounds annoyed with me, which I've noticed is a common reaction when I ask her to do something. A good friend wouldn't react that way, which is another clue that makes me think our friendship wasn't as close as she makes it sound.

"Slow down," I tell her. "It's right here."

"Tell me again why we're doing this?"

I don't answer, focusing on the feeling I'm getting. It's strong and familiar, but I don't think it's because I used to live here. That was years ago. The feeling I'm having now is making me think I was here more recently. I feel relaxed, almost happy, being here, which is odd since I don't feel that way when I'm home.

"Pull over," I say as Rachel drives past the rental office.

"What for?"

"Just do it."

She sighs, sounding annoyed with me again. She pulls over and stops. "Okay, now what?"

"I'll be right back." I get out of the car.

"Wait! Avery, where are you going?"

I ignore her and go into the rental office.

"Can I help you?" the woman at the desk says, her head down as she types on her keyboard. She stops and looks up at me, smiling. "You're back."

"You know me?"

"You were here a couple of months ago. You wanted a studio, but all we had was a one-bedroom. It's Jennifer, right?"

"Jennifer?" I ask, thinking she must have me confused with someone else.

"Jennifer Baxter? From Seattle?" She gets up from her desk. "I think I still have your application, but if not, it'll only take a few minutes to fill out a new one."

Jenny Baxter was a girl I knew in grade school. Then she moved the summer before middle school, and I never saw her again.

Why did I fill out an application for this apartment? And why would I use a fake name?

"That's you, right?" the woman says, getting up from her chair. "Jennifer?"

"Um, yeah," I say, deciding to go with it. This woman

seems sure that I'm Jennifer Baxter, so I don't doubt that I gave her a fake name. But why?

"We have a studio opening up next month. Would that work, or do you need something right away? I know last time you were here, you weren't sure about the timing. Is that still the case?"

"Yes," I say, playing along. "I'm still not sure. I thought I'd just check and see what you had available. So, um, what did I tell you last time I was here? I looked at so many apartments that week that I can't remember who I talked to and what I said."

"You mentioned something about being new to town and not sure if you were going to stay. That's why you wanted a shorter lease. I believe you asked for three months, which is doable but will cost more."

A three-month lease? Why would I move here for three months? Were Logan and I separating? Maybe that's it. Maybe we were having problems, and I decided to move out for a few months. But why wouldn't Logan tell me that? Or why wouldn't Rachel? If we were friends, she'd know if Logan and I were having marital problems. And why the fake name? Did I not want people finding out that I was here? Or was it Logan's idea? He's very concerned with his image. He wouldn't want people knowing our marriage was in trouble. He'd insist I use a fake name.

"Did I say anything else?" I ask.

"Why are you asking?" the woman says in a suspicious tone. "I don't mean to sound rude, but I find it odd that you—"

"I can't remember," I blurt out. "I had a traumatic brain injury." I show her the incision on my head, which is no longer covered with a bandage but is starting to be concealed as my hair grows around it.

"Oh my," she says, staring at my head. "I'm so sorry. I guess that explains why you haven't been back."

"It's also why I'm asking so many questions."

"Well, I wish I could tell you more, but I think that was it. You asked about the studio, filled out the application, and said you'd be back if you decided to rent the one-bedroom, which is all we had available."

"Could I see the application?" I ask.

"If I still have it." She wakes up her computer, then clicks on the keyboard. "Looks like I no longer have it. We only keep them for a limited time. Would you like to fill out a new one?"

"Not right now." I look back at the street, making sure Rachel is still in the car. She is, and she's on the phone. "I should get going," I tell the woman. "Thanks for your help."

As I'm leaving, I hear the woman talking again. "I do remember you brought someone."

I turn back. "The last time I was here?"

"Yes, you brought a friend. She was very pretty. Tall, thin, dark hair. Maybe a year or two older than you?"

It wasn't Rachel. She has blond hair.

"Do you know her name?" I ask.

"Let me think." The woman pauses. "I'm usually pretty good at remembering names. I can picture her in my head." She pauses again. "Paige. Does that sound right?"

"I'm not sure. I mean, it's possible. I just can't think of anyone I know with that name."

"Maybe I got it wrong. But I'm almost positive it was Paige. You seemed like good friends. I'm surprised you haven't heard from her."

"Yeah, me too."

"Avery," Rachel says, racing into the office, "what's taking so long?"

"Avery?" the woman at the desk says, looking confused.

"We have to go." I smile at the woman and hurry out of the office.

"What were you doing in there?" Rachel asks as we get in the car.

"Talking," I say as Rachel pulls back on the street. "That lady knew Logan. She was going on and on about all the work he's done around the city to help the homeless."

"How'd Logan come up?" Rachel says.

"I told her my name, and when she heard Fairmont, she asked if I was related to Logan."

"It's a common name. The fact that she immediately thought of Logan tells you how well known he's become." Rachel glances at me. "It's like you're married to a celebrity."

"Not really. Only local people have heard of him."

"So why'd you want to go in there?" Rachel asks. "You're not looking for an apartment."

"I wanted to see how much the rent was. I was curious."

Rachel glances at me. "That's an odd thing to be curious about, especially when you're not looking to rent an apartment."

"It's not odd when your husband works in the housing business. He's always talking about rent prices in the city, which made me wonder what our old apartment would cost now."

"And? How much is it?"

I laugh. "She never told me. We were talking about Logan and she forgot. And then you came in, and we left."

We're waiting at a stoplight and Rachel's looking at me

like she doesn't believe a word I just said. I don't care. If she's been lying to me, I can lie to her too.

I can't prove that she's lying, but if I go by how I feel, I don't think we were close friends like she claims. Maybe we went out a few times or hung out at each other's houses, but that's just something neighbors do. It doesn't mean we were best friends. And if we were, she was faking it. I don't think she even likes me. We have nothing in common. We struggle to keep a conversation going.

So what's going on? Why is Rachel faking a friendship with me?

CHAPTER THIRTY-ONE

"I don't want Rachel coming over anymore," I say to Logan when we're having dinner that night. I asked him to bring home a pizza so we wouldn't have to make anything.

"Did you have a disagreement?" he asks, pouring himself more wine.

"No, I just don't like having her here all the time. I don't need someone watching over me. I'm a lot better now."

"You said the same thing before you collapsed on the kitchen floor. We even had plans to go out that night. You were looking forward to it." He sips his wine.

I don't know if he's telling the truth or just saying that so I'll fear being alone and go along with his insistence that someone stay with me. Either way, my decision stands. I don't want Rachel here.

"It's different now," I say. "You heard the doctor. Everything looks good, even my blood work. I don't need someone to stay with me."

"Rachel isn't just here as your caregiver. She's your

friend. She's company, so you're not bored all day with no one to talk to." He takes another slice of pizza from the box and sets it on his plate.

"I can have other friends over. It doesn't have to be Rachel."

"What other friends?"

"Friends from my old job. Like Maureen." I take a bite of the pizza, keeping my eyes on Logan.

"Maureen moved to Sacramento."

"She did? When?"

He shrugs. "About a year ago? She sent an email to everyone, including us. I could probably find it if you want to see it."

"Okay, so Maureen's gone, but I had other friends at work."

"That you haven't spoken to in years. And you weren't good friends with them. In fact, I remember you complaining about them." He picks up his wineglass and takes a drink.

I set my pizza down and wipe my hands on a napkin. "What about Paige?"

Logan coughs, almost choking on his wine. "Who?"

"Paige. You know her, don't you?"

He clears his throat. "Yes. I know Paige. I'm just surprised you mentioned her. You met her during the time you can't remember."

How do I explain this? I can't tell him about the apartment.

"I found a birthday card she gave me," I say. "If she sent me a card, I'm assuming that means we were friends."

"You were," he says, setting his wineglass down, "but she wasn't a good friend to you. She only saw the negative side of things, and it was starting to affect you. You were becoming more stressed just being around her. She's a very unhappy woman and can't help but spread that unhappiness to others. It's really rather sad."

"When's the last time I saw her?"

"You spoke to her the week of your accident, but I don't know when you saw her last. It was probably at a committee meeting."

"What committee meeting?"

"The past year or so, you've been volunteering on committees that plan fundraising events to raise money for charity. That's how you met Paige. She's on one of the committees with you."

"So I haven't heard from her for over a month? She hasn't called or stopped by?"

"No, but that doesn't surprise me. You two hadn't been getting along for months. You decided you needed to take a break from her, and I agreed. The stress she was causing you was getting to be too much. You stopped calling her and even took her number out of your phone."

"I deleted her number? That doesn't sound like me."

"The woman was a detriment to your health. You didn't have a choice but to end your friendship with her."

Something about this doesn't add up. Even if I was angry with Paige, I wouldn't delete her number, especially if we were friends.

"I want to talk to her," I say.

Logan shakes his head. "No. I don't want you starting a relationship with that woman again."

"You don't get to decide that. I do, and I want to talk to Paige."

"Avery, you don't remember what you went through with her. What we both went through. Trust me, it's best if Paige is not in our lives."

I don't trust what he's telling me. I found a note that said not to believe him. I wouldn't have written that note if I trusted that Logan was telling me the truth.

"Where can I find her number?" I ask. "Did I write it down somewhere?"

Logan sighs. "I have her number, but I don't want you calling her. I'm serious about this, Avery. The woman is not the type of friend you want."

"How do you know I don't want to be friends with Paige? You think Rachel and I should be friends, and I don't even like her."

"You don't like Rachel? You've been friends with her since she moved in."

"I don't know why. We have nothing in common. And honestly, I don't feel comfortable around her."

"Why? Did she do something?"

"No, I just feel like she's putting on an act. Like she's pretending we're friends but we're not."

Logan gets out his phone, swipes through it, then shows it to me. "I don't know, Avery, but to me, this looks like two people who are friends."

He's showing me a photo of Rachel and me in her backyard, sitting at her patio table with drinks in front of us. I have my arm around her, and we're laughing. We do look like friends, but photos can be deceiving.

"When was that taken?" I ask.

"A few months ago." He sets his phone down. "Rachel has been a good friend to you. I think whatever you're feeling about her now is because you can't remember what she was like before. You need to give her a chance."

"Maybe, but I still don't like having her here. I feel like she's babysitting me. She's always telling me what I can and can't do, which is making me not like her."

"I'll talk to her about that."

"No. I don't want you stepping in to fix this. And I want you to support me when I tell her not to come over anymore."

"I'll think about it."

He can think about it all he wants, but it's not going to change the outcome. I'm telling Rachel I don't need her coming over here anymore. It's time I take charge and stop letting Logan make decisions for me.

"I want Paige's number," I say. "If you don't give it to me, I'll find it myself."

"Fine." He was about to bite into his pizza but drops it on the plate and picks up his phone. He's angry, but I don't care. I need to talk to Paige and find out what really happened between us. "I just texted you her number."

"Thank you," I say, pleased that he actually did what I asked.

Logan wipes his hands on a napkin and leans back, his arms folded over his chest. "Do you want to know her history? Because I really think you should before you get involved with her again."

"What history?"

"She's been arrested. More than once. And she's served time."

"For what?"

"Drugs. Shoplifting. Forging checks."

"Did this happen recently?"

"It was when she was younger. She had a rough past. Grew up in and out of foster homes. Had a kid at sixteen, dropped out of high school, dealt drugs." Logan's brows rise. "Does that sound like someone you want to be friends with?"

"She's obviously turned her life around if she's volunteering on charity committees. The rich, old ladies who run those committees wouldn't accept Paige if she was still selling drugs."

"Just because she isn't doing those things anymore doesn't mean that she's changed. I know you only want to see the good in people, but I don't trust her, and I really don't want you being friends with her again."

"I'm still going to talk to her," I tell him. "I want to know what happened between us."

Actually, I want her to tell me why I was looking for an apartment. What does she know that I don't?

"Do what you need to," Logan says. "But remember, Avery, I warned you about her."

"You know, when I first met you, you believed in giving people second chances. You said people shouldn't be judged for their past."

"Yes, well, I was wrong." He laughs. "Or I might've just said that to persuade you to go out with me. The truth is, people don't change, and everyone's looking out for themselves."

"That's a cynical view. Do you really believe that?"

"It's not a matter of believing it. I know it. I see it every day. It's how the world works, and if you don't accept that and play along, you won't survive." He gets up, taking our plates. "I'll clean up dinner. You can rest or watch TV. I need to do some work. I'll be in my office if you need me."

I leave and go into the guest room. I'm surprised Logan

hasn't asked me to move back into our bedroom. If he does, I'm going to make up an excuse for why I can't. I don't want to share a room with him, or a bed. Until I know what's really going on here, I'm keeping my distance from my husband.

CHAPTER THIRTY-TWO

"Hello?" a woman's voice says.

"Is this Paige?" I ask, my heart beating faster as I realize I haven't figured out what to say. I was going to call her last night but then decided to wait until this morning, after Logan went to work. I should've planned out what to say, but instead I just called her, like we're still friends even though we're not. According to Logan, I haven't spoken to her in over a month.

"Avery?" she says, in a cautious tone. "Is it really you?"

"Yes. You know what happened to me, right?"

"Your brain injury? Yeah, and I'm so sorry I haven't been by to see you. I went to the hospital right after it happened, but Logan told me to leave. He said he didn't want me near you, so I've been staying away, hoping he'd let me see you after more time has passed."

Why did Logan do that? Why does he hate Paige so much? Why is he so determined to keep us away from each other?

"I know this sounds strange," I say, "but could you tell

me what happened? I can't remember much before my head injury. All Logan said was that we stopped talking, but he didn't really say why."

He did, but I'm not going to tell her that. I want to hear her side of the story.

"I don't have time to get into it now," she says. "I'm at work and need to be at a meeting soon. Could we talk later? Like after five?"

"Sure. I could call you at six. Does that work?"

"Actually, why don't we get together? I'd love to see you."

"I'm not able to drive yet, but—"

"I'll pick you up. We could go somewhere for dinner." Her voice rises, like she can't wait to see me. She doesn't seem angry or resentful for whatever happened between us.

"That sounds great! What time can you be here?"

"I'll head there after work, so maybe five thirty?"

"Okay, I'll be ready."

"I'll see you tonight!"

Logan won't like that I'm going out with Paige. Maybe I shouldn't tell him, but then how will I explain why I'm not home? I can't drive, so he'll know someone picked me up.

This is ridiculous. I'm not going to lie. I'm going to tell Logan the truth, and if he doesn't like it, that's his problem, not mine.

The doorbell rings. Rachel's here. I texted her last night and told her not to come over today. She either didn't see my text, or she's ignoring it.

"Hi!" she says when I open the door. "I brought coffee!"

"Thanks," I say, taking the cup from her. "Did you see my text?"

"Yes, and I'm not staying. I just wanted to bring you the

coffee." She smiles at me. "But now that I'm here, can I come in for a few minutes?"

I let her in, knowing if I don't, she'll never leave. She's so pushy, which is another reason I don't like her.

"Can I ask what happened?" she says, sitting down on the couch. "Why you don't want me here anymore?"

"Nothing happened. I just don't need someone watching over me." I sit down across from her on the chair.

"Are you sure that's all it is?"

"Rachel, this isn't about you," I say, although it is a little about her. "It's about me needing more independence. I want to be able to do stuff on my own. Have a life again. Go out and do things."

"But you can't drive."

"I can have someone pick me up. Like tonight. I've decided to go out with a friend for dinner."

"What friend?" she asks, sounding hurt, as if I should only be friends with her.

"Her name is Paige. You don't know her, but I'm sure I told you about her."

"Paige Ballard?"

"Yes, that's her."

"I thought you two weren't friends anymore."

"That's what Logan said, but she was really nice when I talked to her on the phone. I don't know what happened between us, but she seems to be over it. We'll talk tonight and straighten everything out."

"And Logan's okay with that?"

"It doesn't matter. Logan can't tell me who to be friends with. He doesn't even have to see her."

"He sees her every day. She works with him."

"You must be thinking of someone else. She doesn't work

with Logan. I don't know where she works. I can't remember."

"She works at Brickhowser Development. Didn't Logan tell you?"

"No. What's her job?" I ask, unable to remember what she does. It's so frustrating when you can't recall the most basic facts about someone.

"I don't know her exact title, but she's like a liaison between the company and the community. It's a new position. She works with groups in the community that help the homeless and matches them up with housing at one of the Brickhowser properties. You can read more about it in the press release on their website."

"And Logan is her boss?" I ask, wondering why Logan didn't mention any of this when he was telling me about Paige.

"He's not her boss, but I've heard him talking about her with Connor. It sounds like he doesn't get along with her, but I think she's doing well at her job. She's been on the news a few times, talking about all that Brickhowser is doing to benefit the community. She's getting them a lot of press, and she's good on camera."

Maybe that's why Logan doesn't like her. Maybe he's jealous that she's getting all the attention. He doesn't like other people stealing the spotlight, especially at work.

"What did Logan say when you told him you're seeing Paige tonight?"

"I didn't tell him yet. But I told him last night that I was going to call her."

"And what did he say?"

"He told me not to. He doesn't want me being friends with her."

"I can see why. It could be awkward to work with her and then come home and find her at his house, hanging out with his wife."

"He'll have to get over it." My phone rings, and I look to see who's calling. "It's Logan. Checking to see if I'm still alive."

"Don't even joke about that," Rachel says, getting up. "I'll go now, but remember I'm right next door if you need me."

"I'll be fine," I say, walking her to the door. "Thanks again for the coffee."

By the time she's gone, my phone stops ringing. As I shut the door, Logan calls again.

"Hey," I answer. "Rachel was here, so I missed your call."

He sighs. "I thought something happened to you. You should answer your phone even if someone's there."

"And you should be working. You don't need to keep checking on me."

"I have to now that you won't let Rachel do it. Did she stay long?"

"Just a few minutes. She told me something I didn't know. Something you should've told me."

He's silent a moment, then hesitantly asks, "What did she say?"

"That Paige works at your company."

"Oh, that," he says, like he thought I was going to say something completely different. It makes me wonder what else Rachel knows about him that I don't. "Yes, she left her job at the law firm to come here."

"She's a lawyer?"

"A paralegal, but she was bored with it. So now she's here, unfortunately."

"Why is it unfortunate? Rachel said she's been getting the company a lot of press. I would think you'd be happy about that."

"Let's not talk about this. I don't have time, and I'd rather not talk about Paige."

"I'm having dinner with her tonight. She's picking me up."

The phone is silent.

"Logan? Are you still there?"

"I told you I don't want you seeing her," he says in a harsh tone.

"And I told you I'll be friends with whoever I like."

"You really think this is a good idea? To ignore what I'm telling you?" He's angry, but I'm not backing down.

"I'm going out with Paige. I don't need your approval."

"If you do, I promise you, you'll be sorry you ever got involved with her."

"I'm not worried. In fact, I'm looking forward to seeing her. I should let you get back to work. Bye!" I end the call.

He really hates Paige. And he really wants to keep me away from her. I don't know why, but I'm going to find out.

CHAPTER THIRTY-THREE

"It's so good to see you," Paige says as I get into her SUV. Her new job must pay well. It's a very expensive SUV.

"It's good to see you too," I say.

"You look great!" She pulls out of the driveway. "How do you feel?"

"Pretty good. I still get headaches and don't have a lot of energy, but the doctor said my blood work shows that everything is back to normal."

"Wow, so your autoimmune thing just disappeared?"

"I guess. I don't really know. I'm hoping it doesn't come back."

As I look at Paige, I feel like I remember her, even though she's part of the memories I can't seem to access.

"I'm really glad you called," she says. "I've been wondering how you're doing."

"Have you asked Logan? I heard you work with him now."

"Yeah, it's weird, isn't it? I never thought I'd be working

at Brickhowser, but I was tired of doing the paralegal thing, and this job kind of fell in my lap."

"Really? You didn't apply?"

"I did, but only as a formality. I kind of made up the job, not thinking I would be the one getting it." She stops at a light. "I was at this charity thing and was talking to Steve, the owner of Brickhowser. I was saying how they need to better connect with community groups to match the homeless up with housing. Steve thought it was a great idea, and the next day he called and offered me the job." The light turns green and she continues down the street.

"I bet Logan was surprised when he saw you there."

"Surprised and angry." She glances at me. "I hope you don't believe what he says about me."

"He hasn't really said much."

"Yeah, right," she says with a laugh. "He hasn't told you about my past? Tried to make you think I'm still messed up like I was back then?"

"He might have, but I didn't listen to him."

"Good, because you know he's only saying those things to turn you against me."

"But why? What does it matter to him if we're friends?"

"You really don't remember what happened?"

"No. My memory of the past couple of years is gone."

She pulls into a parking lot and turns the engine off. "I don't know if I should tell you this. I'm afraid if I do, you won't believe me and will believe all the awful things Logan says about me."

"Tell me." I take my seatbelt off and turn to her. "I want to know."

She nods and takes a breath. "You ever feel like Logan is trying to control you?"

"Sometimes I do," I say, but the truth is, I always feel that way.

"Does he get angry when he doesn't get what he wants?"

"Yes, but he's been getting better," I say, thinking about how he agreed to stop having Rachel come over. And he didn't forbid me from seeing Paige tonight. He's not happy about it, but he didn't stop me from going.

"Does he ever take his anger out on you?" she asks. "Physically?"

"No. Never," I say, but her question reminds me of the day he blew up at me for letting Edith come over. How he screamed at me and threw her fresh berries in the trash.

"He used to," she says. "You wouldn't tell me, but I could see it. I saw the marks, the bruises on your skin, even through all the concealer you wore to cover them up."

That's why I have all that concealer? To cover up where Logan hit me? No, that can't be right. He wouldn't hit me.

"I think you saw things that weren't there. I wouldn't stay with Logan if he was abusive."

"You would if he threatened you. And abusive husbands love to make threats."

"If Logan was abusive, I would know," I insist. "That side of him would've come out by now."

"It didn't happen all the time. It was usually after you'd had a big fight. I'd see the mark on your face where he'd slapped you or the bruise on your arm where he grabbed you and wouldn't let go."

As she says that, I can almost see it happening in my head. But is it a memory, or am I just imagining it the way she's describing it?

"But I never told you about it?"

"No, but it's common to try to hide it. A lot of women do."

I don't know if I believe her, but why would she make up something like this?

"Did you go with me to look at an apartment?" I ask.

"Yeah, a few months ago."

"Why did I want an apartment?"

"You said you and Logan were having issues. I knew by 'issues' you meant the abuse, but I also knew you wouldn't admit it was happening, so I didn't mention it. I was just glad you were leaving him. But then we went to the apartment and you wouldn't sign the lease. You almost did, but then changed your mind."

"Do you know why?"

"I think you were afraid he'd find you there."

"So I was really going to leave him?"

"You never came out and said you were, but you were obviously considering it, or you wouldn't have filled out the application for that apartment."

"Logan doesn't know about any of this, does he?"

"About the apartment? No, at least I don't think he does. I can't imagine you would've told him."

"And you haven't said anything to him, you know, about how he treated me, right?"

"No, but he knows I don't like him. That's why he doesn't want me seeing you. I'm surprised he let you go out with me tonight."

"He tried to talk me out of it, but I wouldn't back down. I told him I'm going even if he doesn't approve."

"And what did he say?"

"That I'd be sorry for getting involved with you."

"So he's turning it around. Making you think that I'm the

one you have to worry about instead of him. That's so Logan. I hope you don't believe him, because I guarantee it was him who gave you those bruises."

Did that really happen? Because if it did, then why am I still with him? Thinking about this, trying to figure out what's true and what's not, is making my head hurt.

"I'm not feeling very good," I say. "I think I need to go home."

"You don't want to have dinner?"

"Not tonight. I'm not hungry."

"Avery, I didn't mean to upset you," Paige says, her voice full of warmth and concern. "I only told you all that because you said you wanted to know."

"I did, but now I feel sick. I need to go home."

"Do you feel safe there? Being with him?"

"He's not going to hurt me," I say, but I don't know if that's true. I don't know anything right now. I'm so confused. "Just take me home, please."

Paige doesn't say much on the ride back to the house. I don't either. I'm too focused on what to do about Logan. If I tell him what Paige said about him, he'll deny it. So how can I ever know if it's true?

"Do you want me to go inside with you?" Paige asks as she pulls into the driveway.

"No, I think I'll just go to bed."

"Are you mad at me?"

"I'm not mad. I'm frustrated that I can't remember."

"Yeah, I'm sure that's tough." She reaches over and grips my hand. "If you need me, for anything, just call, okay?"

I nod.

"I mean it, Avery. Even if it's the middle of the night, call me. I'll do whatever you need."

"Thanks, Paige." I get out of the SUV, and she drives away.

She seems nice, so why did I stop talking to her? It had to be because of Logan. He must've forced me to end my friendship with her. But why did I go along with it?

"Logan?" I say, going into the house. "Logan, I'm home."

He doesn't answer. He must still be at work. I go to the kitchen and see the key fob for his car sitting on the counter.

"Logan, where are you?" I call out, walking back to the living room. I glance out the side window and see Logan next door. He's in Rachel's house. What's he doing there? He's not there to see Connor. He doesn't live there anymore.

I decide to go over there and see what's up. As I'm crossing through our yards, I spot Logan again through the side window. I sneak up to the house and peek inside. Logan's talking to Rachel. She looks upset, her eyes puffy like she's been crying. Logan says something to her as he takes her hand. He keeps talking and steps closer to her. Too close. Closer than he should be standing to a woman who's not his wife.

Are they having an affair? Is that why I feel so uncomfortable around Rachel? Is she pretending to be my friend while sleeping with my husband?

As I watch, she grabs the front of Logan's shirt and says something to him. Her expression is tense, urgent—like she's desperate for him to go along with whatever she's saying. I wish I could hear them, although their body language is enough to tell me this isn't an innocent conversation between neighbors.

Logan leans down to her and she backs away and races toward the window. I duck down, hoping she doesn't see me.

I wait a moment, then glance up and see the drapes are closed.

What do I do? Should I knock on the door? Catch them in the act?

It's all suddenly making sense now. The reason Rachel is so fake around me. Logan's insistence that Rachel hang out with me and pretend like we're friends. They're trying to throw me off the scent so I don't suspect they're having an affair.

CHAPTER THIRTY-FOUR

LOGAN

"It was never supposed to become more," I say, walking away from Rachel. "We agreed on that when it started."

"Yes, Logan, but then it changed." She races up to me. "You can't tell me you don't have feelings for me. Not after everything we've been through."

"You haven't been through anything. I'm the one with the sick wife. You have no idea what I've been going through."

"How could you say that? I was with you the whole time she was in the hospital!"

"You were with me at night. In my bed. And, hey, I enjoyed it. It was a good way to relieve some stress. But that's all it was."

Her lip quivers. She'd better not cry again. If she does, I'm out of here. I didn't sign up for this.

"It was more than sex," she says. "It still is." She grips my arm. "I care about you, Logan, more than she ever did."

"Leave my wife out of this," I say, yanking away from her. "What we did has nothing to do with her. I love Avery."

Rachel huffs. "Are you kidding me? You don't love her! You don't even like her!"

"If I didn't love her, I wouldn't still be with her."

"You're with her because she's sick!" Rachel almost screams. "Just admit it, Logan. You wanted to dump her as soon as you found out she wasn't the type of wife you wanted, but then she got sick and you were stuck with her. You couldn't leave your sick wife and allow your perfect image to be tainted." She throws her hands around in a dramatic gesture as she continues her rant. "Just imagine what the media would say. Logan Fairmont, Humanitarian of the Year, Mr. Save-the-World, has decided to walk out on his sick wife just when she needs him the most. With no family around, poor little Avery will be left with no one to care for her."

"Are you finished?" I say, folding my arms over my chest.

"Admit it, Logan. Admit that's why you're still with her."

"I'm not admitting anything. What you're saying is nonsense. You're just looking for an excuse to explain why I'm with her and not you."

"Then tell me, Logan. Why are you choosing to be with Avery? She doesn't want you. She'd be happy to divorce you."

"Did she tell you that?"

"She didn't have to. It's obvious she's miserable with you."

"You're seeing what you want to see, not the truth." I walk past her. "I need to go. She'll be home soon."

"Logan, wait!" Rachel runs up to the door, blocking it. "I'll tell her. If you end this, I'll tell Avery what we did."

"Go ahead." I chuckle. "It won't make any difference."

"Of course it will! She won't stay with you when she finds out you've been screwing her best friend."

"You're not her friend. And definitely not her best friend. She doesn't think of you that way. Just the other day, she told me she thinks you're fake and that she doesn't enjoy spending time with you. That's why she told you to stop coming over."

Rachel's jaw drops, then snaps shut. "You're lying!"

"I'm not. Ask her yourself, although knowing Avery, she'll deny it so your feelings don't get hurt. Now get out of the way. I need to go home."

Rachel steps aside. "Tell me this isn't the end. Please, Logan."

After the way I've treated her, she still wants me. It's sad, yet what I expected. She's become attached to me, addicted to the thrill of our affair. I came over here to tell her we're done, but maybe I shouldn't be so hasty. She's right next door. She's ready and willing whenever I want her.

"I'll think about it." I smile, giving her a sliver of hope.

As I walk away, I hear her sobbing, then the sound of something smashing against the wall. She's angry at me, but even angrier at my wife. Avery has what Rachel wants, but she doesn't appreciate it, which makes Rachel truly despise her. I'm surprised she can still be friends with Avery. I was shocked when she agreed to be her caretaker. But she didn't do it for Avery. She did it for me. She thinks if Avery gets better, I'll finally divorce her.

"You're home already?" I say when I go into the house and see Avery on the couch.

"We decided to skip dinner. I wasn't hungry." She smiles. "So how's Rachel?"

How did she know I was with Rachel? Did she see me

there? It doesn't matter if she did. I can talk my way out of this.

I walk over to my wife and sit beside her. "She's not doing well. Have you spoken to her?"

"No, but whatever's wrong with her, I'm sure you made her feel better." Avery smirks. "So how long has it been going on?"

"What are you talking about?"

"You and Rachel. I know you're sleeping with her. I saw you." She points to the window. "Right there. A few minutes ago."

"You think Rachel and I are—" I laugh. "Honey, there is nothing going on with Rachel. We were talking. That's it."

"Yeah, right. I saw you with her. I saw you touching her. That's not the way you act with a neighbor."

"I touched her hand. I was trying to comfort her. She was upset and crying because she'd found out Connor is seeing someone else."

"Why would she care? He moved out. They're getting divorced."

"Yes, but it's still difficult to find out the person you loved has moved on with someone else."

"She doesn't even like Connor. She was only letting him live there because he bought her stuff and paid the rent. She's not upset. She was faking it so you'd go over there and give her attention."

"Avery, that's not fair," I say, making sure to keep my voice steady and reasonable. "We don't know what their relationship was like, just like they don't know about ours."

"I'm pretty sure Rachel knows you're cheating on me since she's the person you're cheating with."

"I am not cheating on you." I slide up next to Avery and

hold her hand. "Why would I want to be with someone else when I have you?"

"I don't believe you. The way you looked at her—"

"Was the way I look at someone I feel sorry for. Even if I were single, I wouldn't want a woman like Rachel. She isn't my type. I'm not attracted to her."

"How could you not be? She's beautiful, and she always looks perfect."

"To me, the woman I'm looking at now is perfect. And the most beautiful woman I've ever seen."

"Yeah, okay." Avery rolls her eyes, but I can tell she's a little bit flattered.

"I'm serious. Why would I say that if I didn't mean it?"

"To make me forget I just saw you with Rachel."

I let out a frustrated sigh. "There is nothing going on with Rachel." I cup Avery's chin and lift her face to mine. "I love you. You know that, right?"

"I want to believe that, but..." She looks down.

"But what?"

"But then I see you with Rachel and I have Paige saying that you—" She stops and takes a breath. "I don't know who to believe. I wish I could remember what our life used to be like."

"Our life was wonderful. It still is."

"It couldn't have been that wonderful if I was sick all the time."

"You couldn't help that. And I was here for you, caring for you." I rub her hand, entwine her fingers in mine. "Let's not talk about the past. What matters is right now." I keep hold of her hand and lean back on the couch. "So what did Paige say?"

I keep my tone light and casual, like I'm just making

conversation, but inside, I'm trying desperately to control my rage. Paige was never supposed to speak to my wife again. I demanded she stay away from her, but she clearly didn't listen. She never does. I should've known she'd work her way back into Avery's life.

"She told me about her new job," Avery says. "And about her kids."

That's a lie. Paige spent the whole time telling Avery what to do and what to believe. Pretending to care about her. It's what Paige does. She's a manipulator. I know how she operates because I'm just like her.

"Be honest, Avery. She told you not to listen to me, didn't she? She knows I don't want you being friends with her, and she told you to hang out with her anyway."

"It doesn't matter what she said. Or what *you* said. I'll do what I want." She gets up. "I'm going to my room."

"Avery, wait. We should talk about this."

"I can't, not until I figure out what's going on."

"What do you need to figure out?"

She looks down, then back up at me. "I don't know if I trust you, or anyone else. I don't know if anything I've been told is true. And until I find out, I can't make any decisions."

"Decisions about *what*? Us?"

"I can't talk right now." She walks off and goes into her room, shutting the door behind her.

Going into my office, I close the door and take out my phone.

I make the call, pure rage coursing through my veins. I'm furious I still have to deal with this. It was supposed to be over by now. It should've been over weeks ago!

"What do you want?" the voice answers.

"This needs to end," I say, tightly gripping the phone as I pace the floor.

"I agree."

"Oh, now you agree?" I scoff. "You said you—"

"I know what I said. But I'm tired of it. I want to be done with this."

"It needs to happen soon," I say, still pacing the floor. "She wants to know what happened, and she's determined to find out."

"Has she remembered anything?"

"No, but there's a chance she might, which is why we can't wait."

"So when do you want to meet?"

We decide on a place and time. I make it clear that this is final. No more second chances. If it isn't done right this time, I'll do it myself. That's how desperate I am to finish this.

CHAPTER THIRTY-FIVE

AVERY

Logan was very convincing last night when he told me he's not sleeping with Rachel. I wanted to believe him, and part of me does. The part that desperately wants to believe that Logan wouldn't betray me like that. Just seeing him at Rachel's house doesn't prove anything. Maybe he really was just talking to her. As for Logan saying how much he loves me, I wanted to believe he meant it. He seemed so sincere. But I can't let myself be swayed by his words, knowing they may not be real.

Last night, hearing Paige tell me that Logan was abusive, then coming home and having Logan tell me how much he loves me—after I'd seen him and Rachel—I was left more confused than ever. I have to find out the truth. I'll scour the house for clues if that's what it takes to get even a tiny piece of my memory back.

"Are you sure you'll be okay being alone here all day?" Logan asks, coming over to the table where I'm having breakfast.

"For the millionth time, yes," I say, smiling at him.

He leans down and kisses me. "Call me if you need me."

"What time will you be home?"

"I'm not sure. I'll let you know later." He grabs his keys from the counter. "You're not planning on having any visitors today, are you?"

"No. Why?"

"You need to rest, not entertain company."

"I'm sure Rachel will stop by, even though I told her she doesn't need to come over anymore."

"If you don't want to see her, then don't answer the door. It's probably best if you stay away from her. She's not in a good place right now."

Is that why he doesn't want me around her? Or is it because he's afraid she'll tell me about their affair? I'm still not sure if anything happened between them, but I'm not ruling it out.

"You should get to work," I tell him, wishing he'd hurry up and leave.

"Yes, I'll see you tonight." He goes out the door to the garage, then I hear his car as he drives off.

I'm finally alone. I get up and take my dishes to the sink, then refill my coffee. I'll need the caffeine boost. I have a busy day ahead.

After a quick shower, I get dressed and head to the master bedroom. I start with the nightstands, Logan's and mine. I take everything out and hold it in my hand, but not a single memory comes back to me.

Next, I search the dresser. I go through Logan's drawers, then my own. When I come to my lingerie drawer, I see the lacy white teddy I wore on my honeymoon. Logan was shocked when he saw me in it since I'm not someone who wears stuff like that. But I knew Logan would like it, so I wore it for him because I loved him and wanted that night to be special.

We were so happy back then. I really thought I'd found my perfect match, the man I'd be with forever. As I take out the white teddy, my eyes tear up, remembering those times, wanting them back.

What happened to Logan and me? When did things change? Was it when I got sick? That's when our sex life slowed down. Is that what made us grow apart? It can't just be that. Our relationship was about more than sex.

I return the teddy to the drawer, shoving it to the very back, knowing I'll probably never wear it again. I should throw it out. As I go to grab it, I notice something in the back of the drawer. I pull it out and see it's a photo, like from one of those instant print cameras. It takes me a moment to figure it out, but then I realize it's a picture of me. A closeup of my face. My cheek is red and looks inflamed.

Turning over the photo, I see something written on it in my handwriting. It reads:

LOGAN HIT ME ACROSS THE FACE. HE MADE ME COVER IT WITH CONCEALER AND THREATENED TO HURT MIA IF I TOLD ANYONE.

A date is written below the words. It's during the time period I can't remember.

"No," I whisper, gazing at the photo. He wouldn't do that. Logan wouldn't hit me. He wouldn't threaten my sister.

But he did. I'm holding the evidence in my hand.

Paige was telling the truth. Logan was abusive. He hit me. Was it just once, or did it happen all the time? I feel nausea rising in me as I think about the likely answer to that question.

I take out the drawer and dump it upside down, searching for more photos, but the one of my face is the only one I can find. If there's more, they're not here.

Yanking out the other drawers, I dump them all out and frantically search for more photos, but there aren't any. Either there was only one, or I hid the photos somewhere else.

Going into the bathroom, I search the area under the sink where I keep extra soap and all my hair products. Logan keeps his stuff on a shelf. I doubt he ever looks under the sink, which makes this a good hiding spot. I take everything out. But I don't find a single photo.

Exhausted, I lie down on the floor and stare up at the ceiling. Logan hit me. The man who claims to love me hit me across the face, then threatened to hurt my sister if I told anyone. That doesn't sound like the man I married. Logan has his faults, but I would've never even thought he was capable of doing something like this.

I think back to one of the last memories I have of Logan and me. It was a few weeks after John died. Logan and I were in bed, and he was telling me how sorry he was that John had died. He said my brother wouldn't want me to spend the rest of my life grieving and that it was time to move on. I remember being angry at Logan, feeling like he was rushing me to get over the loss of my brother. But I don't think Logan's intentions were bad. He thought his words would help me. He loved me and didn't like seeing me so sad.

That's the Logan I remember. That Logan would never

hit me. So what happened? Why did he do it? Was he drunk? Even if he was, that doesn't excuse his behavior.

I should clean up the mess I've made. I look over at the empty cabinet, thinking I should wipe it out before putting everything back. I'm about to get up when I spot something under the sink. There's a photo taped to the underside of the counter. I move to get a better look and see not just one photo, but several.

I carefully peel off each one, then line them up on the floor. They're all pictures of me, or I assume it's me. Some are closeups of my arm, showing dark bruises that look like someone grabbed me hard and wouldn't let go. There's a photo of my face with a red mark on my cheek like the picture I found in the bedroom.

Turning over the photos, I find more dates, along with writing that says:

LOGAN FAIRMONT DID THIS

.
It's odd I wrote out his whole name. It's like I was telling someone else.

It's like I was telling the police.

That must have been what I was doing. I was documenting what Logan did so if anything happened to me, the police would know it was Logan who did it.

My pulse races as I realize what this means. Logan was hurting me. I was afraid of him. I was afraid he might kill me.

Is that why I can't remember? Was Logan's abuse what caused my memory loss?

Dissociative amnesia. That's what my neurologist called it. He said it could be caused by something going on in my life that I wouldn't want to remember. A trauma so horrific that my brain hid it from me.

Seeing these photos, I'm thinking that has to be it. My mind didn't want to remember. My memory loss had nothing to do with my brain injury. I can't remember because I didn't want to.

CHAPTER THIRTY-SIX

LOGAN

"You're late," she says, her arms folded over her chest, glaring at me as I make my way toward her.

"I was in a meeting. I couldn't just walk out." I stumble on the uneven ground, catching myself before I fall.

She laughs. "Walk much?"

"Not in the woods. You know I hate meeting out here." I stop in front of her and notice the dirt covering my leather loafers. "Now my shoes are filthy. How am I going to explain that?"

"Just wipe them off. And stop complaining. Anywhere else we meet is going to have cameras. Do you want to risk us being seen together?"

"Let's hurry this up. Did you find someone?"

"No. I'm going to do it myself."

I look at her, not sure if she's serious. "You? You're hiring yourself?"

"No. You are. I want half the money now, the rest after. And I want double what you paid before."

"I'm not paying double," I scoff. "I already paid you more

than I wanted to, and I got you a job at my company. That was way more than you deserved. And then you didn't even finish the job!"

"Because I trusted someone else to do it. That's why this time I'm doing it myself."

"I don't believe you," I say, challenging her.

"You don't think I can?"

"I think you can. I just don't think you will."

"You don't know me very well, then. I've done worse."

"I'm sure you have, but not to someone you like. Someone you feel sorry for."

"I don't feel sorry for her. It's her own fault for getting involved with someone like you."

"Someone could've said the same thing about your choice in men."

"I was smarter than her. I didn't wait until he—"

"I don't have time to argue. Just tell me the plan."

"It's the same as before, only this time I'll be doing it instead of someone else."

"The same as before?" I huff. "That's your plan? In case you forgot, it didn't work. Avery's still very much alive. I need her to be dead! Do you understand me? I want her dead before you leave the house!"

"Yeah, I know that."

"Do you? Because last time I was very clear on what needed to be done only to get home and find that she's still alive."

"You shouldn't have called for an ambulance. If you'd left her there, she'd be dead right now."

"I couldn't leave her. That stupid woman who lives behind our house saw me. She saw me come home. Saw me in the kitchen. If I'd left Avery there and not gotten her help, the old woman would've turned me in. She can't mind her own damn business. I can't stand her. I might have to kill her next."

"You won't need to. Didn't you say you're moving after this?"

"Yes, but not right away. There needs to be a grieving period of at least a few months, and then I'll sell the place."

"And tell everyone you had to because it's too painful to live there without your wife."

"Exactly." I smile at her, thinking how similar she is to me. Our backgrounds are nothing alike, yet we think the same and are both willing to do whatever it takes to get ahead. I should've married someone like her instead of Avery.

She's not bad looking. Actually, she's extremely attractive, even more so than Rachel, but I haven't let my thoughts go there. I've been too focused on what I hired her for. But now, knowing it'll be over soon, I'm seeing her differently. And I have to say, I'm a little turned on knowing she wants to do the job herself.

"So do we have a deal?" she asks.

"Yes. I thought we already decided that."

"You haven't agreed to my payment."

I take a moment to consider it. "Okay, fine. I'll double the fee."

"With half paid up front."

"Yes, I'll leave the cash in the same place as before."

"Then I guess we're done here."

She goes past me, but I stop her, grabbing her around the waist. "Not so fast."

"Why? What do you—"

I don't let her finish. Instead, I kiss her, pulling her body against mine.

She shoves me away. "What the hell was that?"

"Come on," I say with a smirk. "Just admit it."

"Admit what?"

"That you're attracted to me. That you want to move this beyond a business relationship."

"Are you joking?" She laughs. "Or maybe you're delusional. You seriously think I want you?"

"Why else would you be doing this?"

"For the money. That's the only reason I'm doing it." She steps closer to me, placing her hand on my chest and looking up at me. "I hate to break this to you, but not every woman wants you. I, for one, have zero attraction to you."

"You're lying, but it's fine. We wouldn't have worked out anyway. We're too similar."

"I'm leaving. Have my money ready by tomorrow." She walks off.

"Wait! When is this happening?"

"When I'm ready," she yells, continuing down the trail.

I race up behind her. "Stop! I need to know when."

She turns back. "I have to gain her trust first. That takes time."

"I don't have time."

"Then find someone else." She takes off again.

"Paige!" I catch up to her. "Just tell me it'll be soon. We can't wait. Every day that passes, there's more of a chance she'll remember."

"Has anything come back to her yet? Any memories?"

"Only a few, but nothing significant, and I convinced her she made them up. And I've been saying things to confuse her so she'll think she can't trust whatever her mind is telling her. That way if she does get her memory back, she won't know if the memories are real or fake."

Paige laughs a little. "She must think she's losing her mind."

"That's the intention. So anyway, when is it happening?"

"Get me the money and I'll get it done." She walks off, and this time I don't follow her. There's nobody out here, but I'm still worried someone might see us coming out of the woods together.

Paige had better do this soon, like this week. Any day now, Avery could remember what I did to her. If she does, there's a chance she'll go to the police, and then everyone will know. It'll be all over the media, maybe even the national media. I'll be ruined. I might even go to jail, although I doubt it would come to that.

I've been very careful to keep my hands clean in all this. That's why I hired Paige. We met last year at a fundraiser for the children's museum. I assumed she was yet another wealthy housewife doing charity work to fill her time and socialize with other wealthy women. But after asking some people about her, I found out Paige had a dark past, including a history of arrests and prison time.

She claimed she'd turned her life around, but I didn't buy it. If someone has a dark side, it never goes away. You just learn to hide it. You tell people what to believe about you and create an image that matches that. Like with me. I grew up without money, and my parents kicked me out at eighteen. They called me a bad seed because I was always lying and skipping school and because I got in a few fights. Most parents would excuse that behavior, saying it's what boys that age do, but my parents were very strict and controlling. They wouldn't tolerate my rebellion and made me leave home the day after I graduated high school. I haven't spoken to them since.

My story isn't as tragic as Paige's, but it's still a good story. My own parents abandoned me and left me to fend for myself, and I still became a success. After my parents kicked me out, I used my sad story to convince a local businessman to put me through college. The guy was extremely wealthy and well-connected. He knew celebrities, politicians, tech billionaires. Every semester, we'd have lunch and he'd give me advice. He was always telling me to give back. I told him I had nothing to give. I was broke. So he told me to give my time. I had no interest in volunteering until he told me what it could do for me. He said it was the best and fastest way to get people on my side. Add in a big smile and a tragic story like mine and people would be falling over themselves to help me out and make me a success.

It was the first time I'd heard someone talk about volunteering in a self-serving way, and I liked it. It was cunning and manipulative, yet nobody would see it that way. They'd just think I'm a nice guy. Someone who's trustworthy, selfless, and kind. I'd never been that guy, but I liked the idea of making people think I was, so I tried it. The summer after freshman year, I volunteered to build houses. I actually liked it. I got to be outside, and all that physical labor helped me put on muscle, which helped me get girls.

To make money, I got a job at a country club, parking cars for all the rich people. That's when I started making connections, ones that would eventually lead to a job after college. My first job wasn't anything great, but it led to the job I have now, working directly under the owners of a company that's projected to triple their profits this year. A lot of that is because of me, using my city council role to win us multimillion-dollar contracts.

I'm at the top of my game. There's only one problem. My sick wife. She's dragging me down when she's supposed to be building me up. After her illness lingered on for weeks, then months, then years, I knew I had to get rid of her. But I wasn't going to risk doing it myself. I needed someone to do it for me.

That's where Paige comes in. I hadn't talked to her since that first time we met, but I hadn't forgotten about her. And I was seeing her at more events. She was like me, trying to work her way into high society. But to fit in, she needed to look the part, wearing designer clothes and driving a luxury car. Paige's job didn't pay nearly enough to afford those things. She needed money, and I was willing to give it to her if she'd take care of my problem.

When I offered her the job, I made it sound like I was joking. It was late, and we'd both had a lot to drink. We'd been at this charity event for five hours and she was ready to go home, but I convinced her to stay for one more drink. I told her about my wife and why she wasn't there. I explained how sick she was and that she wasn't getting better. I made a comment about putting her out of her misery, using a tone that was more joking than serious.

Paige smiled, then asked how much. And that was it. She was hired.

The plan was to kill Avery right away, but then I changed my mind. I needed to find out if Avery had told anyone about me, about what I'd done to her or to John. I didn't trust that my threats against her sister were enough to keep Avery quiet. And that's why I had Paige become friends with her. I got Avery on one of the committees Paige volunteered on too, so they'd have an excuse to spend time together. Avery quickly fell for Paige's fake-friend act, but never told Paige what I'd done. Even when I told Paige to ask Avery about the bruises on her arm or the marks on her face, thinking it would make Avery tell her how it happened, she didn't. And if she wouldn't tell Paige, her closest friend, she wouldn't tell anyone else. Avery was either silenced by my threats or too ashamed to admit she was still with me after what I'd done.

Whatever the reason, it didn't matter. I had my answer. Avery had kept quiet. I was ready to follow through on the plan. Paige hired a guy and gave him a key to our house so it wouldn't look like a break-in. He was supposed to sneak up behind Avery, knock her on the head, then arrange her body so that it looked like she'd fallen and hit her head on the granite counter. The week before, I'd made sure to tell her doctor how bad Avery's dizzy spells were getting so that no one would suspect foul play. They would just assume she got dizzy and fell down.

It all would've gone perfectly if the guy had hit her hard enough. But no, she survived his attack, and I was forced to call for help because that nosy neighbor lady was watching me through the window.

This time, that won't happen. Everything will go as planned. It has to. I can't keep playing along as the devoted husband. She's holding me back. Taking up my precious time.

Avery needs to die.

CHAPTER THIRTY-SEVEN
PAIGE

I can't believe that idiot thought I wanted him. He disgusts me. I don't find him even a tiny bit attractive. I see why other women do. He's handsome if you're into the wealthy businessman look. The neatly trimmed dark hair. Clean-shaven face. The expensive suits. I don't like that look. Never have. I like a bad boy with a scruffy beard, covered in tats, and with a few scars to prove he's not afraid of a fight.

I just described my ex, but we know how that turned out. That's why I'm done with men. I'm sure there's a few good ones out there, but I'm not going to take the time or effort to find them. I don't need a guy. I'm good on my own. Now that my kids are teenagers and will be leaving the nest soon, it's time to focus on me and what I'm going to do with the rest of my life.

I've already made great progress with my career. The paralegal gig didn't pay well, but the law firm I worked at had a lot of wealthy clients. That's why I chose it, to get close to people who could help me get ahead. I told my story to whoever would listen, saying how grateful I was to escape my old life and how I hoped to someday give back. Soon, I was being invited to have lunch with wealthy women who saw me as a charity case. The poor single mom, struggling to make ends meet after her abusive husband landed himself in prison and left her with nothing. Add in my horrible childhood and I had those rich women with their pearls and cashmere sweaters bawling their eyes out.

Then, when I told them how I went back to school, working nights as a janitor to pay for it, and became a paralegal, I really won them over. I had drive, I had ambition, and I had a tragic backstory. They saw my potential. I was a project to them. They'd mold me into a polite, refined young woman who fit into their high-society world, then take all the credit when they showed me off at events. And I was fine with that. In fact, it's what I wanted. I've now spoken at several women's conferences in the area, and I've been asked to serve on committees for three prominent charities. I'm getting my name out there and making connections.

Logan would say we're alike in that way, but I am not like Logan. I'm insulted to even be compared to him. He's so full of himself. Sometimes I wonder if he really thinks he's as wonderful as he pretends to be. He's got everyone fooled. His bosses love him. They keep giving him raises and promoting him. That's why I knew Logan could convince them to create a new position at their company, a position that I would later fill. It was part of our deal, and surprisingly, Logan followed through. I didn't think he would after Avery survived.

He'd paid me the money up front, but the job position was supposed to come after Avery was gone. When she survived, I thought he'd tell me the job at his company wasn't happening. But then I got it. I think he was afraid of what I'd do to him if he didn't follow through. He knows what I'm capable of, and he knows what could happen if he got on my bad side.

I've got Logan exactly where I want him. I know all his secrets. I could ask for whatever I want and he'd have to give it to me. He knows if he hired someone else to kill his wife, I'd come after him. I know people, and they're not the kind of people Logan wants to meet. One call and he'd be dead.

That'd make things a lot simpler, but it's not what I want to do. It's good to have the option there if I need it, but I don't want to rely on that as a way to solve my problems. I'm trying to create some distance between my old life and the one I'm living now.

There's risk to what I'm doing. It could easily backfire and I could end up back in prison, but I'm choosing not to think that way. I've been lucky so far, and I have a feeling my luck will continue.

"Hello?" Avery says, answering my call.

"Hey, it's Paige." I smile as I say it. I read an article online that said if you smile while talking on the phone, it makes your voice sound pleasant and upbeat.

"I can't talk right now," Avery says, her words rushed, her voice higher than normal.

"Why? What's going on?"

"I—I don't know." She's breathing fast, like she's been running or racing around. "I'm trying to figure it out."

"Avery, talk to me," I say in a steady tone. "Tell me what's going on."

"What you said the other night." She pauses. "Everything you told me is true."

"You remembered?"

"No. I found pictures. And some notes. About Logan and what he did."

She did what I suggested with the photos and the notes. I didn't think she would. I'd only just met her when I told her that. I didn't think she'd actually do it.

I try not to laugh, but it really is kind of funny.

"I'm coming over," I tell her.

"No! You can't! Logan will be home soon. You can't come over."

"Then I'll come get you. You can tell Logan we're going out. Text him now before he gets home."

"Yeah, okay," she says, like I'm the only person in the world she can trust. She's so gullible. "What time can you be here?"

"I'm heading there now, so maybe twenty minutes? A half hour?"

"Okay, I'll be ready. Bye." She ends the call.

Poor Avery. She sounds scared for her life. As she should be. Her husband's plotting to kill her.

Traffic is bad, and it's a good thirty minutes before I make it to Avery's house. She's waiting out front on the porch, wearing white linen shorts and a checkered blue-and-white, button-down shirt with the sleeves rolled up. She looks like she's dressed for lunch at the country club, which is exactly how Logan wants her to look. She told me how he cleaned out her closet and replaced it with a whole new wardrobe filled with clothes he picked out. She tried to make it sound like that was a good thing, but I could tell it annoyed her. What woman wants her husband choosing her clothes?

"Sorry I took so long," I say as Avery climbs into my SUV. It's a white BMW, top of the line. I paid it off with the money Logan gave me.

"He didn't text me back," she says, nervously chewing on her nails. "What do you think that means?"

"It means he's in a meeting and didn't see your text."

"It's almost six. He should've left work by now."

"There's some big project he's working on with Steve. He probably stayed late to meet with him." I glance at Avery as we wait at a light. "Why are you so worried he didn't text you?"

"Because of what I found. What if he knows?"

"Knows what?"

"That I hid that stuff. What if he was waiting for me to find it?"

"Why would he wait for you to find it?"

"So he could punish me for hiding evidence I could use against him." She turns to me. "He hit me, Paige. More than once."

"I know. And I know you don't remember, but I tried to help you. I tried to get you away from him."

"Why didn't you tell me? After I got out of the hospital, why didn't you tell me?"

"Logan wouldn't let me near you. He deleted me from your phone. Told me never to call you."

"You still could've got in touch. He didn't need to know."

"It was too risky. I was afraid if he found out I'd called, he'd blame you and then punish you for it."

Avery leans back, staring straight ahead. "I don't know who I'm living with. This isn't the man I married."

"What are you going to do?"

"I don't know. What do you think I should do?"

"Where are the photos? And the notes?"

"In here." She holds out her purse. "I was going to hide

them again, but I was too worried he'd find them. But what am I going to do with them when I get home?"

"Give them to me. I'll take them."

She doesn't say anything. She's just staring straight ahead, her leg bouncing up and down as her foot nervously taps the floor.

"Avery, did you hear me? I said I'll take them."

"Yeah, I heard you. But I don't know if I want you to have them."

"Why? If I take them, you won't have to worry about Logan finding them."

"But they are all I have. The only evidence to prove what he did."

"Yeah? So? You don't trust me to have them?"

"I... I don't know."

Well, that's not good. I thought I'd earned her trust back. I need it to finish the job. I also need those photos and the notes. I can't risk her turning them into the police.

"Avery, you know you can trust me. I've been through this. My ex did the same thing to me, only he didn't just slap me. He punched me, again and again." I reach over and grip her hand. "I'm trying to help you. So let me."

She nods and reaches into her purse. She takes out a stack of photos and some small pieces of paper.

"What's on the paper?" I ask.

"Things he said to me. Threats he made. Lies he told me." She looks down at them in her hands. "I wrote them down. Where are you going to keep them?"

"I'll hide them somewhere at my house. Probably my bedroom so my kids don't find them."

There's a restaurant just up ahead. I pull into the lot and

find a space to park. I can't drive and concentrate on keeping my story straight. One slip-up and this is over.

Avery sighs. "What am I doing? Why am I hiding these? I should just give them to the police."

"No. Avery, that's the worst thing you could do. A few photos and scribbly notes aren't enough for the cops to do anything."

"Maybe not the notes, but the photos are proof of what he did."

"Or you did it to yourself and blamed Logan."

"What are you talking about? I would never do that."

"Logan could tell them that's exactly what you did. And they'd believe him. One, because he's a man, and two, because he's a good liar. He could convince people of anything. And he's on city council and active in the community. People trust him. You're a housewife with an injured brain who can't remember anything. Who do you think the cops will believe?"

"What are you saying?" Avery holds up the photos. "That these are worthless?"

"No, but they're not enough to do anything." I take off my seatbelt and turn to her. "If it were me, I'd go home tonight and pretend everything is normal. You can't act nervous or he'll know something's up."

"I don't know if I can go back there. Now that I know what he did, I'm afraid of him. I'm afraid of what he'll do."

"He won't do anything if you act normal. And don't do anything to make him angry, like argue with him. Have you two been fighting at all?"

"We did the other night, after you dropped me off. I accused him of having an affair with our neighbor."

"Why? Did you catch him with her?"

"Yes, but they were just talking." She looks down at her hands, clearly embarrassed and confused. "I thought there was more going on, but I think I was wrong. Anyway, he didn't really get upset when I accused him. He was more hurt than anything. He went on and on about how much he loves me."

He was overcompensating to cover up his lies. I can't believe Avery bought all that love crap. He's definitely sleeping with the neighbor. When a wife gets a feeling that her husband is cheating, it's almost always true. And with Logan? I'm sure it is. The guy's not getting any action with his sick wife, so he found someone else to meet his needs. And that someone is right next door. How convenient.

"You can do this, Avery. You just need to relax. Act normal."

"And then what? I can't keep living there. I need to get away from him."

"You will, but not yet. If someone's violent and has a temper, you can't make drastic moves. You have to be cautious and move slowly. You need to first figure out where you're going to live."

"I could go back to that apartment we looked at and fill out an application. Would you take me there?"

I let out a sigh. "Avery, I think we need to stop seeing each other. It's not what I want, but it's better if we're not friends, at least for now."

"But why? I need your help."

"Logan's made it clear he doesn't want me being friends with you. If you ignore him and do it anyway, it'll just anger him and he might hurt you."

"So this is it? I can't see you anymore?"

"Not right now. You need to show Logan you're on his

side. Tell him he was right about me and that you decided we shouldn't be friends. It'll prove that you're loyal to him and have no idea what went on during the time you can't remember."

"Okay, but what does that mean for you and me? When will I hear from you?"

"I'll call you when I've figured out what to do next. Can you give me a few days to work on this?"

"Yes, but don't take longer than that. I need to get away from him. I won't be able to sleep until I do."

"I'll do what I can." I hold out my hand. "Give me the notes and photos."

She hesitates, then gives them to me. I put them in my purse.

"You want to have dinner?" I ask.

"No. I'm too sick to eat." She looks out the window, her expression blank. "Just take me home."

I drive her back to her house and wait for her to go inside.

It worked. I got the evidence from her. Got her to trust me.

Now I just need to finish this.

CHAPTER THIRTY-EIGHT

AVERY

"Good morning," Logan says, coming into the kitchen, a big grin on his face.

"Good morning." I look back at him and smile. "Would you like some coffee?"

"Please." He walks over to me as I pour him a cup. He puts his hand on my lower back and leans down to kiss my cheek.

My muscles tense up at his touch, but I tell myself to relax. Act normal.

I hand him the cup of coffee. "Do you have time for breakfast? I could make you something."

"I don't want you going to all that trouble. The coffee's enough." He takes a sip of it, eyeing me in a way that makes me think he knows something is up. Or maybe I'm being paranoid. "I'm surprised you'd want to make breakfast. You must be feeling better today."

"I am. I got a good night's sleep. Thanks for not waking me up last night."

When Paige dropped me off, Logan was out, presumably still at work. I went to my room and shut the door. When I heard him come home later, I got into bed and pretended to be asleep. He opened the bedroom door, saw me sleeping, and left.

Logan leans back against the counter, holding his coffee. "So how was your dinner with Paige?"

"It didn't go well." I walk past Logan and pick up the loaf of bread from the counter.

"Why? What happened?" he asks, watching as I walk to the toaster.

"I didn't like what she was saying."

"About what?" he asks, setting his coffee down.

"Everything." I put a slice of bread in the toaster and push down the lever. "She was being so negative, just like you told me. I didn't want to believe she was like that, but you were right. So I told her I don't want to see her anymore, which is too bad because I could really use a friend."

"Honey, I'm sorry." Logan comes over and pulls me in for a hug. "I tried to warn you, but it's better you found this out for yourself. Paige may seem like a nice person, but she has a lot of issues, one of which is jealousy." Logan pulls back but keeps his arms around my waist. "Paige doesn't like seeing you happy when she's not. She'd rather you were miserable like her."

I nod. "That's how I felt when I was talking to her last night. Like she wanted me to be like her. Like she was angry that I had you and she has no one. It's really sad if you think about it. She has so many things going well for her in life, like her job, her kids, yet she's still not happy."

"It's best not to be around people like that. Their negativity can be contagious. You made the right decision by ending your relationship with her."

"I'm kind of surprised we were ever friends."

"You weren't friends for very long. You got tired of her negative comments and stopped going out with her."

"I'll still have to see her on that committee I'm on."

"You're no longer on it. I spoke to Deloris when you were in the hospital and we agreed it'd be best for someone else to fill your committee spot so you could spend your time recovering."

"Oh," I say, disappointed. "That's too bad. I was looking forward to the next meeting."

I wasn't, but it's what Logan wants to hear. I'm being the obedient wife, making sure I don't upset him.

"You can join another committee once you're able to." He gives me a kiss. "I need to get to work. Do you have any big plans for today?"

I laugh. "Yeah, shower and take a nap. And then I might try making something. I'd like to get back to cooking. You might be sitting down to a homemade meal for dinner tonight."

"That's great, honey." He smiles, pleased that I'm getting back into my role as the dutiful housewife, here to serve his every need. Is that what I was like before? Did he force me into that role with his threats and abuse?

"Do you have any requests?" I ask. "I want to make something you like."

"Surprise me. I'm sure I'll like whatever you make." He kisses me again. "Have a good day."

"You too."

If anyone witnessed that interaction, they'd think we're a normal, happy couple. I would've thought the same if I hadn't found all those photos and notes. There were moments over the past few weeks that I've felt something was off between Logan and me, but I ignored it and moved on. Even when he got angry and threw out those berries from Edith, I excused his behavior and told myself to forget about it.

But now that I know the truth, I'm thinking back to every moment, every word, every feeling I had that told me something was wrong, and I'm seeing them as warnings.

"Knock, knock!" a voice says.

Looking over at the glass slider, I see Rachel standing there, holding a white paper sack and cardboard tray with two cups in it. I don't want to let her in, but I feel like I have to when she's standing there, staring at me, eagerly waiting for me to let her inside.

I go over to the sliding door and open it. "Hi, Rachel."

"Hi! I hope it's okay if I drop by. I saw Logan leave and thought you might want some company." She frowns. "Actually, *I* need the company. Do you mind if I come in?"

"Go ahead." I step aside, and she comes into the kitchen, setting the tray and the sack on the center island.

"I brought you a coffee. And I got us some pastries. Do you want to try one?"

Going over to her, I look inside the sack and see an assortment of flaky, buttery pastries that must've come from a bakery. The ones at the grocery store never look that good.

"I've made some toast, so maybe I'll have one later."

"Forget the toast. These are so much better. Personally, I love the almond croissant, but they're all delicious."

"Okay, I'll try one." I take a small, cheese-filled pastry from the sack. "Thanks."

"You're welcome! I originally got them for me, but if I eat

them all myself, I'll gain ten pounds, which will only make it harder for me to find a date."

"You're dating?"

"Not yet, but I will be." She looks over at the kitchen table. "Could we sit down?"

"Sure. Let me get some plates for the pastries."

"Oh, I'm not having any," she says, taking her coffee and going to the table. "I've already had three."

I get a plate for myself, grab my coffee, and join her at the table. "So what's going on?"

I'm not in the mood to hear about her problems when I have enough of my own, but I know she won't leave until she tells me.

"Connor filed for divorce yesterday," she says with a sigh.

"I'm sorry," I say, trying to sound sincere. But really, what did she expect? She kept telling him she didn't want to get back together with him.

"He's found someone else, and now he's rushing to get divorced." She sniffles and wipes her eyes. "How could he just replace me like that?"

I keep quiet, not sure what to say. It's hard to be on her side when she's been telling me for weeks that she wants a divorce, and now she's saying she doesn't.

"What am I going to do?" she asks. "I can't afford the rent on my own. My freelance jobs don't pay enough to cover my expenses."

"You might have to find somewhere else to live."

"I don't want to live in some run-down apartment. That's for college kids, not someone my age."

"There are plenty of nice apartments," I say. "Maybe you should go check some out."

"No." She shakes her head. "I shouldn't have to change my lifestyle just because my husband found someone else." She huffs. "I can't believe I married that loser. Now I'm alone and have to start over again." She looks at me. "You should be grateful you have a man like Logan. He'd never leave you for another woman."

"I'd like to think he wouldn't, but it's possible," I say, remembering the other night, when I saw Logan with her. I'm still not sure what's going on with them.

"Logan wouldn't leave you," she scoffs. "Believe me, that man is never getting divorced."

"Why do you think he wouldn't get divorced?"

"Well, for one, it wouldn't look good. He has an image to uphold. Staying with his sick wife and being her caretaker shows he's compassionate and loyal. Imagine what people would think if he left you during your time of need."

"True," I say, "but he could leave me when I get better."

She cocks her head to the side. "Is there a reason you think he might leave you? Are you two having problems?"

"No, I'm just talking hypothetically." I take a drink of my coffee.

"Would you ever leave Logan?" she says. "If you found out he'd been unfaithful?"

"I don't know. I've never really thought about it."

"Every woman's thought about it. We all know our husbands might cheat. You can't tell me you've never even considered it."

"I don't like to think that way. Logan hasn't done anything, so why think about him cheating? It's not good for our relationship to think that way."

"Well, aren't you the little optimist?" she says with a smirk. "The rest of us choose to live in the real world."

That was rude, and unusual for her. She's usually throwing compliments my way, not insults, but I decide to let it go. She's upset about her impending divorce and not herself today. Or maybe this is the real Rachel, the one I don't usually get to see.

"Enough about me," she says. "How are you?"

"Good. I'm feeling better, so I'm going to try to get some things done around the house."

She takes a long sip of her coffee. "Have you had any memories come back?"

"No, not yet."

"How strange that must be to not remember. But at least you're still alive. I've heard stories about people with head injuries who die almost immediately. Something about bleeding in the brain? I don't know all the details. But it can be very serious."

"Yeah, I was lucky."

She checks her watch. "I should go. I have a hair appointment I need to get to." She stands up. "Sorry for barging in and telling you all my problems. But I feel a little better now. Thank you for listening."

"Thank you for the pastries," I say, getting up.

"You can keep the rest. I shouldn't have any more." She walks to the slider. "Tell Logan I said hi. And save a pastry for him!"

"I will! Bye!"

As I watch her leave, I realize she talked a lot about Logan today, which makes me think something really did happen between them. Or maybe she *wants* something to happen. That could be what I saw the other night. Maybe Rachel tried to make a move on Logan and he told her no.

Maybe that's why she kept insisting he'd never cheat on me. I think he would, but maybe not with her.

    Then again, maybe I'm wrong. Maybe he *would* be interested in someone like her. It's hard to say since the Logan I thought I knew didn't actually exist. Those photos I found prove that he's someone else. Someone I never would've married.

CHAPTER THIRTY-NINE

RACHEL

"Can I help you?" the young woman behind the desk says. She's a beautiful blonde who can't be more than twenty-five.

I smile at her. "Are you Logan's assistant?"

"Yeah, I'm Bree," she says in a voice that sounds more like a preteen girl than a grown woman. "How can I help you?"

"I need to speak with Logan Fairmont."

"Do you have an appointment?" She looks at her computer. "Because I don't see anything on his schedule."

"Actually, this is a personal matter, and it's rather urgent, so if you could just show me to his office."

"It's over there." She points to it. "But he's on a call right now. He doesn't like it when people go in there while he's talking."

"Yes, well, he won't mind if it's me. I'll just go knock on the door."

As I walk past her, Bree pops up from her chair. "Ma'am, I really don't think you should—"

"Trust me, he'll be fine with it." I glare at her. "And don't call me ma'am."

I continue to Logan's office. The door is closed, but I can see him through the glass, pacing back and forth, the phone held to his ear.

Pushing my shoulders back, I do a quick check of my dress, making sure it's not pulling or puckering anywhere. It's rather form-fitting, some would say tight, but that's what I'm going for. I need Logan to see what he's missing out on so he'll change his mind about our little affair. I know he's not getting any action at home, so it makes absolutely no sense for him to end things with me. I'm sure my visit today will change his mind.

I knock on his door, then open it.

Logan does a double take when he sees me, but his expression gives nothing away. I can't tell if he's surprised, angry, or aroused at the sight of me in this dress.

"Frank, I need to go," he says, watching as I walk into his office and shut the door. "But count me in for golf on Saturday. We'll talk later. Have a good day." He ends the call. "Rachel, what the hell are you doing here?"

"I thought I'd surprise you." I smile and slink over to him. "Are you surprised?"

"You shouldn't be here," he snaps. "People will see us together."

"And? We're neighbors. Maybe I'm here to complain about your lawn. You really should mow it. It's far too long."

"What's the real reason you're here?" he says in a hushed tone, even though I doubt anyone would hear us with the door closed.

"To talk to you." I run my hand down his chest. "About our situation."

"We don't have a situation. I told you. It's over."

"I know you said that, but you didn't really mean it." My hand wanders lower, down the front of his pants.

"Stop it!" he whispers, yanking my hand away. "I'm at work! What is wrong with you?"

"Are you saying you'd like to continue this later? Because I could leave the back door unlocked."

That's what I would do when I knew Logan was coming over. He'd wait until Avery was asleep, then sneak in through the back. Connor had no idea. That man sleeps through anything, and he was upstairs with the door closed. Logan and I would remain on the first level, making love on the couch, the floor, or against the kitchen counter. Now that Connor is gone, we're free to go anywhere in the house and be as loud as we'd like.

"I'm saying I want you to leave," he says, gripping my arm.

"I'm not leaving until we work this out."

"There's nothing to work out. I'm married. I'm not leaving my wife."

"Why? Because it would look bad?"

"I need you to leave," he says, his eyes locked on mine. "I mean it, Rachel. Go."

There's a small couch in his office, and I walk over to it and sit down.

"Avery and I talked today." I smile, a coy smile that I know will make him curious.

"Talked about what?"

"You." I cross my legs, causing my dress to rise up higher on my thigh.

"What about me?" he snaps.

"We discussed whether or not you'd ever cheat on her." I

watch Logan's face for a reaction, but his expression doesn't change. And he doesn't say anything. "Avery thinks you'd cheat."

"She said that? That I would cheat on her?"

"She thinks it's possible. She doesn't know it's already happened."

"And she never will. I already told Avery there's nothing going on with us."

"Why?" I raise an eyebrow at him. "Did she suspect something?"

"Yes. When she saw me with you the other night."

"That's interesting. I wonder why she didn't tell me."

"Because there's nothing to tell. We were talking. That's it."

I slowly stand up and make my way back over to Logan. "Why would you want her when you could have me?" I lean up to his ear. "I know I please you so much more than her."

He backs away. "I don't have time for this. I need you to go."

"I'm not done." I turn and walk away, letting him see the back of me in this dress. "What if Avery weren't an issue? What if you weren't married? Would that change your mind about us?"

"We are not discussing this. You're wasting my time."

I turn back to him. "Just answer the question. Would it change anything?"

"Rachel, I told you, what we had was just a fling. And now it's over. Accept it and move on."

"I am not moving on!" I storm up to him. "Not after all that I did for you! You at least owe me an explanation as to why you would choose a plain, boring woman like Avery over me. I'm a million times better than her and you know it! I know you do."

"Avery is my wife," he says through gritted teeth. "You're just a woman I slept with."

"How dare you!" I slap him across the face.

His eyes narrow and he leans down to me. "Get out, or I will have security drag you out."

"It's because she's sick, isn't it? That's the only reason you're still with her. You feel trapped. Like you can't leave her. I can only imagine how horrible that must be for you. That's why I tried to help you. It didn't work, but I could try again." I'm talking fast, getting breathless, as I desperately try to get him to see that I'm on his side. That what we had was more than a fling. And that I love him, and deep down, I know he loves me.

"What the hell are you talking about? What did you do?"

I smile at him, excited to finally let him know how far I'm willing to go to be with him. The risk I'm willing to take for our love.

"I hit her. With a frying pan." I laugh a little. "She didn't even see it coming. I used the key you gave me to get inside, then I snuck up behind her and whacked her on the head."

"Wait—when did you do this?"

"The day you found her. I made it look like she fell, which she did, but that was because of me. Because I hit her. I knocked her out and she hit the floor. I positioned her to make it look like she did it herself. Like she slipped on the floor, hit her head on the counter, and knocked herself out. Then I scattered the clothes from the laundry basket around her so it'd look like the basket flew out of her hands when she fell."

Logan is staring at me, his jaw dropped. He's speechless,

shocked that I would go to such lengths to be with him. I tried to tell him how much our relationship means to me. Maybe now, he'll finally understand.

"I assumed she was dead," I say. "But I didn't want to stick around to make sure, so I left. I was worried nosy old Edith might've seen me go into your house, but if she had, she would've said something by now. And just in case she did happen to see me that day, I told Avery that Edith is losing it so she won't believe anything she says." I grip Logan's hand. "Now do you see how much you mean to me? What I'd do so we could be together?"

"You did this the day I found her?" he says, like he's confirming that's what I said. "The day she went to the hospital."

"Yes. I did it that morning, just before noon."

"That can't be right." He rips his hand from mine. "It can't be."

"What do you mean? I was there. I know what day it was."

"Did someone call you? A woman? Did she tell you to do this to Avery?"

"I don't know what you're talking about. What woman?"

"Nobody called you. You did this on your own. Is that what you're telling me?"

"Yes. Why? I don't understand."

"It's nothing. Forget it." He walks away, cursing under his breath, pacing in a circle.

"Logan, what's going on?"

He races to the door and opens it. "I need you to go. Now. There's something I have to do, and it can't wait."

"What is it? What do you have to do?"

"Rachel, I swear, if you don't leave right now, I will call security."

"Fine, I'm going." I meet him at the door and smile. "I'm free tonight if you want to come over."

I walk out of his office, feeling his eyes on me as I go. He didn't agree to be with me, but he will. Once it sinks in that I tried to kill his wife so we could be together, he'll realize how much I care about him, how much I care about us. And he'll finally admit how much he loves me.

CHAPTER FORTY

PAIGE

Today's the day. I was going to wait a little longer, play it all out in my head a few more times to make sure I didn't miss anything, but I'm getting impatient. I want to be done with this so I don't have to deal with it anymore.

I call Avery, putting on a smile so my voice sounds pleasant.

"Paige?" Avery says in a hushed tone.

"Yeah, it's me. Why are you so quiet? Is someone with you?"

"No, I'm just nervous," she says, raising her voice back to normal. "I thought we weren't going to talk until you had a plan."

"I have one. That's why I'm calling."

"Oh, okay. So what's the plan?"

"I don't want to tell you over the phone. Can I come over?"

"Here? To the house?"

"Yeah. Logan won't know. He's at the office. I just saw him go into a meeting."

"What if he comes home for lunch?"

"Does he do that?"

"No, but he could. Why don't we go somewhere else?"

"I'd rather do it there. I want to do a quick search of the house to make sure there aren't any more photos or notes you might've missed. And then we'll go over the plan."

"Um, yeah, I guess that'd be okay."

"How did this morning go?"

"I told him I wasn't friends with you anymore and he seemed to buy it."

"Good. See? I knew you could do this."

"I was so nervous. I can't believe he couldn't tell. What time will you be here?"

"I'm leaving in a few minutes, so probably around noon." I look up from my desk and see Logan coming down the hall, heading straight for my door. "Avery, I have to go. I'll see you soon. Bye."

My office door swings open and Logan strides in, slamming the door behind him.

"We need to talk." His eyes are dark and narrowed, his jaw so tight it looks like it might snap.

"I can't right now. I'm busy." I get up and go around my desk toward the door.

He grabs my arm. "I need answers. You're not leaving until I get them."

"Let go of me," I say, staring back at him.

"Not until we talk."

"I'm not talking if you're touching me. Now let go of me, or I'll scream and file a harassment suit."

That was one of the many reasons I wanted a job here. So I could sue Logan for harassment if he ever threatened me or tried to blackmail me. Even if I couldn't prove it, filing a suit against him would harm his precious reputation.

Logan lets go of my arm. "You lied to me."

"About what?" I say, keeping my cool. Unlike Avery, I don't get nervous. I've trained myself to stay calm in most any situation.

"You said you hired someone. You said they went there that day. But I just found out that wasn't true."

Okay, now I'm getting nervous. How did he know that? Did Avery get her memory back? Did she remember the day it happened and tell Logan? That's the only way he'd know that nobody was there that day. That she was never hit on the head because I never hired the guy to do it.

"I don't know what you mean," I say, forcing myself to remain calm.

"A woman came into my office less than five minutes ago and confessed that she went to the house that day and hit Avery on the head with a frying pan, hoping it would kill her."

"I never said the person I hired was a man."

Logan leans down to me and hisses in my face, "You didn't hire her. She said nobody called her or set it up. She did it on her own."

"Who was the woman? Did she tell you her name?"

"It was Rachel. She lives next door. I had an affair with her. She wanted to get rid of Avery so she could be with me." He glares at me. "What she did had nothing to do with you."

Is he serious? How is that even possible? What are the odds this woman just happened to try to kill Avery on the exact same day I was supposed to send a hitman to do it?

"She's lying," I say. "She wanted you to think she did

some grand gesture to prove her feelings for you so she made up that story."

"Trying to murder someone is not a grand gesture," he snaps.

"It is to a crazy person, and she's obviously crazy. Why did you get involved with this woman?"

"Because she's right next door. It's easy sex. Who the hell cares? The point is that you lied. You said you'd do the job and you didn't. The question is, why? Are you trying to extort money from me? Or is something else going on here?"

I sigh. "Okay, fine. Here's what happened. My guy went over there to do the job, but when he got there, she was already on the floor. He assumed she was dead, so he left. He called me and said it looked like she slipped on the floor and fell. I didn't tell you because I didn't want to give the money back. And why would I? I did what I said I would. I hired the guy, and I'd already paid him. How was I supposed to know he'd get there and she'd already be dead?"

"But she wasn't dead."

"She would've been if you'd left her there."

"I had to get help. I told you, that old lady was watching me."

"Well, that's not my problem. But next time it'll work. Because I'm doing it, and I'll make sure she's dead."

"I don't think I trust you to do anything, not now that I know you lied to me."

"You want this done or not? Because it's happening today. So if you're calling it off, you'd better—"

"Today?" he says, and I can tell he's struggling to keep his voice down. "It's really happening today?"

"Yeah, if you'd get out of here and let me leave."

"You're doing this now?"

"Not now, but soon. I'll text you when it's done. The text will be something about work, like that I can't make the meeting. That's your cue to go home and find her."

"Why wouldn't I just wait until tonight?"

"Because I don't want someone else finding her. Like your old lady neighbor or the crazy woman you're sleeping with."

"I'm not sleeping with her. That's over."

"Fine, whatever. Now would you get out of here? We shouldn't be seen together right before—"

"Yes. I'm leaving." He slips out the door and hurries down the hall.

That was close. I'm good at thinking on my feet, but I did not expect to have to come up with a story to explain why my hitman didn't do the job. I really thought Avery just fell down that day, which was a big coincidence, but it worked out great for me. Logan assumed the hitman took her down, I was able to keep the money, and Avery was fine. But now it turns out the crazy neighbor tried to kill her.

If she hadn't done that, things would've turned out a lot differently. My initial plan for Logan didn't work. And if he found out I didn't do the job, everything would've fallen apart. He would've known that I lied, and I wouldn't have had another chance at him. Now I do. I just hope this time it works.

CHAPTER FORTY-ONE

AVERY

"Hey!" I hear Edith yell in her gravelly voice. She's at the slider door, waving at me to let her in.

I don't have time for this. Paige will be here any minute now. I don't want Edith seeing her and asking all kinds of questions.

"Hi, Edith," I say, sliding the door open just a crack. "I can't talk right now. I have something I need to do."

"This will only take a minute." She shoves the door open and lets herself in. She really doesn't take no for an answer. "That day you hit your head, did that husband of yours mention you having any visitors?"

"No, I was alone that day."

"And nobody said anything about coming over? Before you hit your head?"

"Edith, what are you getting at?" I ask, trying to hurry her up.

She holds up her phone. "I got something to show you."

"Will it take long, because I—"

"You know those cameras my son put up so I could keep watch on the critters in my yard?"

"Yeah."

"Well, apparently, they record whenever they sense movement. I didn't know how to look at the videos, so I kind of forgot they were there. Anyway, my son was over last night, and he showed me this app he'd put on my phone that has all the videos." She swipes through her phone. "So I was going through them, and look what I found."

She gives me her phone, which shows a video of our shared backyards. Rachel appears on the screen at the door that goes into my garage. She uses a key to unlock the door and goes inside.

"Why was Rachel in our garage?" I ask Edith, not really able to make sense of what I'm seeing.

"I think she was trying to get into your house without you knowing. It happened the day you hurt your head. Check the time." Edith points to the top of the video, showing the date and time it was recorded. "Just before noon. Isn't that when you fell?" I can feel her eyes, sharp on me.

"I'm not sure. I can't remember, but the doctors estimate it happened sometime before noon based on the amount of bleeding in my brain."

"Look at this, taken a few minutes later." Edith pulls up another video. It shows Rachel leaving out that same door in the garage, but this time she peeks out, looks to see if anyone's around, then sneaks out the door, locks it, and goes back to her house.

"That must've been before it happened," I say. "I probably fell right after she left."

"Or she's the reason you fell," Edith says, her brows rising. "You ever consider it wasn't an accident?"

"It was an accident," I insist. "Logan told me I was feeling really dizzy that morning. He said I got dizzy, lost my balance, and fell."

"How would he know what happened? He wasn't even home."

"He's guessing, based on how I was feeling that morning. And when he found me, the way I was positioned, he said it looked like I slipped, hit my head on the island, and fell to the floor."

"So explain why Rachel was here," Edith says in a conspiratorial tone. "And why she didn't tell anyone."

"I don't know. I'd have to ask her."

"She's not going to tell you the truth. Not if she was up to no good."

"What are you saying?" I look at Edith, my head spinning. "That Rachel pushed me?"

"Or hit you over the head. Who knows?" Edith walks over to the kitchen island. "You'd have to be at just the perfect angle to hit your head on this. And you'd have to hit it pretty hard to knock yourself out like you did." She walks back to me. "I think she did it. I think Rachel showed up here, whacked you over the head, and left you to die."

"Edith, that is not what happened," I say with a laugh, but now part of me is wondering if it's possible. I have to admit it's very odd that Rachel was here that day, close to the time I fell, and never told me.

"How do you know what happened? You can't remember."

"Why would Rachel want to kill me?"

"Because she's messing around with your husband."

"Wait—what? Do you know this, or are you just guessing?"

She pulls up another video. "This one isn't as clear because it's at night, but you can still see him." She points to someone in the video leaving my house and going to Rachel's. "I can't get a really good look at him, but I'd guess that's your husband. Wouldn't you?"

I replay the video. "It's hard to see who it is, but it has to be Logan. He left from our house."

"At two in the morning. What do you suppose he's doing at that time of night at the neighbor's house?"

I look away from the video and let out a sigh. "I had a feeling something was going on with those two."

"I've seen him over there a lot, but I thought he was going to see her husband." She points to the video. "I'm guessing he wasn't going to talk golf with Connor at two in the morning."

"No, probably not," I mutter. "Are there more videos?"

"At least three that I saw. I didn't look at all of them, but the ones I saw were all in the middle of the night."

"So this has been going on for a while," I say, wondering when it started.

"My guess is that she wanted him for herself but decided she had to get rid of you first."

"No." I shake my head. "Rachel's not a killer."

"Anyone can be a killer with the right motivation. Don't you watch those crime shows? On almost every episode they got a jealous mistress going after the wife. It happens all the time."

"Okay, but that's not what happened. Rachel wouldn't do that. We're friends."

"That woman is not your friend." Edith's tone shows just

how absolutely clear she is on this. "She's a fake. She's putting on the friend act to throw you off the scent so you don't find out she's fooling around with your husband."

The doorbell rings. That must be Paige.

"Edith, I have to go. Can you send me those videos?"

"Sure, but I'll have to ask my son to help. I'm not good with tech stuff."

The doorbell rings again.

"I need to get that."

"Yeah, I'm going," she says, heading back out the slider. "If that's Rachel at the door, don't answer it!"

"I won't. Bye." I shut the slider and lock it, then race to the front door. "Sorry it took so long," I say to Paige, letting her in. "My neighbor was here, and she wouldn't leave."

"What neighbor?" Paige asks.

"The older lady who lives behind me. She showed me these videos of Rachel, the woman next door, and she was—well, I don't need to get into it. We have other things to worry about."

"No, tell me. What videos?"

Why does she care? She doesn't even know Rachel. I'm a little suspicious she's asking about the videos, but it's probably Edith making me that way. Her suspicions about Rachel have me thinking I can't trust anyone, not even Paige.

"They showed Rachel going into my garage the day I fell. I don't know what she was up to, but I can't worry about it right now. We need to talk about Logan. So what's this plan you came up with?"

"About that. I don't really have one."

"I don't understand. You said—"

"Avery, I need to tell you something," she says, her face

deadly serious. "And I need you to believe me, or this isn't going to work."

"Believe you about what?" I ask, backing away from her. I'm getting a bad feeling about this, and about Paige.

If she doesn't have a plan, what is she doing here?

CHAPTER FORTY-TWO

AVERY

What Paige just told me sounds like fiction, or like one of those crime shows Edith was talking about.

My husband hired Paige to kill me?

But then Rachel showed up and tried to kill me?

"I don't understand this," I say, pacing the floor, my head hurting, my stomach in knots. "Why does everyone want me dead?"

"Rachel wants Logan," Paige says. "And since he won't divorce you, she had to try to kill you."

"But why won't Logan divorce me? If he's not happy, we could get a divorce. He doesn't have to kill me."

"He can't divorce his sick wife. You know that, Avery. Think how bad that would look. It would ruin his image." She rolls her eyes. "He's such a fake. When's the last time he actually helped anyone?"

"I could've divorced him. Then he could've blamed me. Said I left him."

"He'd still look bad, because why would you leave him? People would wonder what he did. Why you didn't stay with him. Rumors would start, and people always believe rumors over the truth."

"So Logan's solution was to kill me," I mutter, still shocked that my own husband, the man who claimed to love me, would want me dead and would actually hire someone to make that wish a reality.

"I was never going to do it," Paige says. "I never even considered it."

"But you've, um... done this before?" I ask. "You've—"

"No," she says, shaking her head. "I've done some bad stuff, but not that. I've never killed anyone. Logan just assumed I'd do it because I spent time in prison."

I sigh in relief. "Okay, good. I mean, I didn't think you would, but—"

"You don't have to explain. I get it. People assume all sorts of things about me because I've been to prison, but I promise you, Avery, I'm not that person anymore. I'm really trying to turn my life around. And I swear, I never for one second considered taking Logan's offer. When he asked me to do it, I immediately called my old parole officer, and he connected me with Chad, the detective I've got helping me take down Logan. Trust me. There's no way he's getting away with this."

"You really think they'll arrest him?"

"Yes. I recorded him asking me to kill you. The whole conversation, and we were outside, in a public space, so it's all legal. I didn't need his consent to record him."

"And Chad has the photos I gave you?" I ask.

"Yes, and the notes. He also has the recording. He said that's enough to arrest him, but to me, an arrest isn't enough. I want the jerk locked away, which is why we're playing this out till the end. Logan has one last chance to call it off, but he won't, which will prove he wanted you dead."

"What if he shows up here before the police?"

"He won't. I'll text Chad first and let him know to send the cops over. Then I'll text Logan. He'll assume the job is done, which is his cue to come home and do his part of the plan."

"Which is to call for help and pretend to be shocked that I'm dead."

"Yes, exactly. He'll turn on the tears and say how much he loved you and how his life won't be the same without you, blah, blah, blah."

"What about Rachel?" I ask, taking a deep breath as I try to process all this.

"The cops won't be able to prove she hit you that day, but you have video of her sneaking into your house, and I can testify that Logan told me she admitted she tried to kill you. Logan might testify against her too in exchange for a shorter sentence." Paige checks the time. "We have to hurry. I told Logan it's happening soon. He's going to be expecting a text from me."

"So what's next?"

"Is there anywhere else you might have hidden evidence? I know you can't remember, but can you think of any place you haven't checked where you might have hidden something?"

"No, but you can look around if you want."

Paige heads to the bedroom. I follow her in there and see her looking through the dresser.

"I already went through every drawer," I tell her. "And I checked under each one to make sure I hadn't taped any photos there."

"What about this?" She points to the jewelry box on top of the dresser.

"I looked in it. I didn't find anything."

Paige picks up the jewelry box, brings it to the bed, and starts taking stuff out.

"I told you, I already looked in there."

"But did you look inside everything?" she asks, opening an earring box.

"Yes, I checked everything in there."

She lifts up a cardboard insert in the jewelry box, and behind it is a folded-up piece of paper. "What's this?"

"I don't know." I take the piece of paper from her and carefully unfold it. It's another note I wrote, covered on both sides. I quickly read it.

"No," I mutter. "No, no, no."

"What?" Paige says. "What is it? What does it say?"

"He killed my brother. Logan killed him." I hold up the note. "He admitted he did it. I wrote it down."

"I thought your brother died in a fire."

"He did, but Logan set it up. He was there that day. He wanted my brother to die."

"Why didn't you tell the police?"

"The note says he threatened to hurt Mia—my sister—if I told anyone." I look at Paige. "He killed John, and now he's trying to kill me."

"He won't. I'm texting Chad." She gets out her phone. "We're finishing this."

I hear a noise. "What was that?"

"What?" she says as she sends the text. "I didn't hear anything."

"Avery?" a voice yells.

"It's Logan!" I whisper, gripping Paige's arm. "What is he doing here?"

"I don't know. Wait here. I'll deal with him."

"But what if he—"

"Lie down on the floor. You need to play dead in case he comes in here."

"Avery!" Logan yells. "Where are you?"

Paige races out of the bedroom, shutting the door behind her.

"Logan," I hear Paige say, "what are you doing here? I told you to wait until I texted you."

"I didn't trust you to get it done."

"Yeah, well, it's done," she snaps back. "But you shouldn't be here. You've just put yourself here at the time of her death."

Paige told me to play dead, but I can't do it. I have to face Logan. I have to tell him I know what he did to John and what he's trying to do to me. It's probably a stupid move, but what's Logan going to do? Try to run away? The cops will be here any minute now.

"She's really dead?" Logan asks as I sneak out of the bedroom. "You're sure?"

"Yeah," Paige says. "I checked. She's dead."

Paige and Logan are in the kitchen. I slowly walk there, hoping they don't hear my footsteps.

"I want to see for myself," Logan says. "Where is she?"

"Right here," I say, coming into the kitchen. I look directly at Logan. "Surprise."

His eyes bounce between Paige and me. "What the hell's going on? Why isn't she—"

"It's over, Logan," Paige says. "I was never going to kill her."

"I knew it," he says. "I knew you couldn't do it. I should've done it myself from the beginning."

He reaches behind him and pulls out a gun, pointing it at me.

"Logan, please, put it down," I say, staring at the gun. "Where did you even get that?"

"From your friend Paige here. She got it from some thug on the street. That's where people like her go to get a gun."

"He's lying," she says, glancing at me. "That's not mine."

"But the police will believe it is," Logan says. "Criminals get guns off the street. You're the criminal, Paige, not me. I came home to check on my wife and found that you'd shot her."

"The police won't believe you," I say. "They—"

"Avery, stop," Paige says, her eyes on Logan. "He's right. The cops will think the gun is mine. I have a record. I've served time. He's going to make it look like I did this."

I look at Logan. "Don't do it. You don't need to. We can get divorced. I'll keep quiet. I'll never tell anyone about this."

"You really think I'm that stupid?" He aims the gun at me.

"Logan, please. Don't—"

A shot fires and I recoil, just as I feel Paige yank me hard to the floor.

"Stay down," she whispers.

"What happened?" I say, noticing I don't feel any pain. "Did he miss?"

"He didn't shoot you. Someone shot him."

"What? Are you sure?"

"Yes. The shot came through the window. They might shoot again, so stay down."

"It must've been the cops."

"Or Rachel."

What? Why would Rachel shoot Logan? Or was she aiming at me and hit Logan by accident?

As I'm trying to figure out what the hell is going on, loud voices ring out from the other room.

"Police!" a man yells.

"In here!" Paige yells back.

I am beyond relieved when two burly officers appear and race over to Paige and me.

"Either of you injured?" one of them asks.

"No, we're okay." I slowly stand up as he reaches out his hand to help me.

Another officer is going around the center island to Logan. "This one's been shot," he says. "He's going to need medical help."

"He's alive?" I ask.

"Yeah, but he's out cold," the officer says. "And losing a lot of blood." He gets on his radio and calls for help.

"Who shot him?" Paige asks.

The officer next to her points at the window behind the sink. "It was a woman. Our guys got her. They'll take her in."

I move so I can see out the window. Two officers are handcuffing Edith as she yells at them and fights against the restraints.

"Edith?" I say, shocked. "Edith shot Logan?"

"Why would she do that?" Paige asks.

"She must've been watching us through the window and saw that he had a gun." I turn to the officer. "You can't arrest her. She shot Logan to save me."

"The woman shot a man, regardless of motive," he says. "We have to bring her in."

"What about Rachel?" I ask. "The woman next door? She tried to kill me. She admitted it. You need to arrest her."

"I already told Chad about her," Paige tells the officer.

"You're the one who's been working with Chad?"

"Yeah. He said we didn't have enough evidence to arrest Rachel, but now Avery says there's a video."

"Edith has it," I say. "She was going to send it to me."

Sirens blare outside the house.

"Ambulance is here," another officer announces, striding into the kitchen.

Moments later, the paramedics have taken Logan away. Paige and I are brought to the police station. We tell them what happened, but it's mostly Paige talking. I'm having a hard time talking or even listening. I'm in shock, feeling like this can't be real, like it didn't actually happen. But it did.

Logan tried to kill me. He was tired of having a sick wife. Tired of pretending to care about me. Pretending to be the doting husband. So he decided to get rid of me. Divorce wasn't an option. He wanted me dead.

CHAPTER FORTY-THREE

AVERY

"I'm nervous," I say to Paige. "I don't know if I can do this."

"Sure you can. It's just talking."

"To a room of three hundred women."

"Just pretend you're talking to me."

"I don't think it works that way." I look back at the ballroom. Every table is filled. Paige said the tickets to this event sold out within hours. Apparently, everyone wants to hear my story. I don't mind sharing it, but I'm nervous to speak to an entire room of people.

My phone alerts me to a text. I smile when I see it's from Mia. The text reads:

> Sorry I can't be there today. But I know you're going to do great!

I text back.

> I don't know about that. I'm really nervous.

> Don't be. You've got this! I love you and I'm so proud of you!

I wipe my eyes, her words making me tear up.

> I love you too.

"Was that your sister?" Paige asks as I set my phone down.

"Yeah, she feels bad she can't be here."

"But she's still planning to visit, right?"

I nod. "She'll be here in a couple of weeks. I can't wait! I'm already planning all this stuff for us to do."

"I'll be right back," Paige says, getting up.

"Where are you going?"

"To tell them to close the raffle. We're doing the drawing right after your speech."

Today's event is to raise money for women who've escaped their abusive husbands and partners and are trying to rebuild their lives. The money will go to several charities in the area, some that provide housing, some that give out clothes, and some that provide free childcare. Paige helped plan the event and keeps running off to make sure everything's getting done.

"Drink some water," Edith says, returning from the bathroom. She sits beside me. "The throat gets dry when you're nervous."

I pick up my glass and gulp down some water. "My throat's still dry. And I'm still nervous."

"Why?" She looks around. "None of these people care if you stumble on your words. They just want to hear your story."

"I know, but I still don't want to mess up."

It's been six months since Logan tried to kill me. He was accused of attempted murder but didn't go to jail right away due to his injury. The bullet went through his back and chest, causing him to need several surgeries. He was in the hospital for weeks. Nobody went to see him. He didn't get any cards or flowers or well-wishes. His perfect image was destroyed. No one wanted to even be associated with him.

It's not just because he tried to kill me, but because of all the other stuff he did. The abuse that went on for years. I finally remembered. It took months of therapy, which included some hypnosis, to unlock the memories my brain had tried to hide from me. The neurologist was right. It wasn't the injury to my brain that caused my memory loss. It was all the trauma I went through. Losing my brother. Finding out about Logan's role in his death. The mental abuse, physical abuse, the threats and mind games. My mind hid all those memories away until I was able to access them again.

My doctors think the stress of what I went through is what caused my autoimmune disease. It's the only way they can explain how my health is back to normal. When I lost my memory, my symptoms improved, and now, with Logan out of my life, my health is great. My headaches are gone, I no longer have joint pain, and I have more energy than I've ever had. It's ironic, really. Logan tried to kill me because I was sick, yet he was the cause of my illness.

I haven't spoken to Logan since his arrest, and I don't plan to. I have no desire to see him or talk to him. His trial comes up later this year. I'm hoping he's found guilty and gets locked away for a very long time. I wanted him to get charged for what he did to John, but unfortunately, there's no evidence to prove what he did. It's his word against mine. I wasn't there to witness his actions.

Rachel's trial is also coming up. She was arrested a few days after Logan was shot. As Paige expected, Logan told the cops what Rachel did to me, hoping it would benefit his own case. Then Edith turned in the video showing Rachel at my house the day she tried to kill me. The cops showed it to Rachel and she broke down and confessed.

As for Edith, it was decided that she shot Logan for the sole purpose of saving me. She told the police she was out working in her garden that day, heard a commotion, looked through my kitchen window, and saw Logan holding a gun, aiming it at me. She raced into her house, grabbed the gun she legally owned, and shot him. She said she had no intention of killing him, but I secretly think she did. She hated him from the day she met him. She's one of those people who can immediately sense when someone is bad. He never had her fooled.

"Are we still going out for a drink later?" I say to Edith. "Because I could use one after this."

"As long as you don't make me go to one of those wine bars," Edith says. "It's gotta be a place that sells beer."

"Must have beer. Got it." I smile at her.

Edith has become like a mom to me. She's not at all like my actual mom, who didn't drink beer or grow pot and definitely didn't own a gun. But Edith cares about me like my mom did. She's always asking how I'm doing, checking on me, looking out for me. She treats me with the sort of genuine kindness that anyone would be grateful for.

"Do you mind if Paige comes with us?" I ask, watching as she races up to the stage to talk to the woman who will be introducing me in a few minutes.

"Does she have to?" Edith says. "I was hoping it'd just be us."

I turn to Edith. "You don't like Paige?"

"I don't trust her. You know how much trouble that girl's been in? How many times she's been arrested?"

"That was a long time ago. She's not like that now."

"That's what she tells you, but do you really believe her?"

"Yes. Think of all she does for the community, like helping to put on this event. And she saved me from Logan. She could've taken his money and killed me, but she didn't."

"I still don't trust her," Edith mutters, watching Paige move around the stage.

"You know, people can change. Their past doesn't have to determine their future."

"Yeah, but a bad seed is a bad seed. You can give it all the sun, water, and fertilizer you want. It's not going to turn a bad seed good."

"Maybe, but that's not Paige. She's really turned her life around. She's a good seed now, Edith," I say with a smile.

Paige leaves the stage and comes over to me at the table. "Okay, they're ready for you."

"Yeah, but I'm not," I say, getting up, my heart suddenly racing, my palms sweating.

"Relax. You're going to do great!"

This is one of my biggest fears. Speaking in front of an audience. A year ago, I never would've thought I'd be getting up in front of a group of women, talking about my marriage. But if my story helps someone, someone who feels trapped like I did, I'll do it.

CHAPTER FORTY-FOUR

PAIGE

"You did great!" I tell Avery, joining her at the table after her speech.

"Do you mean it? Or are you just saying that to be nice?"

"I mean it. You did great. You're going to get all kinds of speaking gigs after today. People were listening to your every word. I didn't see a single person looking at their phone."

"Because it's such a crazy story. It's more about that than my speaking skills."

"Stop putting yourself down. You were great up there. Honestly. You didn't stumble on your words once."

"I did a couple of times."

"Nobody even noticed."

I feel sorry for Avery. Logan really messed her up. His years of abuse destroyed her confidence. Made her feel like she's not good enough. I wasn't lying when I said she did a great job today. She really did, but she doesn't believe it. It'll take years before she recovers from Logan's abuse and sees herself the way she really is rather than how he saw her.

"I'm just glad it's over," Avery says. "Hey, Edith and I are going out for drinks later. You want to come along?"

"I can't. I have some stuff I need to get done." I look over and see Carl coming into the ballroom, wearing his janitor uniform. "I need to go talk to the guys cleaning up. I'll see you later."

"Okay, bye!" Avery smiles as I leave. I hope she's proud of herself for doing what she did today. It takes a lot of guts to get up there and tell a room of strangers your story.

"Hey," I say to Carl, going up to him at the back of the ballroom. It's still mostly full, but a few people are starting to leave.

"Is that her?" he says, looking over at Avery.

"Yeah, that's her."

I can't help but smile when I see Avery these days. She's so much happier now that she's free from Logan.

"You broke the golden rule," Carl says.

"It's not like I planned on it. I took the money. Set up the job. I just couldn't finish it. Avery's a good person. Unlike Logan, she really does want to help people. I knew that the first time I met her. If it'd been someone else, I would've let you do it. But Avery was different. I felt the need to save her."

The first time Logan hired me to kill his wife, I was going to actually do it. Well, not me. I hired Carl to do it. I saw it as just another job. A way to make money. But then I met Avery at that committee meeting. I knew right away that Logan was abusing her, and I knew she didn't have the strength to fight back. I also knew Logan by then, and knew he didn't care about anyone but himself. All his charity work was only done to make himself look good and get people to vote for him. I couldn't stand him, and I didn't want him getting what he wanted.

So I called off the hit. I told Carl not to go to Avery's house that day. I hadn't figured out what excuse to give Logan, but then I didn't have to. He got home, found Avery on the floor, and assumed I'd done the job. He was angry she wasn't dead, but like I told him, she would've been dead if he'd left her there instead of calling for help. I convinced him it was his fault she survived, not mine.

When he asked me to try again, I saw it as a chance to take him down. I got connected with Chad and told him what Logan wanted me to do. I pretended it was the first time, that the other time never happened. I wasn't sure we'd trap him, but it all worked out perfectly. I have a feeling Logan will be locked away for a long time.

"You're getting soft," Carl says, nudging me. "You can't be that way if you want to keep doing this."

"Like I don't know that?" I glance at him. "It was one time. And because of this, now the cops think I'm on their side."

"Until they catch you doing a hit," he says with a snicker.

"The hit's going to be on you if you don't shut up."

"So what do you got for me? What's the job?"

I watch as Avery gets up from the table. She's getting ready to leave.

"I'll tell you later," I say to Carl. "I want to go tell her goodbye."

"Softie," he says.

I turn back and give him a dirty look.

I'm not getting soft. I still do plenty of bad stuff. Just last week I killed a guy, but he deserved it. He killed his own mother so he could get his inheritance. His sister hired me, and I did the job without any remorse.

So yeah, I'm still on the wrong side of the law, but in a good way. I'm only taking out people who deserve to die. Or that's how I see it. And if Avery knew? I think she'd agree.

ABOUT THE AUTHOR

Rowen Chambers writes gripping psychological thrillers packed with unexpected twists to keep you reading late into the night. Her stories involve everyday characters with seemingly normal lives that take a dark, often deadly, turn.

Rowen lives in the Midwest and spends her free time reading, enjoying the outdoors, and dreaming up ideas for her next shocking thriller.

Did you enjoy *Love You to Death*? Please consider leaving a review to help other readers discover the book.

Visit Rowen Chambers on her website:
https://rowenchambers.com

Printed in Great Britain
by Amazon